C000148149

The Assassin's Wedding

wilf morgan

To Claire

Hope you enjoy
the book!

88 TALES PRESS

Wilf ☺

By the same author

That Time in Honduras

The Greatest Show on Earth
(Short Stories and Wonders vol. 1)

For Younger Readers

The Cotton Keeper

The Arilon Chronicles :
Book 1 : Arthur Ness and the Secret of Waterwhistle Pt 1
Book 2 : Arthur Ness and the Secret of Waterwhistle Pt 2
Book 3 : Teresa Smith and the Queen's Revenge Pt 1

Tales from Arilon
Trust Me, I'm a Thief

88TALES PRESS
Southwell, Nottinghamshire,
NG25 0DF
www.88tales.com

First published in Great Britain
in 2008 by 88Tales Press

Third Edition

This edition published in Great Britain
in 2018 by 88Tales Press

Copyright © Wilf Morgan 2008
Cover Illustration Copyright © Wilf Morgan 2008
The right of Wilf Morgan to be identified as the author of this
work has been asserted.

This book is a work of fiction and any resemblance to actual
persons, living or dead, is purely coincidental.

This book is sold subject to the condition that it shall not, by way
of trade or otherwise, be lent, resold, hired out, or otherwise
circulated without the publisher's prior consent in any form of
binding or cover other than that in which it is published and
without a similar condition, including this condition, being
imposed on the subsequent purchaser. All rights reserved.

A catalogue record for this book is
available from the British Library

ISBN 978 1 9997590 0 1

www.88tales.com

For my wife, children
and almost-married
men and women everywhere.

The music at a wedding procession always reminds me of the music of soldiers going into battle.

Heinrich Heine, 1797 – 1856

one :
or forever hold thy piece

"YOU KNOW WHAT, Michael," the Rev says to me as we stand at the front of the crowded church, listening to the pipe-organ quietly play Moonlight Sonata, waiting for my bride to arrive, "I don't believe I actually know what it is you do for a living."

"I'm an assassin," I say, making sure my cuffs are even. "I kill people for money. I like this church, by the way, it's nice."

The Rev doesn't quite know what to do. He just stands there, looking at me.

"Actually, funny story," I say. "I was back Stateside this time last week. Y'know. Working."

"It was a strip joint, downtown Chicago. Lovely little place called 'Spike' on Dearborn Street, south, right in the heart of the theatre district. Keeps itself hidden from casual view by being below street level, 'Cheers'-style. Place like that, though, I guarantee Norm would *never* have gone home. It's not some seedy, sawdust on the floor type place, either. Dead presidents literally ooze out from between every brick, you don't even get through the door without making yourself a good c-note lighter. Looking at the clientele and the location, it's obviously a place for the city's wealthier and more morally lateral tourists. I know you know what I mean, Reverend.

So anyway, I'm sat at the bar; it stretches right round the place in a huge circle. The guys serve you drinks from behind it and behind them, up on a raised, circular platform are ten or twelve of the hottest bodies you'll see in this part of town. Unless *Chicago*'s on at the Schubert Theatre, obviously. I'm thinking some genius of an enterprising individual finally realised the best way of keeping men at a bar and buying drinks was to wrap it around naked, gyrating females.

The music is some indeterminable, thumping dance tune. The genius who put this place together obviously also realised that when you have naked, gyrating females, you've already got ninety-eight percent of the lure. Shelling out good money for a license to play real music becomes pretty unnecessary when you have a fifteen year old nephew with a computer.

Every so often round the circle, the bar makes way for mini catwalks that connect us lowlifes to the heavenly bodies up on the stage. Just to rub our noses in to how close we are to a paradise we can never have (unless we want to take on some very mean looking bouncers), the hotties amble back and forth along those catwalks. Getting closer to us, then pulling back, bouncing toward us then jiggling away; making us think of the age old saying about hating to see a woman go but loving to watch her leave.

And there's Laurel shaking her moneymaker in my direction, giving me the come to bed eyes that are as seductive as they are fake. I don't know that her name is Laurel, you understand, but then I don't know it isn't. At the end of the day, strip joints are built around the basic tenet that a man can fantasise that he is good looking enough for a sexy woman wearing little or no clothes to be attracted to him over every other guy in the place. So as long as I'm Tom Cruise, she's Laurel.

Anyway, Laurel shakes her moneymaker in my direction, giving me the come to bed eyes and tweaking the elastic on her G-string. I rise from my seat, lean drunkenly against the bar, let out a hearty 'whoo' and swing my arms up like I'm some kind of frat boy at a toga party. And like a frat boy at a toga party, I send some guy's drink flying.

"Hey watch it, buddy!" he says.

I turn to the guy next to me. He's tall, thin, kind of geeky looking. He's wrapped in a couple gee's worth of Armani, easy, but it's creased to hell - like he's been sleeping in it. He is definitely the worse for wear. Unshaven. Shirt half out. Tie pulled halfway down. And very, very drunk.

"Hey sorry, guy, my fault totally," I slur. "These women, y'know? They drive you crazy in here like they drive you crazy in real life."

"Who gives a shit? My drink!"

So I offer to get him another one and I ask him what he's having.

"Anything over eighty proof," he says.

So I turn to the nearest barman. "Two bourbons." I look back at the guy then turn back to the barman. "Two double bourbons."

The drinks land on the bar in front of us quicker than Laurel's G-string filled with fifties. That genius again - don't give the clientele time to sober up between drinks. I grab both glasses and start to slide one of them toward my drunk friend. He reaches out to his drink but with my hand still over the top of the glass, he pauses and looks at me.

"What's your name, mac?" I say.

"Look, pal, I don't swing that way," he says.

"And I do, Einstein, that's why I'm ogling naked women. Just being civil is all," I say and I let him have the glass. He pounces on it like it's the last drink in the world and downs it before whoever's chasing him catches up. I turn back to Laurel as he slams the empty back on the bar but she's already promising some other guy the world. Floozy.

"Payne," the guy says.

I'm looking at Laurel's ass. "Ain't it, though."

"No, my name. Ronald Payne."

"Oh, right. Bob, Bob Brent. Life Insurance." I extend my hand to him. He wipes his hand down his silk tie and then shakes mine.

"Hey, me too!" he says with that suddenly excited air drunk people have when they find the slightest commonality between themselves and someone else. All of a sudden we're long lost brothers. "Boring job, huh?"

"Hey," I say, "what I don't know about life expectancy re-evaluation…"

The guy snorts and drains the absolute dregs out of his glass.

"Sorry I knocked your drink over. But now you know why I get so easily excited."

"Hey, don't worry about it. There's always more." He catches the bartender's eye with his glass. The barman has the glass out of Ronald's sweaty little hand and a new, better glass back in his hand in the blink of an eye. A better glass, of course, on account of it being full.

I nod at his new drink. "Either you've had a very good day or a very bad day."

He downs the entire glass in one gulp.

"Bad day," he says. "Very, very bad day."

"What happened? Someone have to make a claim?" Damn that Laurel. All curves and me with no brakes.

"No, I made a … bad investment."

"Oh? What, you dabble in the shock market on the side?"

"Something like that. This guy …" he pauses, like he's trying to figure out whether or not to go on.

"Hey, man, I didn't ask for your life story."

He shrugs, looking forlornly into the bottom of yet another empty glass. That's the thing with drunks. You never know if they're sadder at the start of the drink or the end. I guess it depends on how slaughtered they are and how slaughtered they aim to get.

"Well, let's just say I paid for something but I wasn't specific enough about what I was buying."

"Didn't get what you thought you were getting?"

"Something like that."

"I take it you got something worse, rather than better."

"Definitely something worse. Well, I haven't got it yet. Sure is gonna come soon, though. One way or another."

"Yeah," I say, the realistic part of my mind finally telling me that Laurel's probably working her way through law school in the day and is about as interested in bedding anyone here as I am in pretending I'm drunk any longer. "Probably come sooner than you think."

I drain my glass, give Laurel one last wink as she looks briefly my way and get up from my seat. "Got to go pray to the old porcelain god. Back in two."

I don't really look at Ronald but I see him nod as he raises his hand to order yet another drink. I time my walk to perfection - as soon as I get to the other side of the crowded room, I turn and lean back against the wall and watch.

Back at the bar, Ronald suddenly grabs his arm, his eyes start bulging and his mouth makes this big 'O' but no sound comes out. No-one notices a thing at first, they're too busy looking up at the stage or talking in groups or just being unconscious. He staggers backward off his stool and, left arm still outstretched, his right hand now starts grabbing his chest like he's trying to pluck his heart right out of there. He bumps into a group of Japanese businessmen and they turn around and shout at him. Only for a second, though, because they very quickly see a man having a major heart attack.

I decide now's the time to leave, before everything gets too hectic, before he actually croaks and they stop the music and call an ambulance and turn the lights on and all the rest of it. You might call it unprofessional not waiting to confirm the kill but trust me, I've been doing this a long time. And I know exactly how powerful - and untraceable - the amoxycetalene was that I slipped into his drink. I know for a fact he'll be dead before I even get to the entrance and pick up my coat. I also know how long it takes people to react to things like this and I know I'll be round the corner and long gone before everyone starts raising cain.

It's kind of a pain, killing for free. Not cost effective at all. But when self-preservation comes into the equation, it's pretty hard to put a price on things. At the end of the day, Ronald Payne contacted the Agency and put out a hit on the wrong man. I was the one got assigned the job, ergo I end up killing someone who didn't really need killing. Now that doesn't really bother me; not my screw up so I get paid regardless. Only problem was, the guy I should have killed was a no-good swindler. The guy I actually killed was the no-good swindler's twin brother; businessman, organised crime prodigy and favourite nephew of Ira Giordano, maddest, craziest, most powerful mob boss in Chicago. Now sooner or later, Ira was going to figure out who put on the hit, something Ronnie was clearly already aware of. Which means sooner or later, Ira's men would have been tap dancing on Ronnie's skull. And if I know how these mob guys think (and I do), I know that Ira would have wanted to find out exactly who it was that pulled the trigger on his favourite nephew, the son he never had. The chances are slim, real slim, that he would ever have gotten through the Agency and all the way to me. But slim chance ain't no chance.

So a quick drink with a stranger and Ronnie speaks to no-one. And I'm gone. A faceless nobody who vanishes into the crowd and who no-one ever remembers.

Well, except for Laurel, of course. She'll regret not getting with me the rest of her days."

I finish up and the Rev's still looking at me. Not moving, not talking, just staring.

Well, okay, he would be if I'd actually just said all that stuff. What do you think I am, crazy? I'm not about to blab all about my secret life to dear old Rev Mann here. Guy'd have a coronary.

The last few seconds actually went;

"You know what, Michael? I don't believe I actually know what it is you do for a living."

"I'm an insurance salesman. Life, Equity, mostly. Mainly, I sell into corporates, blue chips. Premiere services. High premiums but big payoffs, you know? APRs to die for."

The Rev's eyes start to glaze over. That's why I do it. Stops people asking questions. They move onto another topic, they don't get bored, I don't have to kill them…win, win, win.

"Ready for the off?" Rev Mann asks. Topic changed. Mission successful.

"Certainly am," I say, scanning the congregation. A woman in a broad-rimmed hat smiles at me. I nod back. "I can't wait to become George to someone's Mildred."

"Well, Emily and her father should be pulling up any minute now," he smiles that kindly smile that all elderly, Anglican Reverends must go on some kind of course to learn. "You've only got about eight minutes to relish being young, free and single." He pats my shoulder and wanders off to go and memorise his lines or whatever.

Eight minutes. Not a long time. I mentally pat the loaded Beretta .45 with silencer that's snuggled in my inside jacket pocket, a couple inches behind my pastel yellow buttonhole flower.

Eight minutes to figure out which upstanding member of this congregation I have to kill.

And once that unpleasant business is out of the way, perhaps I can finally concentrate on getting married.

two :
dramatis personae

BREAKFAST. THE MOST nutritious meal of the day. Unlike most males in America, I always make sure I eat a good, healthy meal first thing in the morning. In my line of work, you have to be in shape. So it's fruit, cereal, yoghurt, juice, toast all that good stuff. Sometimes a boiled egg. In order to relieve other people of their lives, I have to make sure I take good care of mine.

Today, though, screw all that.

I'm having a Full English breakfast which is the exact spiritual, conceptual and physical opposite to a healthy start to the day.

I put the menu down and look up at the steel blonde waitress, her pen and pad held ready like it's an Olympic event. I give her the starter's pistol.

"Okay, I want the Full English but with the following modifications; I want three rashers of bacon, crispy but not blackened, not even a little bit. I need a fried egg - no, better make it two - not over easy, don't flip them at all. What I need you to do is fry them in lots and lots of oil and just keep flicking the oil onto them with the spatula. Make sure the white's cooked right through but the yolk has still got to be plenty runny. Give me three fat, pork sausages. If you don't have pork, beef will do in a pinch. Now when it comes to the sausages, they have to be cooked in the same oil as the eggs and they have to be cooked long. I want to see them black and hard, but the inside still has to be soft. If you overcook them, they'll just be dry and you won't be able to feed them to a hungry dog. On the side, I need some baked beans - I know you won't have Heinz, just do the best you can - and some plum tomatoes. Mushrooms too. Again, lots of fat. The whole thing's got to be swimming in it. Apart from the bacon, remember, the bacon's got to be crispy. I think that's it."

The waitress' pencil is smoking.

"Um, anything to drink?"

"Big bucket of tea. No sugar, lots of milk."

The waitress takes my menu, half-smiles like I'm some kind of nutcase and clacks off in her high heels to tell the Mexican cook in back everything I just said using the eight words of English he knows. I'm not holding my breath.

I turn back to the other four people round the table.

"Nobody wanted anything else, right?"

I'm met by a bunch of shaking heads and shrugging shoulders which I take to mean 'no', so I'm about to go back to my paper when Jody pipes up.

"Getting used to being a Limey again?" she asks.

"Once I've reacclimatised to the food, the vocab's next," I say, "You can keep your sidewalks and pants - for the next couple weeks, I'm going back to pavements and trousers."

"I don't get why you guys gotta have different words anyway," Whilce says. "Why you couldn't just stick with the ones we gave you…"

"Hey, I know some more, too," Lianne says like a kid with a new dictionary. "Soccer is football, truck is lorry and Santa Clause is Father Christmas. Come on, Mike, test me, I know 'em all."

I fold up my paper, seeing as it looks like I won't be reading it. This is a company breakfast Shepard Insurance Sales style. My little outfit is only five people light. I'm not really that bothered about starting an insurance sales empire, I just need a mask. Superman has his day job at the Daily Planet, Mike Shepard has this.

Okay, let me introduce you around. I mean, it'd be rude not to. Jody is my office manager. She keeps folks in line, writes up reports on how well they're doing, makes sure the trains come in on time, that sort of thing. The kind of person the whole thing would fall apart without. The others are my sales force; Whilce (walking food disposal), Bud (God's gift to women) and Lianne (also God's gift to women). Then, obviously, there's me. I'm the kind of boss that's in some days, out some days, you know the type. You've had that kind of boss. Maybe you *are* that kind of boss. If you are, I can almost guarantee what you do when you're not in the office and what *I* do when *I'm* not in the office ain't the same thing at *all*.

My cell beeps. Text message. It's my revered employers.

Last kill not necessary. Giordano would never have gotten thru us to you. You know this.

"Alright," I look up from my screen and face my Texan salesma'am. "We say 'Fries' and they say…?"

"Chips," she doesn't even pause.

"Cookie."

"Biscuit."

"Jelly."

"Jam."

"Jell-o."

"Jelly."

"Bonus point – what are 'soldiers', and I'm talking about food not the army."

"That's when you slice your toast up into little fingers so you can dip them into food, usually soft boiled eggs accompanied by a pinch of salt and a cup of tea."

"Go, Lianne!" Jodie's impressed and even the guys give her a clap. "You rule, you English muffin, you!"

"Okay, spill, you never worked all that out," I say, my eyes flitting between Lianne and my phone.

Just being thorough. Don't like loose ends. Prefer living.

"Alright, I confess, I've been doing a little bit of research on the internet," Lianne puts on her mock coy face. "I was kind of hoping you were going to invite us to the wedding…"

"Is that so?" I smile. "I guess I'd look like a pretty mean boss if I turned you down now, after you've gone to the trouble of learning English and all."

Not a problem. U being thorough = plenty $$$ for us. Already sent new jobs to yr inbox. Fancy trip to Dubai before yr wedding?

"Well, I wouldn't worry too much about that," Jody says. "We all know you're a mean boss already. You bring us down to Times Square for breakfast every Monday morning and force us to sit and watch you pay. You bastard."

"Be that as it may, England isn't a place for the faint hearted," I give a deadpan glance across the table. "I mean, who here has the mental fortitude to face sitting on the right-side of the car, driving on the left-side of the road and doing battle on a multilane double-roundabout? With stick shift?"

"It's okay - we can take public transport," Lianne says. "Nottingham has an excellent bus infrastructure and we can easily get up there from Heathrow by train, there's one that leaves right out of the airport."

Everyone's looking at Lianne like she just dropped out the sky, most of all me.

"Lemme guess – that's verbatim off of the 'come visit England' website," Whilce is somewhat taken aback.

"I'm guessing Lianne would quite like to go," Jodie says, finishing her coffee.

"And the rest of you?" I ask.

"Yeah, sure."

"Be cool."

"Why not?"

"Lianne and me can go cruisin' for English chicks."

I don't know why I didn't invite these guys in the first place.

"Okay, I guess the world can survive without us selling it insurance for a few days."

"Oh, thank you, thank you!" Lianne wants to hug me but stops herself. Then she hugs me anyway. "You're the best boss in the world! You're not a bastard, don't listen to Jodie."

I'll be in England. Surely someone there needs killing? Pref. someone in the Midlands.

"Thanks boss!"

"You're the man, man!"

"As Whilce says, you are most definitely the man," Jodie smiles. "Even though after the wedding, your wife will be the man, but, y'know, whatever."

Will let u know. [Agency Out]

The waitress puts a plate down in front of me. I look up at her. She's got this nervous smile, like she's waiting on the man from Del Monte.

It's art. Really. Like a Picasso, I'm thinking it'll look better with distance. I drop a couple twenties down on the table as I stand up and reach for my coat. "Tell your cooks, nice try."

A slightly disappointed waitress is about to take away the mutated mess when Whilce, without even looking up from his food, reaches out, picks the plate up and pours the contents on top of what's left of his mixed grill.

"You know, there must be some way we can make money off of this guy," Jodie says, kind of impressed, kind of disgusted.

"I got people to see, I'll see you guys back at the office later. I'll expect you to have pulled in the Smithsonian account by the end of the day if you want me to pay your flights to England."

They all groan as I pull on my coat and leave. The Smithsonian account is the world's biggest pain in the ass. If they pull that in by the end of the day, I'll go out and buy a hat just so I can eat it. But I'll buy their tickets anyway. You know why? Because I'm a good, caring boss. I should win some kind of award.

*   *   *

"Okay, Sarah, what was the very first thing you remember about last night?"

"The first thing, the very first thing I remember is my good friend Catherine picking my drunk arse up out of that gutter."

"The first thing you remember is me wiping vomit off your blouse and chucking you in my car? That was, like, nearly two a.m.!"

"No, wait, I remember right before you got there. I remember lying face down in the alley behind that pub, being fast asleep and wishing I would never wake up."

"You remember being asleep?"

"I know, I'm a freak."

"But you don't remember how you got out to that alley."

"Nope."

"Do you want me to tell you how you got out to that alley?"

"Nope."

"You got so drunk, the landlord threw you out the back of the pub with his own two hands."

"I thought I told you I didn't want to know."

"At least I got to you before you shagged some deadbeat again."

"...yeah..."

"Sarah!"

"No, Catherine, I'm sure you did. Honestly, I don't remember shagging anyone."

"You never remember, that's the problem."

"Catherine, please, not so loud..."

"Sarah, you have to stop doing this to yourself. Look at you, you look pathetic. You're not getting any younger. One of these days, you're going to find yourself face down in one of those alleyways and you're going to get your wish about not waking up. You haven't touched your coffee."

"I'm waiting for it to go away. I'm waiting for you to go away."

"Well, that's another wish you're going to get coming true; I'm late for work on account of not being able to wake you up."

"Should have just let me sleep…"

"For all I know, you'd have dropped into a coma, the amount of alcohol you must have sunk last night."

"Wait a minute, how did you know where I was? How do you know what I was doing?"

"I was looking for you. I haven't seen you in days. Plus I had to pass on a message from one of your clients, they called last night. Apparently, it was urgent. Matter of life and death. By the way, you have got to stop giving my phone number as an alternative contact number for your business. You don't live here."

"I know, I know…"

"You've never lived here."

"How did you know where to find me?"

"There are just three bars and two pubs in all of Nottingham that you go to when you want to drown your sorrows. And you always seem to have sorrows to drown. By the way, she asked for Sarah Jackson."

"Who asked for Sarah Jackson?"

"Your client. Why are you still using your married name?"

"I haven't got round to changing all my stuff back. You know how long it took me to change it all over when I got married? Ages."

"You haven't been married for a long time, Sarah. You're not Jackson. You should go back to your maiden name, that's who you are now."

"It's been a long time since I was a maiden, Catherine."

"You know what I mean."

"Look, if there's a person on this Earth who can tell me who I am, I'd like to meet them. But there isn't. So, really, does it matter what name I use?"

"You know what happened to me a couple of weeks ago?

This guy, white guy, he was shown to my desk and when he saw me, he seemed to go even more white and he said to me 'great – a darkie *and* a woman – I'm going to get *great* financial advice here…'."

"What a dick. I apologise on behalf of the rest of whitekind."

"No need. You know what I did? I referred him to a white, male colleague of mine and I moved on to the next person in the queue. You know what that's called? Being an adult. Moving on. Not wallowing in crap. Not bringing yourself down to the lowest common denominator. Am I getting through?"

"Yes and your noise is making my head hurt."

"That's not me, it's your freaky ringtone. It's calling from the next room. You should answer it, it might be that woman. If it's not, I left her details on the fridge. You can't afford to throw away business, not in your situation."

"Okay, mother."

"I'm going to work, now that I know I'm not going to come home and find you in exactly the same position I left you in but minus a pulse."

"What happened to that guy?"

"What guy?"

"The arse from the bank."

"I think Jamie sold him one of those unethically high interest rate loans. Y'know, as revenge."

"Do you want me to put a hit out on him?"

"Oh right, you're an assassin now?"

"Used to be but I gave up. Do you have any full fat milk in here? All I see is skimmed."

"All I have is skimmed."

"Your pursuit of health knows no depravity. I'm serious, though, about that guy. I'll take him out to some back alley and duff him up for you. You're the closest thing I've got to a best friend. You're the closest thing I've got to a friend, full stop."

"Sarah, do me a favour please? For once in your life, try to sort out the multitude of problems you have before trying to sort out other people's. Okay?"

"Didn't Jesus say something like that?"

"I don't know. He's always swiping my sayings, so maybe. Leave the key in the normal place when you go. And don't make me have to drag you out of an alleyway again. It's murder on my shoes."

"Okay, thanks - oh, hey, I forgot! Want to come to a wedding with me today?"

"A wedding?"

"Yeah, an old school friend I bumped into. Want to come?"

"Sarah, I've got to go to work."

"Nobody *has* to do anything. Come on! We can play that game where we try and guess how long the marriage will last. It'll be fun!"

"I'm already late."

"Excellent reason to call in sick. You've clearly been throwing up all morning and despite your best efforts to make it into work, your bus journey was cut short by an encore performance of 'The Exorcist' so you turned around and came back home. Then you donned your glad rags and came to a wedding with me."

"I don't really like weddings."

"Trust me. This one, as the yanks say, will be a blast."

three :
santa claus, the easter bunny and the queen of hearts

SO HERE I am, walking along Fifth Avenue, chatting on my cell phone to my intended. She says nice things to me, I say nice things to her. She tells me she loves me. I tell her I love her. She means it. I mean it. So why do I feel there's movie credits appearing in the air around me as I walk along? 'Starring Mike Shepard as The Fool Getting Married, Special Guest Star - Ernest Borgnine'.

I mean, I love Emily. I proposed to her and I can't wait to get married to her. And yet, I can't shake two really overpowering feelings;

a - This doesn't seem real.

b - Somehow, this is a really bad idea.

Mr. Cold Blooded Assassin and the fair English Maiden have only been in each others lives for two weeks shy of eighteen months. Is it too soon to be getting married? Maybe that's it. Simple cold feet. I'm used to being a bachelor; a footloose, fancy free, not-a-care-in-the-world killing machine. And now I'm getting married. I'm sure it's completely the same as every other man in the world on the brink of 'you may now kiss the bride' has to contend with.

And yet, on that night we first met, the thought of spending the rest of my life with Emily Coleman was all I wanted to do.

Okay, let's go back eighteen months. Just for a minute.

I'm standing there on the steps of the Roosevelt Hotel on sixth avenue, round the corner from the Empire State Building, thinking that being an assassin is a job with dignity and style. And then I sigh as I realise my giant, pink rabbit suit is riding up my ass again.

"Are you sure you got an invite in there somewhere, Bugs?"

"Bugs?" I repeat, my giant rabbit head looking up at the doorman.

"Bugs Bunny."

"Bugs Bunny isn't pink, Jer, he's grey," the lady doorman next to him says.

"So, what the hell you supposed to be, then?" the guy doorman asks me.

I stop rifling through concealed pockets and hold up my basket of chocolate eggs, covered in multicoloured foil wrappers. "I'm the Easter Bunny, dude."

"Okay, so are you sure you got an invite in there somewhere, Easter Bunny?"

"I got your invite right here," I hand over a small piece of paper; a small piece of paper that I appropriated along with the suit from a guy even now sleeping off a chloroform hangover back in his apartment.

"So is it okay, or do I have to go back to the subway and let that homeless guy carry on peein' on me?"

The guy doorman hands me back my invite. "Have a ball, Mr. Hall."

Tweedledum and Tweedledame open the doors and I saunter on in, soon finding myself in the lavish lobby of the Roosevelt, hotel to the rich and richer of New York. Businessmen on crucial dinners entertaining their Japanese investors, international dignitaries on UN business in New York, celebrities taking advantage of the excellent restaurant while shooting a movie in town. Just a few of the groups of people who look up in bemusement at the six foot, pink rabbit striding through their midst.

It doesn't take me long to find the Damocles Suite and the Fancy Dress Christmas Party for the clients and employees of Pickard, Stayton and Steel, Attorneys at Law.

It's typical Christmas party décor - tinsel, holly and mistletoe everywhere. Loud, cheesy Christmas music, drunk employees dancing, drunk employees drinking and drunk employees making out. And still only 8 p.m.

I scan the room, looking for the man I'm here to kill. I don't know what he's done or who he's annoyed. That's because I never read that section of the brief. Don't see the point. When the man comes out to your house to fix the washing machine, you don't tell him why you bought that leather jacket. You just tell him that the leather jacket has jammed up the machine. He removes it. You pay him. He goes. The fact you were trying to relive your youth as a rocker is none of his business, nor does it enable him to do the job any better.

So, somewhere in here, is a man dressed as Santa Claus who has done something that annoyed someone enough that they contacted the Agency to have him killed. The Agency gave me the brief, since the job fits my skills and psyche profile, and I read the relevant parts. I know his face, his name, his comings and goings, his address, the name of his wife, kids, dogs, fish, his social security number, his job, his car licence plate number, his favourite holiday retreat, what foods make him sick, what books he reads, what music he loves, the name of his mistress, where he goes to drink, what football team he supports and whether or not ET made him cry.

But I don't know why someone wants him dead. And I don't - in case you hadn't got this yet - care.

"Hey, killer suit, man!"

I turn around and see The Matrix's very own Neo and Trinity. They wish.

"Nice suit yourselves," I say. "Hey, can you really dodge bullets?"

They laugh and say something but I don't really catch it because I've just spotted something. My man? No. Something altogether different.

Neo says, "Awesome that you came as Bugs Bunny, man, that is so retro!" My attention clicks back into his west coast drone.

"Seriously, can you dodge bullets?"

Their laughter isn't quite as hearty this time and I walk away from them. The reason I picked Gareth Hall to knock out and replace was because several days of surveillance of PSS employees had revealed that he was keeping his costume secret. That meant I could turn up as him and no-one would know who I was. Funny thing is, I'm finding myself feeling indignant on his behalf - he'd clearly gone to a lot of trouble picking his suit and people just aren't getting it. Bugs frickin' Bunny. My ass.

I walk over to the thing that had caught my attention so completely. A group of four people stood by the buffet table, halfway between the punch and the sandwiches. Zorro's talking to Darth Maul and another guy I don't recognise. He's wearing a regular suit and an eye patch. Really pushed the boat out. Probably management. But it's the fourth member of the group that has my little bunny heart racing. The Queen of Hearts. She looks just like the ranting, raving, beheading woman from the Alice in Wonderland cartoon - but with a much shorter dress, much better legs and a much, much prettier face.

I don't want to sound like some giddy teenager, but this feeling really has never happened to me before. I don't know the woman, I can't even hear her speaking. And yet, I feel like I have to be near her, like all the time I've been alive has been a waste because I haven't spent any of it with her.

Well, at least I'm not sounding like a giddy teenager.

"Can we help you?"

The manager in the eye patch is looking at me. They're all looking at me. I realise I'm stood with them, looking at her. I point to the table.

"You're blocking the punch."

They move aside, shaking their heads, saying something about employees draining the company dry and I go to the table and start ladling out some punch. The initial shock of seeing the Queen of Hearts has passed and I'm feeling something else altogether now. Anger. At myself. How could I lose the plot like that, even for a second? It's never happened before and it will damn well never happen again. The quickest way to get killed in this game is to stop concentrating. You can never -

"Can I get a glass of that? This party is boring the pants off me." The Queen is by my side. I don't know whether the slightly light-headed feeling I'm getting is because she's suddenly there and talking to me or because she's suddenly there and she could have been anyone, including Santa Claus with a loaded .22.

"Have mine," I give her the glass I just poured. "I don't even like punch."

"Cheers."

"You're English."

"You're a rabbit."

"Well spotted."

"Likewise. Cheers again." She raises her plastic glass before taking a dainty, woman-like sip. Followed by a manly, down-in-one gulp that drains the entire thing. "Actually, that's some good punch."

"Thanks, I made it myself. Here, have some more."

She takes the refilled glass but doesn't drink it. She just holds it and looks at me. I have to remind myself why I'm here.

"Aren't you going to get back to Zorro and those guys?"

"No," she shakes her head. "They're talking shop. They were boring me so badly, I decided to come and talk to a six foot, pink rabbit."

"Lawyers, huh? Can't live with 'em, can't shoot 'em unless someone's paying you."

"If my well trained ears aren't mistaken," she says suddenly, with this look in her eye like she's just figured out something, "I'm not the only Limey at the punch bowl."

"Damn, you saw through my disguise. I'm impressed."

"Well, it was the ears," she smiles. "That and the fact you noticed I was English but didn't ask which part of London I was from."

"Well, if *my* well trained ears aren't mistaken, you're from somewhere down South. Kent, maybe?"

"Nottingham."

"Ah, wrong end of the country altogether. Not so well trained ears, obviously."

"I lived in Kent ever since I finished University there, though. I only moved here a few months ago."

"And the rabbit's ears win again," I smile beneath my mask. "You had me doubting myself there, for a second."

"You sound like you've been here for a while, though."

"Since I was a kid."

"Ooh, now there's a story I want to hear. What could possibly have brought a kid from...?"

"Scarborough."

"...to New York when he was a child and then had the bad taste to leave him here?"

"My parents died. I came to live with my Uncle. Then he died."

"Oh..." She looks really embarrassed. "I'm so sorry. I have a tendency to lead with my mouth. I feel a complete arse."

"Hey, don't worry about it. Was all a long time ago, now. Different life."

She's looking at me, now, as though she can see through my mask. It makes me uncomfortable.

"Y'know," I continue, "before I became a rabbit."

She laughs. It's a beautiful sound. Seriously, you gotta be vomiting by now, right?

"So which are you, client or lawyer?" she asks.

"Don't you recognise my voice?"

She shakes her head. "Should I? Oh, wait, Lou, is that you?"

"No."

"Oh," she looks disappointed. Maybe a little too disappointed for my liking. "That was a stupid guess, anyway. Lou's not English, different life or no."

"Who's Lou?"

"This guy in Procurement. You clearly don't work in Procurement if you have to ask who Lou is."

"Oh, *that* Lou," I say. "The good looking one, so the women never get sick of saying."

"So you do know him."

"I do if you're talking about Louis Taylor, Group Procurement Division, worked there eight years, favourite song 'Black Dog' by Led Zeppelin, ET made him cry."

She looks a little bewildered. "What are you, his stalker?"

"No, but I do know he came as Santa Claus tonight. Inspired Lou, as I like to call him."

"Oh, so he did come then?" she starts looking around the menagerie of movie, cartoon, cultural and fantasy characters that pack the ballroom.

"Why are we talking about Lou?" I ask, a little miffed to tell you the truth.

"You sound jealous," she smiles a cheeky smile.

"I thought you were trying to guess who I was."

"I don't think we've ever met before," she says. "And even if we had, you're wearing a mask so how am I ever expected to know who you really are?"

She steps a little closer, my heart rate gets a little quicker. "Why don't you show me your face? You never know, that might start ringing bells with me."

With her free hand, she starts to reach up to my mask. Now, keeping my face hidden is not a cast-iron requirement for this hit, depending on how I decide to take out my guy. For instance, if I do the tried and trusted poison thing, no problems. However, if I end up having to shoot him, investigators'll be combing through the CCTV footage and eventually they'll spot a guy who nobody recognises and who, it'll turn out, was never invited. Bad joo-joos. So professionally, in order to keep all my options open, I really need to keep my mask on.

But I really want her to see my face.

"Emily Coleman, as I live and breathe, if you want my head, you can damn well have it," says the most rugged, good-looking Santa Claus I've ever seen as he whips the Queen of Hearts toward him with a single, fluid motion. Emily - as it turns out she's called - smiles up at him. I might be imagining it, but the smile doesn't seem as warm as the one she used for me.

"Speak of the devil, we were just talking about you!"

I'm mad. Again, at myself. Because this time, Santa Claus - aka Louis Taylor - really did manage to get the drop on me. Luckily for me, he didn't have a .22 in his arms. Instead, he has the Queen of Hearts in his arms and the fact that I can't tell if I'm madder about that or about losing focus again makes me mad. I'm just all kinds of mad.

"I think it's time the Queen of Hearts had a slow dance with old Santy Claus, don't you?" Lou starts to lead Emily away but she stands firm.

"Lou, I'd like you to meet…" and she looks at me with this twinkle in her eyes as if to say, 'Ha! Gotcha!'

It feels like we're still having our little conversation even with Lou present and that feels good so I smile, extend my hand and say, "Derek. Derek Sturge."

"Uh huh," is all he says, sparing me the briefest glance before going back to Emily. "So, come on, that dance…"

"Actually," Emily bristles, presumably at Lou's bad manners, "I'm just having a drink. I'm afraid I'll have to take a rain check."

Lou doesn't seem pleased at the knock back. Guy that good looking probably isn't used to getting them too often. "Well, those checks are only good for about fifteen minutes so finish up your drink and I'll be back to cash it in." He gives Emily a predatory smile and she suddenly looks really shocked, her eyes open wide. It takes a second or two before I realise that he just copped a feel of some royal ass.

"'scuse me, Bugs," he pushes past me and saunters off into a crowd of oompah-loompahs.

"Prick," she says.

I look at her. "Emily Coleman, huh? Pleased to meet you."

She looks at me and her annoyed pout disappears and an annoyed smile takes its place. "Pleased to meet you, Derek Sturge."

"That's not my name."

"It's too late now, the game's up. I know you."

"Seriously? Derek Sturge? What am I, a porn actor? C'mon, I made it up."

"Why?"

"I never like to give up too much on the first date."

Emily raises her eyebrows. "Oh, so this is a date, is it?"

"I've had dates like this," I nod my big rabbit head.

"I see," Emily takes a sip of her punch as 'Paradise by the Dashboard Light' by Meatloaf ends and 'Santa Baby' by Madonna starts. "Well, as dates with rabbits go, this one isn't all that bad."

"Thank you." I realise I'm still holding the ladle so I put it back in the bowl. "This stuff goes straight through me, I have to go visit the little bunnys' room. Will you promise to still be here when I get back?"

She nods and raises her plastic cup to me. "Trying to guess who you really are."

I smile to myself as I walk across the dance floor and through a crowd of gyrating Elvis Presleys. I've done this whole thing before many times and no doubt will again in the future; leave someone holding a drink while I excuse myself to go to the bathroom. Except usually, their drink's spiked and I'm going across the room to watch them and make sure they die. So the reason I'm smiling is that this time I'm actually going to the bathroom and coming back to talk to her rather than going to watch her die. Which is nice.

As I go on my quest, though, I can still see her in my mind's eye; stood by the punch bowl and saying 'hello' and 'how do you do' to any passing work colleagues in her very English accent, sipping her punch and - most of all - thinking of me. I'm a good reader of character, you have to be in this game, so I know we're hitting it off and she's not just being polite.

Part of me is worried, though, about the effect she has on me, on my focus, on my professionalism. I mean, I'm actually on a job tonight! I've never, in eighteen years in this vocation, ever been on a job and spoken a single word to someone that wasn't specifically designed to help me accomplish my task or been part of some fake persona. Tonight is the first time my real self and my 'job' self have even touched let alone overlapped. That's a scary thought.

But then I see her smile.

"That was quick," she says.

"Well, I didn't really go to relieve myself," I reply. "I followed Louis to the bathroom where I know the CCTV cameras aren't working at the moment. Then I waited until we were alone, snapped his neck and left him locked in one of the cubicles. Anyone going in will assume he's passed out drunk. By the time anyone realises he's dead, I'll be well away from here. More punch?"

Okay, okay, I didn't actually say it.

"I didn't want to risk you getting bored and leaving without saying goodbye. More punch?"

I think that's much more likely to progress this relationship.

"Don't worry," I say. "I washed my paws."

"I figured out your name," she says, in a kind of conspiratorial, hushed voice.

"Oh?"

"Yep. Keyser Sozé."

My brain ticks a few cycles, then, "Oh, 'The Usual Suspects'?"

"No one really knew who he was, either."

I smile. "I can see I need to give you a helping hand. One second."

I squeeze through the crowded hall, which seems to have gotten a lot more busy since I came in, and go over to the DJ desk where he keeps all his slips for people to write their requests on. I write something on one of the slips but I don't leave it with the DJ, I bring it back over to the punch table, my brain screaming at me the whole time. I hand it to a bewildered looking Emily.

"Is this what I think it is?"

"I've got to go," I say. "But if you want to find out any more about me, then use it. If not, I'll try to recover from the rejection without reverting back to my previous orphanage-induced alcoholism. But, y'know, no pressure."

"I haven't had a man's telephone number in a long time,"

she smiles. "It's been even longer since I had a rabbit's."

I salute her as I step back, memorising her features one last time in case I never see them again.

She salutes me back. "See you around, Easter Bunny."

It certainly was a night to remember, that one. Nearly eighteen months on and I can safely say she knows my name now. And since she knows my name and I know her name, there didn't seem like anything else to do but get married.

As good an idea as that seemed at the time, though, it came with a pretty obvious problem. One hand; single male, no personal or emotional ties to the world. Other hand; married male, devoted to his wife. Which one of these works better if your occupation is 'hired killer'?

When your intended thinks you met at a party and you actually met at the scene of an assassination you were carrying out, it kind of makes a mockery of the concept of an honest relationship.

As I enter the lobby of Pickard, Stayton and Steel, I think I've hit the nail on the head regarding my cold feet. Being a husband is going to diminish my ability to be a secret killer and being a secret killer is going to diminish my ability to be a husband. Ouch, my head hurts already.

If I had any sense, I'd run for the hills but for two very good reasons; one - I do love her and, more importantly, two - her mother has already started planning this wedding and she is a force only a fool would oppose.

"She on her way down?"

I hear a voice from behind me. "I'm already here."

I turn away from the receptionist to the sight of my beautiful lawyer fiancée getting up from one of those huge, oversize lobby sofas and I think - I'll figure it out.

"So," I say, "there's only one rule and it's a simple one. Anything over five hundred dollars is out. No wedding ring is worth more than that."

"Dear, dear, Michael," she says, hugging my arm with a huge grin, "you just don't know me at all."

four :
lollipops and ass-whuppins

EMILY'S TRYING OUT the mother of all wedding rings right at this moment, so I'll take a couple minutes out to let you in on something I know's been bugging you for a while now.

How does being an assassin work?

Well, okay, since you ask, it's very simple. Here's the Cliff Notes version.

People in the world piss each other off. It happens all the time. It can be over anything. Someone's run over your cat. Someone's slept with your wife. Or your daughter. Or your wife *and* your daughter. Someone's orchestrated a hostile takeover of your company. Someone's not getting old fast enough and you want your inheritance sooner rather than later. Someone's currently ruling a country that has kept your social group oppressed for centuries. Someone's married to a woman you've fallen in love with and you both want to run away together. Whatever.

Now, as you can probably figure, there's no simple right and wrong about a lot of those situations. They're just situations. And situations need resolving. And that's where the Agency comes in.

Wait, I'm getting a little ahead of myself. As Stan Lee used to say, let's take a f'rinstance;

Some guy sleeps with the wife of the CEO of a multi-national oil conglomerate. The CEO finds out about it. Probably slaps his wife around some. Then calls his trusted advisor. Not the one that goes with him to meetings at the White House. The other one. The one that oversees things like security for his seventy million dollar mansion and background checks on the families of any boy his daughter brings home. He says he wants the scum who screwed his wife 'taken care of' (oh, yeah, people use that phrase).

Now, everyone knows a criminal within about three degrees of separation. Maybe less. Ask around your friends and work colleagues. Trust me, it'll shock you. And it's this thin but ever present link between the respectable world and the criminal world that allows people who aren't criminals to commit criminal acts by proxy. So, the CEO's trusted advisor is not a criminal but he goes away and speaks to some people. They're not criminals either. Those people go off and speak to other people, and these people usually *are* criminals. Only a little - you know, shady accountants and like that. But criminals nonetheless. They're less than snow-white clean. Once the request gets into those kinds of circles, it's pretty much a matter of hours before someone's talking to the Agency.

The Agency is just one of many, many brokers out there who gather work for assassins. Don't know exactly how many there are but I'm pretty sure it runs into the hundreds in North America alone. Some are low rent, some charge top dollar. The Agency is the biggest out there by a long, long way and that means the dollar they charge is the toppest there is. Their size also means they're the most secure. Sure, the CIA or FBI or whoever are all over it like a rash from New Year's Day to Christmas, but it's been running for over twenty years straight with no problems. If Uncle Sam was able to put it out of business, he would have done it by now. Besides, you ask me, Uncle Sam's probably placed a couple calls to the Agency in his time. You want to get real paranoid? It wouldn't surprise me a whole hell of a lot if that dearest of uncles had more than a hand in setting the Agency up in the first place. Hey, colour me Mulder.

So anyway, the Agency. Imagine your local temping agency, Office Buns. Now, Office Buns is just some room somewhere with a half dozen people working there - but on their books, they have a whole raft of nice, polite, pretty, young women who sit around all day waiting for news of an accountant's office somewhere in need of someone to type out letters, photocopy invoices and send faxes. But imagine those nice, polite, pretty, young women knowing their way around a Dakota T-76 Longbow assault rifle with model-70 style trigger, adjustable cheekpiece and blind magazine feed. Imagine them turning up to an office in the dead of night and hiding out in one of the cupboards, waiting, perhaps for hours, until one particular person comes along. That one particular person who they've been given a file all about and which holds such tidbits as their place of residence, place of work, general comings and goings and anything else that the Agency has uncovered about that person that'll make the hit go easier. Oh, yeah, and the background to the hit (the bit I never read). And when that person comes along, that person gets dead really soon after. Imagine that. That's basically what the Agency is about. That's basically what we're about. The freelance killers who have the years of experience and success that qualifies us to be on the books of such a prestigious outfit.

Apart from the fact we're not all nice, polite, pretty young women. Okay, some of us, sure.

When a job comes in, it's all pretty slick. The Agency generously provides a whole bunch of hardware and software to each of its workers since their cut of your fee more than pays for the outlay. Their secure computer servers send hit information to our secure email inboxes along with a secure text message to our secure mobile phones and we log in and pick those emails up. Securely, of course.

We look over the hit and decide whether it's our thing. It always is. As part of our initial application to join, we have to undergo extensive skills and psychological evaluation. This assures the agency of our mental state as well as what types of jobs we're competent to carry out. That way, we get the right jobs for our skills - there's no use in sending a low-grade thug-whacker to surgically remove the President of Guinea-Bissau.

So, once we've looked the job over and decided to take it, the target is then what death row prison wardens refer to as a dead person walking.

Which brings us right back to our oil conglomerate CEO and his philandering wife. Once her lovesick young stud has been taken off the scene, there's nothing that ties the deed to the initiator. Not if the assassin has done their job. When we're on our game, we're invisible almost to the point of not even existing. The only thing to mark our passing is a corpse. Sometimes, not even that.

The CEO's pockets suddenly become a good half mil lighter and he has no idea who the money's gone to. And he doesn't care. He had a problem. He had money he was willing to spend. The problem went away. His broken feelings have been fixed. He's happy.

And the Agency? The Agency moves on. It doesn't have time to be happy. It has another fifty sets of broken feelings to fix. That's about the size of it. Being an assassin - at least, an assassin in the employ of the Agency - is a fairly straightforward business. Not glamorous or sexy. I wouldn't be so irresponsible or, well, such an idiot as to claim being an assassin is glamorous or sexy. It's just a job. Like being a milkman. I won't lie and say it's boring. If you have an aptitude for it, you can last a long time; you get to see the world and meet a lot of interesting people. Quite a few of them, you don't even have to kill. And the best part - as least as I see it - is you're fulfilling your place in the universe. Oh yeah, the universe has a place for hired killers too, you know. What, you figure anti-war campaigners and soup-kitchen volunteers got the exclusive deal?

"What do you think to this one?"

"Anything that warrants its own zip code is good enough for you, honey."

"You see, life's so much easier when you start seeing things from my perspective. I'll need your card. And get off your phone, it's so rude."

"Sorry, honey."

As Emily goes back inside the shop with my card, I finish up my text message to the Agency, accepting one of the jobs they sent to my inbox. In a couple days, we're going to be back in the land of Fish n' Chips getting ready for the wedding of the century a week from now. Sometime in the next seven days, some bigshot businessman from Yorkshire is going to discover that me and the Agency have one thing in common. We're both in the market with just two products; lollipops and ass-whuppin's.

And we're all outta lollipops.

five :
glass half full

I LOOK AT the guy holding my passport, he looks at me, I look at him, he looks at my passport and I think to myself that customs guys are a lot like assassins.

The job of a customs officer is to sit in a booth and, for queues and queues of people, look at their passports to determine if who their passport says they are is, in fact, who they actually are. And why's his job like mine?

It's a necessary part of humanity's existence but only complete psychos actually enjoy doing it.

"According to my girlfriend," I say, "that picture of me looks like a young Harrison Ford."

The guy, like all those in his profession, has no sense of humour. He gives me back my passport and looks past me to the next person in the queue.

"Welcome to the country," somehow the words come from his mouth without him actually saying them. I take the cue and move along.

"Will you come on?" Emily says, picking up her hand luggage now that I've finally finished my effervescent exchange of witty repartee with the passport guy. "I want to get to the baggage claim before everyone else gets there and stands in front of the conveyor belt and blocks us off."

"Have you ever considered," I say, almost jogging to keep up with my impatient fiancée, "that it's that precise attitude that actually *causes* people to stand in front of the conveyor belt and block people off? If everyone actually stood behind the damn line like they're supposed to-"

"Look, if I don't do it, someone else will. Excuse me please."

I dodge the frail granny that my sweet English maiden just barged past. I dodge several other people off our plane that natural selection says will not be at the front of the baggage claim herd.

I consider arguing some more. I consider mentioning that if you manage to actually get to the front of the crowd and find yourself literally kneeling on the baggage belt that your bag doesn't come down the chute any faster. That, in fact, you have to put up with people constantly pushing you out the way so they can grab their bags as they go past. I consider saying all this and more but then I remember, I don't actually give a shit about any of it. The only reason I feel like arguing with my fiancée is because I'm about to meet her parents again. And nothing puts me in a bad mood faster than that.

The first time I met the Colemans, the entire clan was out in force. It was Emily's great Uncle Arnold's birthday - I think he was about two hundred and something. It had been my first visit back to England in about three years. Six years if you don't count the trips where I killed someone.

Emily's parents live in a big, old converted farmhouse in the countryside on the outskirts of Nottingham, north end, in a nice little village called Epperstone. Very respectable. Filled with nice people, far as I can tell. So how that cantankerous old bastard and his harpy of a wife managed to make themselves a pillar of the community, I have no idea.

But I get ahead of myself.

The house and grounds were pretty impressive. Old, renovated main building with several smaller outhouses where guests usually stayed. Big, expansive spread of land that used to yield potatoes, apparently. Now it yielded a clay pigeon shooting range, a quad biking area, a couple swimming pools and a big-ass warehouse. According to Emily, her Dad was a self-made import/export magnate. (I ignored the fact that most people who described their occupation as import/export were actually criminals).

Apparently, he'd wanted to pass the business onto Emily. She was so interested in that idea that she became a lawyer and moved to the other side of the Atlantic Ocean. With no other kids, what he was going to do with Guardian Shipping was anyone's guess. Leaving it to the grandkids is out of the question. Why? Because he'll never have any. Why?

I'll tell you why.

Because as soon as Fraser Coleman looked at me on that mild August evening nearly a year ago, and as 'Bob the Builder' played out of a stereo system that cost more than Bob made in a year, I knew he was never going to like me or any other man his daughter brought home. In fact, I got the distinct impression that he'd rather kill any boyfriend of Emily's rather than entertain the fact she'd actually had sex with them.

"Michael," was all he said to me after Emily introduced us. All around us, various members of the Coleman tribe were talking, drinking, eating - one or two enterprising (drunk) individuals were even dancing.

"Good to meet you, sir," I said, humble to the last.

"And what do you do for a crust, Michael?"

"I run an insurance company based out of Manhattan."

"Successful?"

"We do okay," I shrugged lightly.

"Is this your first trip to England? I suppose you're finding everything rather smaller and less fattening than you're used to."

"Actually, Dad, Mike's originally from England."

"Oh, really?"

This is the stock response I always get from English people when they realise the yank they're talking to used to be normal like them. It's kind of like telling people your left arm is actually a prosthetic replacement for the one you lost in an industrial accident. They're surprised. Then shocked. Then, they kind of pity you.

"What made you go over there then?" Fraser jerked his head to his left, as if America was about six yards beyond the edge of the marquee.

"Dad, I'm sure Mike doesn't want to -"

"My folks died, so I was sent to live with my Uncle. Then he died. I ended up in care."

"At least you had the good sense to avail yourself of the American welfare state rather than ours."

"*Dad!*"

"All I'm saying is they've got the money to spare. Over here, he'd have been shoved in with some family on a council estate and probably grown up to be a not very good car thief. On the other hand," he said, taking a sip of his sherry, "at least he wouldn't have had to live in America. All swings and roundabouts, I suppose."

"I can certainly say I didn't grow up to be a not very good car thief," I cast a sidelong half-smile at a fuming Emily to re-assure her I wasn't offended by her father. He was clearly trying to get a rise out of me. Behind us, some guests wandered past trying to figure out, none too quietly, which one great Uncle Arnold actually was.

"You into football, Michael? Proper football, not American Football," the wild Fraser ride took me in a new direction.

"I follow a couple teams, nothing too serious."

"I suppose you're more into American Football."

"We just call it Football."

"Well we call it American Football. Best you do the same or else you'll end up confusing folk."

"I'm actually not into it too much. Watched the Superbowl once."

"Are you into any sport?"

"Not really."

"A man should be into sport. I used to play rugby and football when I was young man. Trains the mind to be more competitive. Men who aren't into a sport, I can't really understand how they think."

"Mike, tell Dad about the book you're reading at the moment," Emily clearly didn't feel things were going too well. Our ace in the hole was supposed to be kept for when needed - it was apparently needed after less than two minutes.

"Oh? What are you reading, Michael?"

"He's reading 'The Invisible Man' aren't you?"

I nodded, a thin smile crossing my lips. I was reading it because Emily had told me it was her father's favourite book. Apparently, it'd give us stuff to talk about.

"Did you understand it?" he asked.

"I haven't finished it yet," I said, not really sure I got what he was asking me.

"What have you made of it so far?"

"It's very interesting."

"Got enough car chases and explosions for you? Kevin Bacon was born for the role, don't you think? Nothing like a Hollywood movie to piss all over a great piece of literary fiction."

Okay, so 'The Hollow Man' was apparently *my* fault...

"This is a lovely house, Mr. Coleman," I decided to try and take control of the ride myself. "It must be worth some serious money, what with house prices so inflated right now."

"Well, seeing as I don't intend on selling it, I don't see how its value is particularly relevant."

Okaaay....

"I built Guardian Shipping up with my two hands, Michael. And this house is an expression of years of hard work. On top of that, my wife and daughter mean the world to me," he put a protective arm around Emily. "An Englishman's home is his castle, have you heard that phrase?"

"Yes, sir, I have."

"Well, this is my castle. And I'm very protective of it. People don't just wander in and automatically take their place at my table, they have to earn the right to do so."

I decided that if he mentioned a 'circle of trust', I was going to shoot him right then and there.

"Enjoy the party, Michael. Excuse me while I catch up with my daughter. I don't really like the fact she lives in America but at least when she comes home, I get plenty of amusing stories. Glass half full and all that."

As I watched Fraser Coleman wander away with Emily and, while talking to her, crack a smile for the first time, I suddenly realised we hadn't even so much as shook hands.

Six months later, Emily and I decided we were going to get married. We decided to fly back to England to tell Emily's parents in person. We decided we were going to have the wedding in their neck of the woods to make them feel more involved.

I decided I was going to start taking valium.

I suddenly realise I'm shoving my bags pretty hard into the trunk of the rental, a black BMW. I have to calm down. This wedding's going to be stressful enough without me letting myself get cranked up by Fraser Coleman, Lord and Master of Coleman Castle. I shut the trunk - sorry, the boot - and get into the driver's side.

"Are you sure you're alright to drive?" Emily asks. "Do you want me to?"

"No, I'm good, Em, really. Besides, I'd rather let your bloodlust die down to normal levels after the carnage you just left behind at that conveyor belt. Letting you loose on the good people of the M42 would probably see this country's first Road Rage Massacre."

"Hey, don't worry about me," she smiles. "If you let emotion rule you at baggage claim, you're asking for failure. That was business, pure and simple. It's already forgotten. As far as I'm concerned, that man's foot broke itself."

It's moments like this that I'm thinking this woman's probably more on my wavelength than I realise. I reach for the gear stick but she takes my hand first. I look at her.

"It's going to go fine," she smiles at me and I remember how much I love her. Then she's suddenly all serious. "You've got your valium, haven't you?"

"Get off me!"

I whip my hand away and we both laugh. I savour the laugh and hold onto the feeling because I know it's the last time I'll be doing it for the next seven days.

Ah well, I think to myself as we pull out of the rental car park and begin to negotiate our way out of Manchester Airport, I may be getting married this week, but at least I've got someone to kill.

Glass half full and all that.

six :
clay pigeons

"GOOD MORNING MICHAEL, my boy. It's been too long!"

"Shut up you pompous prick."

I pull out a Colt Series 70 9mm and blow Fraser Coleman's head clean off.

"Mike, what the hell are you doing?" Emily doesn't seem impressed.

I take a look at my handiwork. I've managed to completely miss our exit.

"Damn it, sorry," I say. "We'll spin round at the next junction."

"What, with all that backed up northbound traffic? Not bloody likely. We'll just come off and take an 'A' road or something. Let me get the A to Z out."

"Sorry," I say again.

"Are you all there? You've been out of it since Stoke."

I've been fantasising about blasting your nightmare of a father all over his imported Italian marble hallway.

"Just preparing myself for a week with your parents."

"Look, Mike, I know you and Dad haven't ever really seen eye to eye but after this trip, everything's going to be different. I can feel it."

"I know. You're right. Of course, you're right," I under-take some old guy doing thirty-five in the middle lane. "This time, it'll be all roses."

We've made depressingly good time from Manchester; I prayed for an overturned melon truck. Roadworks. A freak snowfall. An alien invasion. All simple requests, all denied. Now, just shy of two hours after leaving the airport, we're just a stone's throw from crossing the moat of Castle Coleman.

Now, I feel like I need to explain something. I'm not afraid of Emily's dad. Hell, no. I mean he's a fearsome old bastard and I can definitely see how he's managed to build a million pound company out of the proverbial lemonade stand. I know he doesn't really hate Americans (well, no more than any other Englishman), he just hates any guy his daughter brings home - if I was black or Irish or had one arm, he'd make whatever appropriate comments could be made to force me to go running back up into the hills, crying, my tail between my legs. So yeah, he's a fearsome character but, no, I am definitely not afraid of him.

I am afraid, however, of what I might do *to* him.

I'm not used to having to control my emotions. Before Emily, there were two very distinct parts to my life - the part where I killed people and the part where I pretended to be nothing more than a mild mannered insurance salesman. Both were almost totally devoid of emotion.

The part where I killed people was, as I've already outlined, just a job. A Mike Shepard-shaped hole in the universe that I happen to fit. My calling. I do it because I was meant to, not because I enjoy it. I'm really good at it, so that means I don't tend to feel any fear about any given assignment. No joy, no fear. Just the job.

And the part where I pretended to be nothing more than a mild mannered insurance salesman – well, obviously, that's just not real. I might as well have a painted picture of me and Jodie and Bud and the rest of the guys on a piece of eighteen by twenty-four canvas for all the real-life authenticity of that setup. It was a construct I created to act as a cover for my work. No emotion there either.

My life was blissfully emotion free. Not that I'm a Vulcan or anything, I mean I had emotions. I got real excited when the new Star Wars movies came out and I got as choked up as anyone when Smith & Wesson announced they were axing the Aimster rifle. But I had the luxury of only getting emotional about things that didn't matter. The crap we fill our lives with to keep from getting too bored. All the real important things in life, I didn't get emotional over. Or to be more precise, all the real important things in life were not present to get emotional over.

Then I met Emily and my very carefully crafted emotional scales got screwed all to hell. All of a sudden, I'm in situations that *mean* something to me. If I was on a job and someone said nasty things to me, I knew they didn't know me and so I didn't take it personal. (Besides, it was probably just sour grapes from the fact I was about to kill them, I'd probably be the same). And if I was pretending to be Mr. Boss Man of Shepard Insurance and someone said nasty things to me, well, I don't really care about that company and if the whole thing went south, I'd just set up something else. Some client's upset because they didn't get a big enough discount? Boo-frickin'-hoo.

But when I'm talking to Fraser and he says something nasty to me, I know he's saying it to be personal. I know he's trying to get as personal as possible. He wants me out. But I can't just turn around and walk away because I love Emily. And I can't just shoot him, because I love Emily. So, with the only two options I've ever needed now taken away from me, I have to go with option number three. Just stand there, grin like an idiot, and take it.

"Home at last," Emily says as we pull off the road and trundle up the gravel driveway, past all the big ferns and oaks and on up toward the big house. She sounds excited. I force a smile as I pull up in front of the house and see Emily's mother, Mary, coming out to meet us. I kill the engine and pray that's the only thing within ten miles of this place that gets killed this week.

Okay, scout, here goes. After this week, nothing in your life will be the same again.

"Emily, I wasn't expecting you so soon - you only landed three hours ago!" Mary embraces her daughter before turning to me. "I hope you didn't drive too dangerously, Michael."

"We were really fortunate with the traffic, Mrs. Coleman," I say. "Most of it moved out of my way when it realised I wasn't going to stop."

Mary's about as amused as the passport guy had been a couple hours ago. "Very funny, I'm sure."

I lean forward to give her a very respectful peck on the cheek. "Nice to see you again, Mrs. Coleman."

"Yes, well…" Mary tries to maintain her air of hostility toward me while simultaneously being pleased to see her daughter and just ends up looking confused. "Dinner's not quite ready but

I'll get a pot of tea on for when you've taken your bags upstairs. I've put the orange bed-set on."

"Where's Dad?" Emily asks.

"Oh, yes, do go and see him before you come in. He's on the shooting field."

"Okay, mum, see you in a bit."

"Okay dear. Michael."

"Ma'am."

As we turn to head off down a path that branches away from the house, I'm sure I can see Mary tutting quietly to herself as she looks at the dirt along the bottom of our car.

We head off down the aforementioned path, past the house and through a leafy tunnel toward one of the fields adjoining the property. Emily's saying something about jetlag being an artificial, man-made construct and that it doesn't really exist except in the minds of people who don't know any better. I'm not really listening. I'm too busy making sure I don't have my Colt Series 70 9mm hidden in one of my pockets. I don't. I'm relieved and disappointed all at once.

"Pull!"

Fraser's stern shout is the first thing we hear as we emerge from the leafy canopy that's guided us all the way from the house. The big man's a walking contradiction. He's standing in the middle of a field he owns with the mandatory green Wellington boots, cord pants, polo-necked jumper and flat cap. But then, instead of the customary green body-warmer, he wraps up all that upper-class attire with a big, black and orange miner's jacket.

The man standing just to Fraser's right pulls a lever on something that looks like a camcorder tripod built out of coat hangers and a six-inch disc whips into the air and, within a second, has disappeared to nearly a dot. Fraser makes use of the final part of his upper-class outfit.

He fires his rifle. Almost instantly, the tiny dot in the sky is replaced by a puff of dark red smoke as the clay pigeon is blasted into near-invisible particles.

"Hmph," he says to himself. He put a clean shot on a six-inch target sixty yards away and getting several yards further away every second. And still, he isn't satisfied.

"Not using mum's dinner plates again, are you?"

"Emily!" Fraser hands his firearm to the other guy and embraces his daughter, finally back from the uncouth colonies. "You're early. I hope Michael didn't drive too fast."

Good grief.

"Mr. Coleman," I grin a humble grin but am not so foolish as to extend my hand. "Good to see you again."

"Yes, I expect it is." He nods at the guy holding his gun. "Do you shoot, Michael? I know how you Americans love your guns."

"I've, uh, done it once or twice."

"Here you are, then," he takes the gun from his tall sidekick (the guy reminds me of Lurch from the Addams Family), breaks it open so it's a big inverted 'V' and hands it to me, "have a throw of this."

I take a look at it. It's a twenty-eight bore Holland & Holland 'Royal' side-by-side shotgun. Twenty-five inch barrel, deluxe grade walnut, polished and oil finished with a semi-pistol grip. Even comes with a leather covered recoil pad and customised gold engravings. If none of that means anything to you, then you're clearly not a gun geek like myself or my father in law elect. Instead, just keep in mind this tiny fact; this little beauty wouldn't have cost a penny less than fifty-five thousand Great British Pounds.

"Looks very nice," I say. "Is it, you know, expensive? Couple hundred or something?"

"This, young man," the Old Lord literally bristles, "is a 'Holland & Holland' shotgun. They've been making guns for nearly two centuries. You don't buy them at the dime store with a free copy of 'Guns and Ammo'. You go to exclusive outlets and pay upwards of fifty-five thousand pounds for the privilege of owning one of the finest hunting weapons ever made."

"I see," I smile amiably. "Well, it looks nice."

He takes it off me and Lurch hands him a couple of small, red tubes which he shoves into the two barrels with two loud clacks. Ammo loaded, Fraser pulls the gun shut so it's a straight line again then he holds it out to me.

"Martin," he says. Lurch takes a clay disk from the case next to him and starts loading it into the launcher. With a quick glance at Emily - who is smiling from ear to ear, might I add - I take 'one of the finest hunting rifles ever made' and point the business end into the air.

I'm actually quite good at pretending I don't know how to shoot. As Fraser quite correctly said, Americans love their guns and I have been in situations before where people have handed me guns to hold or to shoot and I've had to feign a level of ignorance. It's not easy at first - try pretending not to know how to work a television. But practice makes perfect and acting is all part and parcel of living a lie.

"Like this?"

"Close enough," Fraser says. "Pull!"

Lurch does the pulling and the clay disk does the flying. It whips into the air so fast that I don't actually see it at first. Then it arcs into my field of view and quickly starts to shrink. I lead the target with the barrel of the rifle and know that if I pull the trigger right now, I get a clean hit. Forty yards. I leave it a little. The clay plate starts to drop towards the ground again and it's now nothing more than a red dot. I could still make the shot, easy. Sixty yards. Sixty five. Screw it. I was going to miss on purpose but I want to see Fraser's face when I blow the thing apart on my 'first go'.

I pull the trigger.

And miss the target altogether.

The clay pigeon drops into a bunch of trees in the distance. A gaggle of birds are, like me, disturbed by my lack of accuracy. They all take off and fly into the air, mocking me.

"Never mind, young man." Fraser takes the gun from me, smiling the biggest smile I've ever seen him throw in my direction. "It's not the same as using a fully automatic machine-gun is it?"

How the hell did that happen? I don't miss. Not shots like that, that was chicken feed to a guy like me. I mean, I've never actually shot the wings off a fly, but y'know what, I bet I could if I tried. It doesn't take me long to realise what it was, though. Arrogance. And you know where arrogance comes from? The same place as being bothered about stuff. And you know how much time me and 'being bothered about stuff' used to spend together before I met Emily?

You get my point.

"Perhaps you can give it another try some other time."

"Never mind, hon," Emily puts an arm around me. "If an intruder ever breaks into our house, you can sell him insurance. That'll send anyone packing."

I can't help but notice Fraser's smug grin fall away a little at this point and I know it's because he was reminded that his little angel would soon be shacking up with a guy. It was almost worth missing just to see that. Almost, but not quite.

"Martin, pack this lot up, will you? I'm going back to the house."

"Yes, Mr. Coleman," Lurch says in a surprisingly high, thin voice. Kind of makes me think of the first time I heard Mike Tyson speak.

"So, my dear…" (I assume Fraser isn't talking to me) "…tell me about your trip. Bad food, squealing babies, in-flight films you'd seen before?"

We have the pleasure of Fraser's company all the way back to the house. I tell Emily I'll bring all the bags in. She offers to help but I would rather make several trips to the bedroom and back all by myself if it buys me an extra couple minutes out of the Coleman family painting.

Leaving Emily and Fraser to go into the house, I start lugging cases. I lug a little under my threshold on each trip so I can extend the overall task time. Also, it gives me the opportunity to do some thinking.

I have a businessman from Yorkshire to kill and these things don't take care of themselves. First, there's the prep time. This starts with the surveillance. Learn the target's patterns, their comings and goings. This leads to the decision on where the deed will take place. You can get them at the most vulnerable part of their routine or at their most protected. You can show your face or you can hide it. Kill them during their normal activities or kidnap them to some other, more isolated location. It all depends on how you intend to do the deed. Gun close up, gun far away, poison, bare hands. It's like going to the candy shop with your gran and being told you can only pick one thing.

Then after you've chosen your method, you have to go out and pick up the appropriate equipment and weapons. I don't permanently own a lot of the tools of my trade for obvious reasons. The last thing I need is someone stumbling into my batcave full of guns, wire-garrottes, laser-scopes, vials of poison and printed-out papers of past kills. Most stuff, I pick up as I go and get rid of when the job's over. Most things I need are pretty readily available in most places so I don't need to bring stuff with me. Lunch is, as they say, provided.

Then last, but not least, is getting away with it. See, being an assassin sounds glamorous to the uninitiated but it's damn hard work. Most people who commit murder even once find it difficult to get clean away with. An assassin, by pure definition, has to get away with it time after time after time. (Although, if we're going to be pedantic, I don't consider what I do as murder. I consider what people do when they hire me as murder. But anyway…).

So all the stages need to be planned out. As I drop the last of our bags onto the orange-covered bed (and *man* is it orange), I know that it'll be a welcome peace to do the planning.

Okay, that's the bags done. Better go down and make nice with the in-laws-to-be. And by 'make nice' I mean 'constantly restrain myself from killing them'.

No, no. Got to stop thinking negatively about all this. Look on the bright side. If I was really just some normal guy - i.e. not secretly an assassin - then I'd still have to take all this crap but without the knowledge that if it all gets too much, I can shoot my way out. That's got to be a plus point.

As I leave our bedroom, shutting the imported French oak door behind me, I realise that's not really a plus point at all, the thing about killing Emily's parents. I obviously can't do that. If it all goes too far south, all's going to happen is me ditching this whole escapade like the bad idea it clearly is and getting on the first plane back to NYC.

Any other bright sides I can look on, then?

Of course there is.

There's my little assignment involving a Yorkshire businessman. That small job that I took on specifically to ease the pressure that this week is surely going to bring. Something that, whenever things start getting a little too stressful, I can excuse myself and go off and work on. Temporarily losing myself in a calm, serene world I know and can control. Away from this madhouse.

"Who's that?" I ask Emily as I come to the bottom of the stairs. The ample living room is spread out before me with big, comfy sofas and, even more impressively, the biggest plasma screen I've ever seen in my life on the far wall. Emily's sat on the nearest sofa to the bottom of the stairs browsing through a paper and sipping a cup of tea. Her dad's talking to some bearded guy at the other end of the room.

"Hey hon, I would have helped you take the bags up, you know. You all done?"

"Don't worry about it, all sorted."

"Cool. That's Geoff. Geoff Waterstone. That's Dad's partner in the business."

No way. Co-incidence. Got to be co-incidence.

"I've never seen him before."

"No, he's usually been at home when we've come over in the past."

"Where does he live?"

Don't say Doncaster.

"Doncaster."

"I've just remembered, I need to take my vitamins, I left them upstairs."

"You're supposed to take them first thing in the morning, every day!"

"I'll be right back. You want I should bring yours down?"

"Nah."

I try not to sprint back up the stairs. I walk fast. It makes me look pretty camp. I get back to our room and pull out my cellphone. A couple seconds later, I've pulled up the dossier and I'm scrolling down the page.

Geoff Waterstone. Yeah, I already knew that.

Address; blah, blah street, Doncaster. Okay, already knew that too. Birth town, Leeds. One kid, seventeen. Picture. Where's his -

Yup, there it is.

My nice, little, get-away-from-it-all sanity check job just happens to be my father-in-law-to-be's business partner.

I suddenly feel just like one of those clay pigeons.

seven :
bad company

OKAY, THINGS MAY not be as bad as they currently seem. Let's make like Mr. Spock and get all logical on this problem's ass.

Why did I take this job?

Am I desperate for work? Am I desperate for money? No and no. I mean, I'm always happy to fulfil my raison d'etre. But it's not like I'm addicted to it or I get the shakes if I don't work for, like, a couple weeks or something. I took this job as a way of winding back the stress dial this week. It was my pressure relief valve.

How would it have relieved pressure?

By taking me physically away from the people giving me the headaches and putting me into an easy job that could calm my mind.

How has that changed?

The guy works with Fraser. That means part of my prep will involve hanging around the very person who precipitated the need for getting away from it all in the first place. Also, the job becomes harder when you're a known factor in the target's environment. Killing them is just as easy but when the murder inquiry ensues, you're one of the people getting questioned. That doesn't usually happen if you drop them from a hotel window half a mile away and are on a plane home before the body starts to bleed.

So, what are my options?

Simple; stick or twist. Go ahead with the job or call the Agency and cancel. Not like I've never cancelled a hit before. It will, however, be the first time my reasons for cancelling have had anything at all to do with the target. On the three occasions I've cancelled in the past, they've all been because I've fallen ill. Cold, flu, stuff like that. I always keep a healthy emotional disconnection from my work so I've never cancelled because I couldn't bring myself to kill person X. That's the whole reason I'm a good assassin. I accept that I'm part of the process of killing, not part of the process of deciding to kill. Cancelling this hit because of who the target is would fly in the face of everything I've followed my entire career. Do I really want to set that kind of precedent for myself?

The answer, of course, is no.

As always, I'm going to put out of my head all thoughts of potential consequences. Even without me, tomorrow this guy could die in a car crash or a house fire or he could slip getting out the bath. People die from stuff like that all the time. And whatever repercussions come from that, Fraser and everyone else would have had to deal with. So, instead of slipping getting out the bath, he slips onto a .22 bullet. What's the difference?

So I'm going ahead with it. And, here come those bright sides again. Think about it, Mike. This is now a pretty difficult job. I have to carry it out in such a way that I'm beyond reproach when Columbo comes knocking. The challenge of this job - that's what'll be my pressure relief. Okay, he's a family friend so it'll put a downer on the wedding. I can live with that. As long as the wedding doesn't get cancelled.

Okay. The world's back on track. Normal service resumes. I close the file and put my mobile back into standby and pocket it. Then I take my vitamins because I actually did forget to do it this morning, on the plane. Then I go back downstairs.

"All vitamined up?"

"I can feel my body fighting off infection as we speak," I sit myself down next to Emily and sink further into the sofa than I thought I would. Damn, that's comfy.

"Your tea's cold, do you want me to warm it up for you?"

"I don't like tea, Em."

"I know you don't like tea but my mum made it 'specially. She'll be offended if you don't drink it."

Fraser and Geoff are still talking at the other end of the room. I can tell straight away that Fraser doesn't like Geoff much. And the feeling looks pretty mutual.

"How long have your dad and Geoff been partners?" I ask. I'm pretty sure that info ought to be in the dossier when I read it, but there's no harm in a little third-party research.

"Since the early days." Emily puts her paper down on her lap and we talk in hushed tones. "Dad started the business but Geoff came into it pretty soon after. Some kind of alliance of resources or something. I don't really pay that much attention to the detail."

"You like him?"

"Who, Geoff?"

I nod.

"Not really. He's a bit of an arse. Bit paranoid. Goes on about immigrants a lot."

I'm surprised to feel a rush of relief at her answer and I realise that the effect of Geoff's death on Emily was the one potential consequence I hadn't completely dismissed. I'm glad she's removed it as a concern. But I'm concerned it was there at all.

"So, he owns half the company?"

"Yep. It's always pissed Dad off, that. He's usually diplomatic when he talks to us about Geoff but I know he resents having to have brought Geoff in on things so early on. Well, at all, really."

Mary Coleman suddenly swings into my field of view as she comes pounding out of the kitchen. I don't think she's pounding on purpose but those high heels she always wears walking across these wood floors makes it sound like Assault on Precinct Thirteen. For some reason, 'Ride of the Valkries' starts playing in my head. She comes straight over to me.

"Michael, you haven't had your tea, it must be freezing cold by now," she says immediately like that's the only reason she even came into the room.

"I'm sorry, Mrs. Coleman, I'll go heat it up."

"If tea was meant to be heated up, it would come cold."

Someone's cell phone goes off. Out of the corner of my eye, I see Geoff excuse himself from his conversation with Fraser and take the call.

"Sorry, again, Mrs. Coleman. I know how long it took you to make it."

"Was that supposed to be a joke at my expense?"

"Mike, I've told you, call my parents by their first names."

Whatever news Geoff's being given, he isn't taking it too well.

"He most certainly will not," Mary says to Emily before turning to me. "You'll refer to me as Mrs. Coleman until after the wedding."

I nod. "Absolutely. Then I get to call you mom."

Mary is unimpressed. But Geoff is even less impressed. You can tell that when he suddenly shouts into his phone;

"Damn it woman, calm down!"

Everyone in the room stops talking and looks at the tall, dark-haired man as he talks to his apparently deliriously-babbling wife.

"You're not making any sense - say it again, slowly."

We all wait as she attempts to do just that.

"What do you mean 'missing'? A seventeen year old boy can't just go bloody missing!"

I'm guessing that Mrs. Waterstone is now telling her husband that their seventeen year old boy bloody has. That's what everyone else is guessing too, judging by the sudden looks of horror on their faces. We all wait in an uneasy silence as Geoff's wife continues telling him whatever she's telling him. This is the point where everyone's running through all the possibilities in their mind - has he been run over, is he lying in a ditch somewhere, has he run away, has he been kidnapped, is Mrs. Waterstone just a paranoid old dear and so on. Me, I'm thinking just one thing. I'm thinking that this may just push my job from 'interesting challenge' into the realm of 'too much trouble'.

"Okay, okay, I'm on my way. I'll be there in an hour. Just … look, I'll be there soon…" and Geoff Waterstone clicks his cell off. He has a kind of faraway look in his eyes, like he can't really believe what his wife's just told him.

"Geoff?" Fraser says, showing more concern for another human being (that isn't his daughter) than I thought he was capable of.

"Jeremy. Jeremy's gone missing. He's just … gone missing," Geoff keeps saying 'missing' like he doesn't understand what it means.

"Are you sure he hasn't just…" Fraser seems to search for the right words, "…run away?"

"Jean says his wallet and all his clothes are still at the house. He left to go to his friend's this morning and never got there. That was over eight hours ago."

"Maybe he got…" Emily seems to share her father's penchant for speaking before she knows exactly what words to use, "…sidetracked".

"He's a very sensible boy," Geoff says, suddenly galvanized into action by some internal switch that has just flicked. He starts gathering up all his papers and piles them into his briefcase. "He doesn't change what he's doing or where he's going without calling me or his mother. He knows better than that."

Geoff suddenly looks up at Fraser in a way that everyone in the room but me seems to miss. It's a weird look. Like a sudden realisation of something. But it only lasts a second. Less than a second. Then it's gone. And Geoff's packing just a little bit faster than before.

"You're not in a fit state to drive, Geoff, let me have someone take you ba-"

"I'll be *fine!*" the last word of that sentence seemed a little hostile to me. More than a little. But everyone else in the room, I think, has just taken it as the emotional instability of a man who's just been told his only son has disappeared without a trace.

He clicks his briefcase shut.

"I'll let you know what's going on when I get some more sense out of Jean," Geoff says. "The old girl's probably had too much sherry, you know how she is."

Fraser nods. "Let us know if there's anything we can do."

Geoff seems to flash that look again, but maybe it's just me. He just nods and walks very quickly out of the room. His quick, heavy footsteps on the wood floor in the hall have transformed into crunching footfalls out on the gravel drive before anyone in the living room even speaks.

"Well…" Fraser says, a little shell-shocked "…I don't really know what to say after that."

"Poor Jean," Emily says, her hand absently on my arm. "She must be beside herself."

"I'll go and make a pot of tea," Mary stops wringing her hands and turns toward the kitchen. Hooray for the salve to treat all English ills - a cup of tea'll find the silver lining to any cloud. I've always been convinced that if, during World War Two, Hitler had ever actually managed to invade and overrun Britain, the English, instead of panicking, would simply have put on a pot of tea. ('Well, really, you have to look on the bright side - all that chocolate and beer').

"Kind of puts what we were discussing into the shade a little bit." Fraser starts tidying up his own papers, a little more orderly than Geoff had.

"What was that?" I ask, not really sure why. Sometimes, a little voice tells me I should be nosey.

"Not that it's any of your business," my loving father in law to be says, "but we were discussing possible areas of expansion for Guardian Shipping, my company. *Our* company." He adds the last sentence on the end almost through gritted teeth.

I remind myself never to share ownership of Shepard Insurance with anyone. If having a business partner makes you that bitter... But then I remember who I'm talking about. Fraser Coleman was probably bitter about having to drink milk as a baby.

"I don't know what I'd do if anyone ever hurt my only child," he says, picking up the last few sheets of paper.

"Dad, stop it," Emily says, partially embarrassed, partially still thinking about Jeremy Waterstone. She sits back down onto the sofa and picks up her magazine again. She starts flicking through the pages but she isn't reading it. Her mind's obviously elsewhere. I realise I suddenly want to put my arms around her and tell her everything's going to be alright, that I'll always be around to make sure nothing bad ever happens to her. Just as suddenly, though, I can feel a pair of eyes burning into the side of my head. I turn.

And sure enough, Fraser is staring at me.

Without averting his gaze, he clicks his briefcase shut. We lock stares for a moment. I don't know exactly what he's thinking, but I know I don't like it.

"Kettle's boiling, tea'll be ready in a minute." Mary clacks back into the room.

Fraser's stone gaze is suddenly replaced by a broad smile.

"Don't let it go cold, this time, Michael, eh?"

eight :
eight a.m.

"WE'VE GOT A busy day ahead of us today, my dear," Emily says, "so you're going to be called upon to display unheard of levels of endurance."

Emily's sat in front of the most over-decorated lady's dressing table I've ever seen. The mirror's surrounded by a golden snake that winds its way up from one side of the table, over the mirror and down the other side. All along its back, there are those little fleur-de-lis symbols you find in the wallpaper of old people's houses. It makes it look like whoever's looking in the mirror's about to be strangled by the campest snake ever. To top that, there are lace doilies and curtain pelmets everywhere. I'm thinking we're at the ground zero blast of a bad taste bomb.

While the light of my life does her hair, I try to gauge how much ammo I can fit into my inside jacket pockets without looking like Santa Claus.

"Where else do we need to go apart from that wedding shop?" I ask.

"Wedding Belles."

"Yeah, apart from there."

"All over the place. We still need to confirm decorations for the top table, favours for the guests, I need to try on my dress, you need to try on your suit…"

"Okay," I wince in what I believe is actual, physical pain, "I know we've got a lot of places to go to make final arrangements and whatever, and that's going to be fun enough. But, seriously, does your mother have to come?"

"She's arranged most of this wedding, so far. She'd rather die than hand it over to us now."

I make no comment.

"Besides," Emily goes on as she holds one bit of dark brown hair in one position and sprays God knows what all over her head, "Auntie Hattie needs a few things and mum promised to show her the best shops in town to-"

"Seriously?"

"What?"

"Auntie Hattie."

"What about her?"

"You have an Auntie Hattie. A real live auntie named 'Hattie'."

"Mike, what's the matter with you?"

What's the matter with me? I'm psychic, that's what's the matter. I can see into the future. I can see Auntie Hattie's name written in an address book with a purple velour cover and a pen attached with a string. The book lives in the drawer of a little coffee-table in the hall. We're not allowed to move it. It lives there. The telephone is on top of the coffee-table. Next to the telephone is a pad and a small cup of pens (in case the string on the address book snaps). The walls are papered with fleur-de-lis of all different shades of orange. Outside, I'm washing the car because it's Sunday. And also because we have to go to the train station later. To pick up Auntie Hattie.

"Nothing, I'm fine."

Emily seems to read the state of my mind because she stops coating her hair (and my lungs, incidentally) with chemicals and turns to look at me like she has something real serious to say.

"Do you want to get married?"

Okay, that's pretty serious.

"What? Of course I want to get married! What -"

"Let me rephrase the question," she says. "Do you want to get married right now? At this point in your life?"

I try and throw over a light-hearted smile. "Whoa, Em, it's a little early in the a.m. to be getting into the deep and meaningfuls, I mean, I haven't even had any cereal ..."

"Mike, I'm serious."

I sigh. She's serious.

"Do I want to get married at this point in my life?" I repeat back to her.

"That's what I asked."

At this point in my life, I kill something like three people a month.

"Of course I want this. I want it right now, how can you even think I don't?"

Emily shrugs. "People quite often go into marriages with massive issues to sort out. And by people I mean men. And by issues, I mean not being able to get laid every night by a different woman before coming home and living off nothing but pizza."

"I hate pizza."

"Mike…"

"Alright!" I hold my hands up. "Sorry. Okay, look, being married, yeah, it'll be a shock to the system. I know that. I don't know what kind of shock, exactly, I mean I have … visions … But I don't know for sure. I don't know what I'll turn into. I don't know what you'll turn into. I don't know where we'll live or what kind of cars we'll start driving. But there's one thing I'm pretty damn sure of …" I walk round the bed and hold one of her hands in mine. "I know that I'm getting married to you. And I know nothing's going to stop me."

I'm so damn sincere.

All the tense energy suddenly seems to drain out of her body, her shoulders slump and she even smiles a little.

"I'm being silly, aren't I?"

"Hey," I kiss her hand, "women are genetically programmed to think too much. And men are genetically programmed to get cold feet before marriage," I shrug. "It's a caveman thing."

"That's your excuse for everything." She kisses my hand then drops it and picks up her hairspray again. "I still cannot believe that copper went for it that time."

"Speeding's a caveman thing, Em, he was a man, he understood."

I go back to picking out what jacket I'm wearing today. Emily goes back to burning a hole in the ozone layer. Inside, I sigh a sigh of relief.

I hate lying to her. I mean, I wasn't lying when I said I was going to get married to her. That's definitely on. I just wish I could just tell her everything about myself. My job, my past, everything. But I know better.

Some people think you have to wipe the slate clean before you go into a marriage. Tell all. Confess your ass off. I don't really go along with that. I mean, if you have anything that needs confessing that bad, all's going to happen is you'll just scare the person off. No, in my opinion, these are the things you release when the time is right. The onus is on you to pick someone who you think'll be able to handle it when it comes.

That's what I realise I've done with Emily. She's strong. Stronger than probably she even knows. Don't get me wrong, I'm not saying she'll take it in her stride. She'll freak. My God, she'll freak. Anyone would if faced with a .22 cross-threaded pistol silencer dropping out of their spouse's pants as they're sorting out the laundry. But she'll handle it in the end.

So, yeah, I'm maybe a little shocked at the sudden realisation that I planned on telling Emily the truth all along. But it's a good kind of shocked. I'll tell her everything. When she's ready. Maybe in a year, maybe in five years. Who knows? Someday. Someday, she'll know everything.

Just not today.

nine :
the sun tzu guide to weddings

I LOOK AROUND me. There are people all over, all with their orders. Their missions are set. They're armed. Ready for battle. There's no room for compassion here. It's them or it's you. And believe me, they will tear you a new asshole before they let you have the last of the pastel pink table flower bouquets.

War is hell.

"Emily, go to the left, Hattie, go to the right. If you see the table cloth we're after in the correct colour shade and with the correct pattern, call my mobile and tell me where you are. I'll be checking down the middle. Find shop assistants to help if you can. Michael, you'd better go with Emily since you clearly have no idea what's going on."

"No complaints from me."

"What was the colour code again?"

"K36, Hattie, do pay attention!"

"Sorry, Mary," Hattie adjusts her headscarf. I swear, it looks like a salute. "K36, got it."

"Come on, then! Let's look lively!" Mary stomps off into battle and her lieutenants fan out into the underbrush.

We go deep into enemy territory. Emily converses with one of the locals in their language. She speaks the tongue fluently, smoothly enquiring about 'overlays' and 'accents' and something that sounds like 'tulip orb'. After the largely unintelligible interchange, Emily turns and starts walking.

"This way."

She doesn't even take the time to look at me, such is the desperate importance of this mission.

'Wedding Belles' is the premiere wedding superstore in Nottingham (so the brochure says) and it'll serve all your wedding-based obsessions under one roof. Well, maybe any regular wedding-based obsessions - but Emily's mother and the word 'regular' don't even belong in the same language. This is just the first stop in a tour of duty that'll take us the length and breadth of Nottingham's city centre looking for all things marital. I'm pretty sure that when Robin Hood and Maid Marian got hitched, all they needed was Friar Tuck, the merry men and a couple trees. There was no mention of ice sculptures, swans bearing silk ring cushions or choreographed butterfly releases.

Yet here we are in 'Wedding Belles' (I love the name, by the way; must've taken someone all of eight seconds to come up with). Our mission; table cloth. Consequences of success; the correct style of table cloth. Consequences of failure; having to make do with something that will look so similar, nobody will know the difference.

You're obviously thinking what I'm thinking - failure is not an option.

We look like we're making progress; the layout of the surrounding terrain seems to suggest we're getting near our target. But it's Hattie, the veteran, that sends up a flare first. Even over the din of all the combatants attending their individual and group assignments, the polyphonic magnificence of 'Land of Hope and Glory' will not be denied.

We adjust our waypoint accordingly and set off on our new heading to rendezvous with our strike partner. When we arrive at her location, though, we find her already engaged in battle. Worse, she's pinned down by enemy fire.

"I saw it first," this young blonde says. She's backed up by another, slightly older blonde. Their fire is relentless but Auntie Hattie's got shots of her own.

"You didn't grab it first, my dear, and that's what matters I'm afraid."

I don't know if Hattie and Mary are related or just friends but one thing's for sure - they both shoot from the hip.

"Look, stop being such a cantankerous old cow and hand it over," the older blonde sprays a short but directed burst toward Auntie Hattie.

"Well since you ask so nicely, I'll definitely hand it over now." Hattie returns before shaking her head. "Who says young people today have no manners?"

The 'it' that everyone's so desperate to get (or keep) their hands on is a big, oblong plastic packet with a beige (everything in this shop is beige) table cloth folded up inside. There are about eight hundred other table cloths on the shelf next to Auntie Hattie that all look exactly the same to me. But then, I don't have my 'FEMALE X100 Filter Visor' on. With that little piece of equipment, the beige table cloth Hattie's holding onto couldn't be more different from the other beige table cloths.

And, as I believe Obi-Wan Kenobi once said to Luke Skywalker, an awful lot of things depend greatly on your point of view.

Emily comes to Auntie Hattie's rescue, all guns blazing.

"Who are you calling a cantankerous old cow? At least her hair colour isn't out of a bottle."

The older blonde fixes this new combatant with a disdainful stare. "Oh right, blue's a natural colour now, is it?"

No weapon is off limits in guerrilla warfare.

One half of me is thinking I need to get involved in this skirmish and help out my fiancée. But the other half (the intelligent half) tells me that I'd be like a kid with a BB gun compared to these Uzi-carrying death maidens out of some John Woo flick, blasting round after round as they fly through the air in slow motion.

And talking about flying through the air in slow motion, here comes the cavalry.

Hattie and Mary have probably been double-teaming like this for decades, maybe ever since shops started selling stuff. Hattie and the blondes are trading shots, swapping blows, no quarter asked for and none given. Emily gets a few double-taps off too but even she knows when to step back and let the professionals play. And playing they are; Hattie holds the Holy Grail of Tablecloths out at arm's length. The blondes think they've won. They think they see the white flag of surrender pop up from over the hill. When in reality, it's a positioning marker to let the air force know where to fly over.

"At least you've come to your senses," the younger blonde is saying as she reaches out for the packet. But she never gets it.

Mary's flight path brings her right through the centre of the clearing and, without stopping, she scoops up the prize and stomps straight out the other side.

"Hey!" both blondes shout at the same time and even Emily's caught off guard with that one. Only Hattie knew what was coming; she's standing there now with the biggest, smuggest grin on her face. The blondes are both stood there not knowing whether to chase this new target or finish off the one they were originally entangled with. But in this game, you hesitate and you're lost.

Mary's got the thing zapped, paid for and bagged so fast, she's even had time to tut at the fact the checkout girl's top button isn't fastened up.

"Come on you three," she calls at us from the door. "We haven't got time to dawdle. Our next task awaits."

Such is the life of the soldier. Victory's only reward is new battles.

And new battles is what we get. The war takes us from the densely populated jungles of 'Wedding Belles', through the desert conflict of 'Till Cakes Us Do Part' and onto the urban, guerrilla warfare of 'Hats R' Us'. No R&R allowed, each victory sees us shipped off to the next theatre. The shops begin to blur into one, long, searing hell until, eventually, I just can't take it anymore.

Some soldiers have been known to blow off a toe so they can catch the next train to the nearest hospital. Not that this doesn't cross my mind, but I'm thinking that's maybe not a 'first base' kind of idea. I think, maybe, something a little less self-deforming to start with. But I will move onto the removal of body parts if and when it becomes absolutely necessary.

"You know what, guys," I say as we emerge from a department store that reminded me a little too much of Libya that time with the broken down manure truck, "I'm going to have to take my leave of you -"

"What?" Mary isn't pleased.

"- temporarily, just so I can … do some stuff …"

"What stuff?" Emily asks.

"Well, since you forced it out of me, I've gotta go pick up a present for your mother."

"Oh, I didn't know you'd-"

"Well, surprise is all ruined now…"

"Well, she doesn't know what it is, so, you know, still a surprise..."

"…suppose…"

"Michael," Mary huffs as I ram a wrench right into the middle of her well-oiled war machine, "we're on our way to choose the streamers for the side of the marquee."

"Just…pick out something I'd like. I'll meet you at the suit place? In an hour?"

Since I'm already moving away from them, Mary admits temporary defeat. "Not a second later! Use that clock up there so there's no excuses." She points at the big, domed, hundred year old clock tower overlooking the Old Market Square. I turn back to her and give a quick salute. I blow a kiss to my fiancée. And I completely blank Auntie Hattie (if you'd spent the morning with her, you'd be the same, don't judge me).

Then I turn and try to stop myself from running for my life.

The hour, like three months in an army hospital recovering from a mysterious toe injury, goes depressingly fast.

I spend most of it up at the castle, talking to Laurent Cissé. Whenever I'm working in Europe and in need of something a little more sophisticated than a hotel window and a sniper rifle, I call on this guy. Me and a whole bucketful of other assassins. For the last fifty years or so. The guy's a legend in our circles. Consultant. Got a million and one ideas on how to carry out any given job under any given situation. As if that wasn't good enough, he also provides the equipment required to carry out his advice (at very reasonable prices, so he tells us). Guy's been a major player for decades and he only does face to face meetings. But discretion, as they say, is his middle name. He don't talk about us, we don't talk about him. He's an institution in our world, everybody loves him. He's kind of like your favourite uncle who you go to for advice about girls or school or how to hit a Head of State in a heavily guarded military installation.

We chat for a while, he's glad to have the opportunity to come to Nottingham, he's never been before. Doesn't really make a habit of coming to England. He says he's happy for me getting married but sad for me having to suffer a wedding day. People in our profession are usually very private characters, he says, so being the centre of attention like that's kind of like someone burning you alive with a giant magnifying glass. But, he tells me, if there's a free bar then there's hope that the day will eventually blur into one of the most memorable days you ever forgot the details of.

Then we wander through the gardens that cover the old castle grounds; the sun beats down on us, tourists are taking pictures of Robin Hood's statue, kids are running around all over the place and Laurent tells me how I can kill Geoffrey Waterstone tonight.

a MIKE SHEPARD film

a DENIAL STUDIOS production

starring
JOSH HOLLOWAY
ELIJAH WOOD
MALCOLM McDOWELL as 'GERALD'

INT. KITCHEN, KING'S SCHOOL, SOI 8, PATTAYA, THAILAND - MORNING
The kitchen is a little run down but homely. A steaming cup of tea sits on the table while a man, around thirty, works languidly over a sizzling hot stove. He's wearing a vest and jeans and is sweating in the Thai heat (working over a stove isn't helping, either). He stops now and again to smell the aroma of the bacon and eggs he's cooking. His name is LUKE. He speaks with a drawling Texan accent. He sounds like George Bush.

A much younger man - maybe seventeen - is sat at the table, sipping a glass of water. He looks pre-occupied.

The door opens and in walks an older man, maybe fifty, fifty-five. He's wearing a bright, clean set of pyjamas under an immaculately pressed robe with some kind of crest on the chest pocket. His appearance is at odds with the run down kitchen around him. His name is GERALD. As he enters the room, he stops for a moment to take in the sight of Luke cooking breakfast and the young man sat drinking water. He 'humphs' under his breath then sits down at the table. When he speaks, he sounds like the well spoken Englishman he is.

> GERALD
> Good morning, all.

> LUKE
> Morning, Ger. Tea's on
> the table. Heard you

comin' down so I jus'
poured it.

>   GERALD
>   Thank you...

>   LUKE
>   Luke.

>   GERALD
>   ...Luke. Thank you,
>   Luke, most kind.

He's about to drink from the cup but pauses and
looks over it at the young man.

>   GERALD
>   What's in it?

>   LUKE
>   The tea?

Gerald nods.

>   LUKE
>   Water. Milk. Two
>   sugars. A teabag.

Luke turns to look at Gerald for the first time
since he entered the room. He has a cocky grin
on his face.

>   LUKE
>   Don't worry, Ger, I
>   ain't gonna poison you.

Gerald smiles thinly, nods then starts to sip
his tea. From his expression, we can tell it's
actually a damn good cup of tea. Luke grins and
returns his attentions to the cooker.

>   LUKE
>   So, what did you have
>   in mind for today, Ger?

>   GERALD
>   Well, marking. Then, I
>   have a class at ten.

                    Then more marking. Some
                    preparation. Maybe a
                    spot of lunch. Then
                    another class at one.
                    Another at two. Then I
                    was going to go into
                    Pattaya. Get a ticket
                    to Bangkok.
                              (beat)
                    I meant to do it
                    yesterday.

Luke smiles at him, briefly. Gerald returns with
another thin, humourless smile.

                    LUKE
                    I love Thailand. Did
                    you see that place in
                    town? 'The Porn Hotel'.
                    I mean, they just don't
                    hide it, huh? The kid
                    thought it was funny as
                    shit. Tell him.

The teenager nods at Gerald with a brief flicker
of a smile forced onto his face. Yeah, I found
it funny as shit. I laughed my ass off. He
returns to his water.

Gerald decides to be a little conversational.

                    GERALD
                    Interesting time of
                    year right now, don't
                    you think? Songkran.
                    Thai new year.

                    LUKE
                    Yeah, I know. I already
                    got jumped by three
                    punk kids with water
                    pistols over on the
                    Sukhumvit.

Gerald seems to be loosening up a little, now.

                    GERALD
          The water, I can
          handle. It's when they
          throw in the flour...

                    LUKE
          Don't get me started on
          that, Ger, just don't.
          This hair don't look
          this good naturally,
          y'know. Takes lots a'
          work. An' when those
          punks take to attackin'
          me with buckets of
          water and bags of
          flour...

                    GERALD (laughing)
          I've taken to carrying
          a gun, now!

                    LUKE (suddenly
          concerned)
          Really?

Gerald nods over to the corner of the room.
Resting against the back door is a Master
Blaster Super Soaker IV.

                    LUKE (relieved
          smile)
          Goddamn, lookit that
          beast! Must be a two-
          hander to lift when
          it's full!

                    GERALD
          One of my students got
          it for me the day
          before yesterday. He
          said 'now you soak them
          good, Mister Banks, so
          they no soak you first
          - you no afford replace
          another suit'!

Gerald and Luke laugh their asses off. The young
man doesn't really move a muscle. Just continues
sipping his water. Gerald puts down his tea,

nearly finished, and wipes a tear away from his
eye as his and Luke's laughter starts to die
down.

                    GERALD
          So, Luke - am I
          actually going to be
          able to eat any of that
          bacon before you kill
          me?

                    LUKE
          Well, I ain't cookin'
          it for myself, Ger.

The teenager blanches and looks like he's about
to be sick. His gaze is still locked on the far
wall. Gerald looks at him, momentarily, but
focuses back on Luke.

                    GERALD
          Well, good. A condemned
          man is entitled to a
          last meal.

                    LUKE
          Well, Xing don't think
          so. But I'm a lot more
          of a nice guy than him.
          Breakfast was my idea.

                    GERALD
          Well I can only be
          grateful that Xing
          employs men of such
          honour.

Apparently satisfied with the quality of the
bacon and eggs, Luke spoons them onto a plate.

                    LUKE
          I'm only a poor
          American, Ger, so I
          can't tell if that was
          a genuine statement or
          if your sophisticated
          British sense a' humour
          was bein' sarcastic on
          my ass.

Luke places the plate in front of Gerald along
with a knife and fork.

> LUKE
> But, under the
> circumstances, I guess
> a little sarcasm can be
> permitted.

> GERALD
> Why, thank you, Luke.
> For the permission and
> for the breakfast.
> (smells the food)
> Now that smells good.
> (eats some)
> My compliments, young
> man. I don't believe
> I've had a better
> English breakfast from
> American hands.

Luke spins a chair round and straddles it. Now
all three are sat at the table.

> LUKE
> Hey, don't thank me,
> thank the kid here.
> He's a Limey, he showed
> me how to make bacon
> and eggs like the
> Limeys like it.

> GERALD
> My compliments, young
> man.

'The Kid' barely moves. He looks like someone
scared witless. Gerald looks at him properly for
the first time.

> GERALD
> Don't worry. I'm sure
> it will all be over
> quite quickly.

Michael looks at Gerald properly for the first
time, too. An expression comes over his face –

but it's hard to tell if he's comforted by
Gerald's words or if they've made him feel
worse.

> LUKE
> Aw, he'll be fine,
> won't you Mikey. He's a
> strong kid.
>> (to GERALD)
> Y'know, it wouldn't
> have made a scrap a'
> difference if you'd got
> that ticket and got
> outta dodge yesterday.
> He'd still a' found
> you. You know that,
> right?

Gerald nods, resignedly, while eating.

> LUKE
> Still, you gotta try, I
> guess.

Gerald nods again, smiling thinly, remorsefully.
Then takes another forkful of bacon.

> LUKE
> Maybe next time, you'll
> keep your nose outta
> the business of people
> who're clearly
> gangsters.
>> (to MICHAEL)
> Almost a year, this
> guy's been annoyin'
> Xing, you believe that?

> GERALD
> If by annoying, you
> mean trying to get him
> to throw some of his
> vast wealth in the
> direction of this
> scandalously
> underfunded school for
> orphans...

                    LUKE
          That's the definition
          I'm usin'.

Gerald smiles, like he's just remembered
something amusing.

                    LUKE
          What's so funny?

                    GERALD
          Oh, it just reminds me
          of a story someone once
          told me. About a
          reporter who was
          interviewing a Jew at
          the Wailing Wall. She
          said what are you
          praying for? He said
          peace between the Jews
          and the Muslims, an end
          to war, wise world
          leaders. She asked him
          how long he'd been
          coming. He said fifty-
          five years. She asked
          him how he felt after
          that length of time. He
          replied 'like I'm
          talking to a bloody
          wall'.

Luke laughs his ass off again. Gerald smiles but
doesn't laugh too much. He's mopping up the last
of the yolk with the last of the bacon.

                    LUKE
          I like that one, man.
          That's a good one. I'll
          have to remember that
          one.

                    GERALD
          My point is, sometimes,
          you have to just do
          something. It might
          work out, it might not.
          But at least you tried
          to do something.

                    LUKE
          Ger, stealin' money
          from a Thai gangster,
          ain't just doin'
          somethin'. It's doin'
          somethin' stupid.

                    GERALD
          It seemed like a good
          idea at the time.

                    LUKE
          Even though you knew
          what kinda man Xing
          was. Even though you
          knew what woulda'
          happened if he found
          out it was you.

Gerald shrugs.

                    LUKE
          You're a decent man,
          Ger. You shouldn't'a
          got yourself involved
          in shit like that. You
          should'a got someone
          else to sort that stuff
          out. Someone suited.
          People like you start
          tryin' to act like
          people like me, only
          one thing's gonna
          happen.
                    (beat)
          Ain't that right,
          Mikey?

Michael suddenly puts his glass of water down
and gets to his feet. He pulls out a Browning 85
with silencer and points it at Gerald's head.
Gerald stands up slowly, with dignity. And
stares right back along the gun at the teenager.

Michael pulls the trigger. There's almost no
sound at all. Gerald falls backward, a tiny red
hole in the middle of his forehead. He falls
back against the wall, sparing us the view of

the back of his head which most definitely did
not get off as lightly as the front.

Michael stands stock still for a moment, the gun
still in the same position. He lowers it slowly.
Luke didn't move the whole time. He's still
straddling the chair backwards, his arms folded
across the chair back, his chin rested on his
hands. When he speaks, he doesn't take his eyes
off Gerald.

>   LUKE
>   You wanna puke, go
>   ahead. Rather you do it
>   here than in the car.

Michael doesn't puke, though he looks like he
wants to.

>   LUKE
>   It would'a been the
>   easiest thing in the
>   world to take you to
>   some of the real
>   scumbags on my joblist.
>   But there's no point
>   one a' them bein' your
>   first. Even folks don't
>   like killin' wouldn't
>   find it too hard to cap
>   one a' them child
>   molestin' drug dealers.
>   You needed someone like
>   Gerald. Someone decent.
>   Someone who didn't
>   deserve to die.

Michael looks at Luke, now.

>   LUKE
>   You kill someone like
>   that, you may just have
>   a future in this
>   business. Work for Xing
>   for a few years then go
>   freelance. Heck, you
>   might even get yourself
>   picked up by one a'
>   them big brokers like

                    the Agency one day.
                    Wouldn't that beat all
                    get out?

Michael swallows, still looking at Gerald's
crumpled heap. He slowly puts the gun away. Luke
sighs, taking one last look at Gerald himself.

                         LUKE
                    Come on, I could go for
                    some noodles.

END OF ACT 3

eleven :
talk radio

"THAT WAS 'SHAKE Down' by Ken E. Great song, great song. Okay, next on the line we have Derek from Stoke-on-Trent. Evening, Derek."

"Hello."

"Now, you've got a problem with your wife, haven't you? Why don't you run us through it?"

"Well…"

"Just take your time."

"…well, me and my wife, Jasminder…we've been married about four years?"

"Now, Jasminder, she's Indian isn't she?"

"Yes…"

"And you're not, are you?"

"No, Alan, I'm caucasian. Jasminder and I met in a bar one night in town? We just really got on. Really clicked? She said she wasn't into Indian men because she was supposed to be in an arranged marriage but, basically, ran away from her family."

"In India?"

"Ashton-under-Lyme."

"Okay."

"So anyway, we eventually got married and things were going really well. We were really happy? Well, I was, but maybe she wasn't because I found out she was sleeping with this Indian guy from her work?"

"Even though she said she wasn't into Indian men…"

"She was really apologetic about it. Really sorry? She thought maybe it was just in her system and she needed to get it out."

"I take it you gave her another chance."

"I took her back, yeah. As long as it was out of her system and everything?"

"But she did it again."

"Five more times."

"Always with Indian men."

"Yes, Alan."

"Well, Derek, I think it's pretty obvious she's not as averse to Indian men as she thinks."

"But Alan, I just don't know what to do."

I'll tell you what to do, Derek. Pack your bags and move to Idaho. Or kick her out the house. Divorce her. Upend her wardrobe out the window. Anything, just don't stay married to her.

"Well, what does your heart tell you, Derek?"

"I can't bring myself to leave her, Alan. I really love her, you know?"

Derek, old boy, you deserve everything that happens to you.

I don't make a habit of listening to night-time radio. For some reason, radio bosses believe that, as soon as it gets dark, we don't want to listen to music anymore. No, we want to listen to depressed losers whine about their sorry, misbegotten lives.

I once read in some Zen book that the answer to any problem is simply the opposite of the problem. I don't get why Derek and his tormented ilk can't figure that out; the answer to any of their problems is staring them in the face. Derek, leave your wife and you'll stop having a wife that cheats on you. Guy from Leeds, stop eating so much and you won't be as depressed about your weight. Woman from Basingstoke whose husband spends all his time working on his car, burn his car. Either he spends more time with you or he leaves you and you can find someone else - either way's a winner.

I reach forward to turn the radio off.

Instead, I turn it up.

Okay, I admit it, these people fascinate me. They wallow and wallow in their emotion until they're paralysed by it. It's not a state of affairs I'm particularly used to. I'm blessed with the ability to see what needs doing and just do it. No muss, no fuss. Emotional turmoil's for the birds. That's why I can do the job I do. There's nothing about the situation of my targets that I'm the least bit bothered about.

Well, at least that's how it normally goes. This job I'm on now, though, well it's hovering on the outskirts of giving me bad thoughts. I mean, it's all Em's fault. If I didn't love her, I totally wouldn't be bothered about Geoffrey being a family friend. Or about him being Emily's dad's business partner. And I sure as hell wouldn't care that his son's just gone missing. A racehorse doesn't care what kind of plant the hedge is made out of, it just gets its ass over it.

But it kind of itches that someone I care about will be affected by me carrying out my job. Hell, it itches that I care about someone period. So maybe that's why I decided to just go ahead and get this job done. No stringing it out, no keeping it for when conversations about the order of service get me too steamed. Just get it done and dusted. Before I start turning into Derek. 'Cause that'd be really bad?

I wind the window down a tad. Even at nearly half past ten at night, it's pretty warm out and this rustbucket I'm sat in's baking me alive. It's got no CD player (hence I ended up listening to the radio), no A/C, no electric windows and - pretty crucially from my point of view - no security. Joyriders love stealing older cars with no security. We don't care how old it is as long as it'll drive us around at eighty miles an hour and as long as it'll burn real nice at the end of the night. And if all that youthful, over-exuberant speeding gets it involved in a hit and run that kills, oh, say, a Yorkshire businessman as he drives home, well that's the way it goes. As long as we remember to keep our gloves on the whole time and dust everything down before we throw the gasoline on - just to make sure. (By the way, I've consulted with Laurent Cissé on several occasions and he's always come up with elegant, foolproof solutions – this time he comes up with 'crash into them with your car'? Seriously? 'Sometimes the best way to disguise a small sound is with a great noise' he says. Me, I just think he's bored and, just for the crack, decided to give me clearly terrible advice and see if I still blindly followed it. Either that, or my French is *not* as good as it needs to be.)

The hardest thing about tailing old-Geoffey-boy from his (very nice, very big) house on the outskirts of Doncaster into the town centre and finally to this movie theatre parking lot was keeping this old heap going in a straight line. I had a go on one of those mechanical bulls in a bar in Texas once - this was a lot like that. Seriously, a lot. I figure after I've finished and put this bucket to the torch, I'll be doing the owner a cast-iron favour for sure.

So keeping this thing on the road was a bit of an ask but tailing Geoffrey, that was easy as easy comes. Almost as easy as excusing myself from Chez Coleman for the evening to go track down an 'old friend' who I suspected lived in the greater Robin Hood area. Dumping the BMW somewhere safe and out of the way and 'picking up' this J-reg heap, that was simplicity itself. And of course, staking out Waterstone Castle and then following Geoff when he emerged about an hour ago wasn't just a piece of cake, it was the whole cake, the icing and the flimsy card box it came in. Yeah, most everything that led to this point was pretty textbook and stuff that I've done maybe a thousand times.

The one thing that was a little bit of a headscratcher was why Geoffrey had pulled into the parking lot of Doncaster's main movie theatre. I didn't think that a man whose son had just gone missing was going to put watching the new James Bond flick at the top of his 'to do' list. But pretty soon, the puzzlement was lifted; no sooner had he killed his engine, he got out of his car and into the bright red hatchback that was parked next to him. He was meeting someone. I force myself not to ask the most burning question; who is he meeting? I don't ask it. I didn't ask it just now. I'm just describing how I didn't ask it. I don't care. As soon as he's finished with whoever it is and he heads off, he has a date with the front end of my car. So who he's meeting is pretty damn irrelevant.

Wonder who he's meeting?

See, this is the problem when you're personally involved, no matter how slight, no matter how many degrees separated. I know this guy, I know what's been happening to him over the last twenty-four hours. And not just from impartial pre-hit observation, but from being involved in his life, even if only by association.

They've been sat in there a while. I can see a little. I can see he's meeting a woman. First thought was 'mistress'. But the body language is all wrong. Looks more like a business meeting. In fact, it looks like they've never even met before tonight.

The woman, far as I can tell from this distance, isn't an unattractive soul. Dirty blonde hair. Practical looking; y'know, no make-up, hair tied back, clothes that are scruffy but easy to move around in. She's got one of those non-threatening faces you feel like you've seen a million times before. A good assassin face, i.e. forgettable.

There's no smiling going on, just talking. Ol' Geoff looks stressed. Probably hasn't slept since he got the news about Jeremy. That's good. His reactions'll be slower. Make it easier to get him in one clean motion rather than draw it out. Less painful for him, less suspicious for me (I mean, how many joyriders accidentally crash into the same car three times in quick succession?).

"So Derek, you promise you'll have it out with Jasminder, okay? Tell her you aren't going to put up with this. She has to make her mind up; either it's you or someone else. She can't have both. Okay?"

"Yes, Alan. As soon as she comes in. Although she said I shouldn't wait up because she was going to be really late."

"Where is she?"

"I'm not sure. Some work thing?"

Hello, meeting's over. Geoff's going back toward his car. I have to hand it to him; this parking lot's the perfect place for a clandestine meeting. You go somewhere too quiet, all it takes is some nimrod to come strolling past and you're discovered. Somewhere too busy and you have increased risk of someone present being nosy enough to eavesdrop your conversation. Parking lots, though, have just the right amount of people - especially at this time of night. And best of all, people are always on their way through, it's not a destination in itself. Good thinking on Geoff's part to choose this place. Unless it wasn't his idea - unless it was the woman's.

He's gunning his engine. I gun mine. There's a half dozen cars leaving the car park at the same time as us so I can stand to follow pretty close without looking too conspicuous. His Lexus pulls out of its space and I slowly begin to move off-

- and then slam my brakes on as a bright red hatchback screeches out and stops right in front of me, blocking me off from following my target.

The bright red hatchback belonging to the woman Geoffrey'd just met.

She jumps out of her car and comes stomping toward me, saying something. I can't really hear her because, apart from having my windows mostly closed, all my attentions are focused on the black Lexus pulling unhurriedly out of the parking lot, indicating and then disappearing effortlessly into the night.

I'm so mad that at first, I can't even move. I'm mad at this woman for intercepting me but mostly I'm mad at myself for letting her. The paralysis quickly lifts, though, and I jump out of my car to have it out with this woman before I realise what an insanely ill-thought-out move I've just committed myself to. Already one or two rubberneckers are looking over at the priceless sight of two drivers getting into a rumble.

I want to say something but I suddenly realise I have absolutely no idea what. It isn't helped by the fact this crazy woman is actually smiling.

"Well, well," she says, grinning like she's bumped into an old college buddy, "you know what, it's been a while since I've been in the presence of a real live assassin. This is so exciting! Hey, want to go for a drink?"

twelve :
vodka before bedtime

"LADIES AND GENTLEMEN, you have no idea the treat you are in for tonight. If you thought you were just goin' to come out tonight to 'ave a few pints, chat up a couple a' birds or fellas and scoff a kebab on't way 'ome, you 'ad no idea what lay in wait for you 'ere, in this establishment, this very night.

"This fella's wowed crowds from Southend to Land's End, from Manchester to Colchester, from Northampton to Southampton and all the 'amptons in between. Fresh from 'is latest conquering raids in deepest, darkest Coalville, Leicestershire, I bring you your new ruler...

"Julius Pleaser!"

The crowd goes wild. A fairly rounded individual jumps up onto the stage with a circle of olive leaves on his head and a toga on and he looks suspiciously like he's going to – yep, there it goes. Now, there's no toga. Just the olive leaves and a union jack thong.

The crowd lose their collective minds.

Welcome to Monday night in Doncaster town centre.

Now, Doncaster, far as I know, is a fine town with a rich coal mining history and respectable people. But like most places in this overworked, underpaid country, as soon as the sun goes down, it don't matter how fine the place is or how respectable the people are, everyone has three very simple aims; Get drunk. Get kebab. Get laid. Usually, but not always, in that order.

Phase one is all but complete for most; the pints and shots have been flowing, spilling and regurgitating for hours. The groundwork for phase three is well underway with levels of sophistication brought to bear that would shock and awe lesser minds.

"Get yer coat, luv, you've pulled. Soon's I've finished this pint, I'll let you call us a taxi."

The romeo on the next table over draws my gaze. Kitted out in his *vêtements du guerre* (black shoes, black pants, white shirt, pint in one hand), the guy's in full tilt hunt mode. He's managed to latch himself onto a group of young ladies and, impressively, separate one from the protection of the pack. Easy pickings if he doesn't strike too early. She giggles and says something about him being funny. He's clearly having trouble focusing.

All these things vie for my attention in the way that things do when you're faced with something so mind-blowingly important that it really should be commanding every thought in your head. Like when a doctor tells you you've got six months to live and all you can think of is how you've been in his office for an hour and he hasn't touched his computer, like, once, so why's he even have it?

I try to get back on-mission.

"Okay, let me go over this again, let me get this straight," I say, "just so's I understand it. Geoff hired you to find Jeremy."

"Correct," Sarah Jane says while trying to decide which of the three shot glasses in front of her to go for first. "He hired me tonight."

"And you spotted me watching him."

"Yup."

"And you managed to pick me out of the background because you used to be-"

"I used to be an assassin." She goes for the centre shot glass. "Damn good one, too."

She sounds proud.

I shake my head, this is so bad. "And, what, you made me straight away?"

"Yeah. Well, no. After you'd been there a while," she gulps some of her chocolate vodka and shudders briefly. "Hooyah."

I really don't know what to make of this woman. She seems like the kind of person who'd stumble across real, live aliens and just ask them if they'd heard tonight's lottery results. Here she is discussing something pretty much life and death – maybe hers – with three different flavours of vodka lined up on the table in front of her.

I look around me again and try to figure out what is very fast turning into the most surreal night of my adult life. I don't know what's more strange – this crazy woman or the fact we're talking openly about being assassins in the middle of a crowded room. She assured me that a packed bar with deafening music and scores upon scores of totally drunk people is 'so the best place' to talk about stuff you don't want anyone to overhear. So far, it seems to be working.

She smiles at me as she holds the half-finished vodka near her mouth. She looks really amused. "You really want to shoot me, don't you?"

"The thought had crossed my mind."

"Don't worry, I won't take it personally. If people don't want to shoot me, I take it as a sign I'm not doing my job properly."

"That's why you told me you'd picked me out, right? To keep me from going after Geoffrey. Keep me with you, figuring out if and how to kill you off."

She winks at me and takes another sip of vodka. "And I'm still alive because…?"

"You know what, I really don't know," I say. "No-one's ever made me before. Maybe I'm still in a state of shock."

"No-one?" she seems genuinely shocked. "Ever? Bullshit."

"Not unless I revealed myself."

"Ever?"

"Seriously."

She looks suitably impressed. I think she whistles but the deafening roar of the crowd as Julius Pleaser shakes his moneymaker drowns it out.

"Holy crap, you're good," she shakes her head.

"Apparently," I say, "so are you."

She smiles again and raises her half-finished chocolate vodka. "I am that." Then she downs the rest of it and slams the empty glass upside down on the table, Indiana Jones style.

She gestures at the remaining two glasses. "You sure I can't tempt you?"

"Positive."

"Good," she goes for the strawberry. "So, now we've established that you're good at staying hidden and I'm good at finding people who are good at staying hidden, shall I get down to brass tacks?"

"Please do, I'm finding it hard to concentrate with my peripheral vision being assaulted by eighty-plus pounds of male flesh hemmed in by nothing but a Union Jack thong."

She cranes her neck round to catch a glimpse of the stage show, turns back and laughs. She sips a bit of strawberry vodka, does that little shudder again then puts the glass down, clasps her fingers on the table in front of her and looks at me.

"Okay," she says. "Brass tacks. I don't want you to kill Geoffrey Waterstone."

"Why'd you give up being an assassin?"

"Don't change the subject."

"I'm not," I say. "How you answer my question'll determine how well you'll understand what I have to say."

"My reason'll make no sense to someone like you, but here it is anyway; I got tired of killing people and decided I wanted to help them instead. Your turn."

"Based on that reason, I predict my answer will make no sense to you but here it is anyway; I have no choice."

"I won't let you kill him."

"And exactly how are you going to stop me? Since the parking lot, I've counted eighteen separate occasions when I could've killed you and gotten away with it."

"Don't try to scare me with that bullshit, there's been six."

Damn. She's been paying attention.

"My point is, I'm going to kill Geoffrey Waterstone and there's nothing you can do to stop me."

"There's plenty I can do to stop you, Mr.Hard-as-Nails Yank Assassin. I could snap your neck like a twig without even getting out of my seat."

"I think you'd find it difficult to do that with a broken collar bone."

"My foot isn't a million miles away from popping your kneecap right off your knee."

"And my hand could push your nose up into your brain before you even blinked."

"Am I the only one being turned on by this?" she says. I'm a little thrown.

She suddenly breaks out into a smile, sits back and picks up her drink again. "Phew!" she says wafting herself with her free hand. "I'm all a-glow!"

I suddenly realise I've moved right forward in my seat and that our faces were almost touching for a minute, there. I sit back, a little embarrassed. She downs the strawberry vodka. The glass joins its pal face down on the table.

"I think we've established that we could kill each other at any time," she smiles, "so let's move on. I've got a lasagna in the oven."

"There's not really a lot to move on to," I say. "Geoff's been booked. I can't give him up. The power to not kill him doesn't rest with me."

"I know," Sarah Jane nods, she understands, I can tell. The only reason she asked at all was because she had to. She knows as well as I do, I can't just not kill him. Even if I did the unthinkable and pulled out of the hit, it'd just get reassigned to someone else.

She looks around the bar, probably figuring out where to take this next. I get the impression she often flings herself into situations she hasn't quite figured how to get out of. She's looking off toward who-knows-what, absently playing with a small ivory piece hanging round her neck and with three vodka glasses in front of her (two empty and upside down). She reminds me of a Jack Vettriano painting or something. Kinda sexy, enigmatic, deadly, vulnerable, all at once.

Julius Pleaser exits the stage to thunderous applause. He's replaced by a rock band who look like they've dropped right out of the eighties. The crowd cheers them on, obviously local favourites.

The romeo on the next table has passed out, his face is marinating in a puddle of beer. The girl he'd snared was clearly charmed right out of her panties to the point that she took off with her pals.

"My husband tried to kill me," Sarah Jane suddenly says. I whip my head back round to her, somewhat surprised at her latest comment.

"He … okay …" I'm not entirely sure what to do with that information.

"He was an assassin, too," she goes on. "I don't think he had a contract on me or anything, he just decided it would be a good way to end four years of marriage."

"What, um…what happened? I mean, he obviously wasn't too successful…"

"We met on a job. We'd both been hired to hit the same person. After laughing at the absurdity of the situation, we killed the guy, ran off and got married." She's talking with the matter-of-fact air of someone who's had a lot of practice at separating herself from the things that hurt. I recognise the tone. I've used it myself.

"Anyway," she goes on, "we both carried on working until I told him I was pregnant and I was going to quit the job and I wanted him to quit as well."

"Okay…" a slight chill passes through me. I can see where this is heading.

"Yeah, so that's when he pulled a Glock on me and put three 'I love you's' right through my chest."

"Ouch. Sorry."

"Don't be. Before he could finish me off, I pulled my Walther and put one big 'I love you too' in between his eyes. He bought me that Walther for our wedding anniversary." She lets out a big sigh. "*Any*way, suffice to say I lost the baby and the divorce was really quick."

"Shit, I'm… I don't even know what to say."

She's crossed her arms, fingering her ivory pendant, leaning forward on her elbows a little and looking over my shoulder with a weak smile. For the first time this evening, she's having trouble looking me in the eye. "It was about then I decided to give up being an assassin, y'know, even though I wasn't pregnant anymore. I thought that maybe, just maybe, killing people was a tad wrong. Instead of taking people away from their loved ones, I thought, maybe, I'd have a shot at bringing them back together instead. Y'know, kind of an atonement thing."

I suddenly feel kind of empty and dry. I nod down at her remaining vodka glass. "Are you planning on drinking that?"

"Hell, yes." She picks it up and downs the entire thing in one go before slamming it down to join its comrades. "You had your chance," she kind of laughs.

"Um…look," I say, "not that I don't appreciate the heart to heart and all…"

"I'm just trying to illustrate to you," she puts on a kind of mock teacher voice, trying but failing to return to her jokey persona, "the absurdity, the futility, the…well, it's just a screwed up business, isn't it?"

"It?"

"Being an assassin. I mean, I don't know how many of your compatriots you've actually met face to face – probably a few?"

"A few," I nod.

"So you know what screwed up psychos they are. Even the nice ones," she smiles at me with her eyes, but her mouth is still serious. "Killing people for a living, it's just…"

"Kind of wrong?" I finish off for her. She smiles, properly, with her mouth this time. She spreads her hands as if to say 'there you go, you see my point'. But her right hand keeps going until it snags a young woman walking past carrying what looks like a three-tiered revolving rack of tiny vodka glasses.

"Blueberry, Vanilla and Liqourice, please, love," she says. Three glasses of clear liquid land in front of her and her empties replace them on the rack. Three shiny pound coins make their way into the barmaid's pocket and Sarah Jane is reloaded and ready to go.

"Look," I say as soon as the young woman's out of earshot, "I'm not totally delusional. I know killing people is wrong. But hey, here's a newsflash, sister; people want to kill people. They've been doing it since, like, page three of the Bible. It's a part of human nature. But you know what's really messed up? As natural as it is for us to want people dead, actually doing it don't come natural at all. Most people that try it, they just make a great big mess – physically, psychologically, socially, you name it. That's where we come in. We're their dark sides – the bits that can do the job right. We keep it clinical, keep it clean. Stop it making any more mess than it has to. You can't stop people killing other people, my alcoholic friend, but you can stop them killing themselves."

Wow. I think that just might be the first time I've ever told anyone else any of that.

Sarah Jane slowly pushes one of the shot glasses toward me.

"I think you might need this."

She's right. I upend about half of it. Liquorice vodka. Nice. Next time, I'll cut out the middle man and go straight to drinking puke.

We sit in silence. The band finishes one number. The crowd cheer. They start another.

The psychopaths aside, every assassin has a nerve. One nerve that they don't like anyone to see. A nerve that helps them do what they do. I think, from the way she's looking at me, Sarah Jane can see she's just touched mine.

I start to get up.

"Geoffrey Waterstone's a dead man," I say, quickly. "Don't get in the -"

"He's a criminal," she says suddenly. I stop.

"What?"

"He runs a criminal empire. Him and his partner. They're what we refer to in the movies as 'crime lords'."

I sit down again. I sit down hard.

"Are you serious?"

Sarah Jane nods. Then she sinks the blueberry.

"Are you…" my mind's racing, "…are you trying to tell me my father in law-to-be is a crime lord?"

Sarah Jane's mouth suddenly drops open like she's just found out the juiciest gossip in the history of man.

"You're getting married?!"

Shit.

"You're getting married…to Emily Coleman?!"

What?

"Do you know her?"

Of course she doesn't. She'll have just read up on her in her background checks and-

"I only went to school with the stuck up bitch!"

In my head, I can just hear Mickey Mouse and pals singing 'It's a Small World After All'.

"You're kidding me."

"I shit thee not. She was in my class all through comprehensive. I hated her."

"Really?" I find it hard to imagine anyone hating Emily for anything.

"She was one of the popular girls. You know the type – the ones all the lads want to get into the knickers of. The pretty ones who think they're better than all the other girls."

"So…" I'm just thinking about this now, "…my fiancée was a cheerleader and my father in law elect is a crime lord… can we go back to that one? The crime lord, thing, can we go back to that?"

Sarah Jane's shaking her head and smiling. She still can't believe Emily Coleman's marrying a Yank assassin. She clearly thinks it's as funny as hell. But she's professional enough to realise that the whole 'you're marrying into a criminal empire' thing, while not as 'Friends Reunited', is definitely more of an issue.

"Well," she says, "they import and export furniture and antiques."

"And by furniture and antiques, you mean-"

"Lots and lots of drugs."

"Right."

I remember my first thought when Fraser said he was in import/export. The thought about him being a criminal mastermind. I almost want to laugh. Instead, I finish the liquorice vodka.

Now, of course, I've come across more criminal masterminds than you can shake a stick at. So the mere existence of people like that is no news to me. But it's another ass-kicking side effect of this whole 'touching normality' thing. Marrying a nice girl, meeting her folks, sitting around drinking cups of tea in the conservatory while they reminisce about that holiday to Portugal where they all got sunburned and had to spend the entire flight back home sat forward in their seats…that's supposed to be stuff that normal people do. It's supposed to be a million miles away from my world. No criminal masterminds allowed.

"You know," Sarah smiles a cheeky smile while she sips her final vodka, "when other dads say 'if you hurt my daughter, I'll kill you', they're only speaking metaphorically. Isn't that funny?"

Oh, yeah. My sides split at the thought.

God, what if he splits my sides open?

Stop it, stop being dumb.

Dumb? Remember Manuelle Ortez? What he did to that fisherman who cheated on his daughter?

Earlier, I said I wasn't afraid of Fraser Coleman. Right now, I'm not sure I could say that without lying just a teeny, tiny bit.

Sarah Jane appears fairly amused by this whole turn of events.

"I'll bet, right now," she says, "that the very uppermost thought in your head is – why is this paragon of virtue in front of me working for a criminal?"

I look at her blankly, "I can think of nothing else."

"Well, although Geoffrey Waterstone hired me, I don't consider that I'm working for him. I'm working for his family as a whole."

I nod. Geoff's old lady sounded a mite agitated on the phone yesterday.

"Turns out he's really close to the lad," she goes on, "If anyone can give me any insights into whatever clues I manage to dig up regarding Jeremy's whereabouts, it'll be him. Basically, he's my best hope of finding his son."

There's something else going on here, though.

"Why'd you tell me about Geoff and Fraser being crooks?" I ask. "I didn't need to know that."

"Well, this is the really interesting bit." Sarah Jane leans forward, a conspiratorial glint in her eye like she's whispering gossip with her school buddies at the back of the class. "See, Fraser and Geoff have worked together for years but they've never really trusted each other."

"So I hear."

"Yeah, so, anyway, Geoff's been saying for quite some time now that he wants to leave his half of Crooks R Us Ltd to his son one day. Wants to start grooming him to take over. Now, according to Geoff, Fraser isn't too hot on this idea. Apparently, he wants to regain full control of the business."

This is so going to a place marked 'Abandon hope all ye who marry into this frickin' family'.

"When Geoff got the call that Jeremy was missing, the very first thing he thought," she says, "the thing he still thinks…"

"…is that Fraser's done away with Jeremy?"

Sarah Jane nods, supremely satisfied with her freshly dispensed gossip. "Now that's one messed up business relationship!"

She's not kidding. But –

"Okay, but still – why are you telling me all this? You're supposed to be convincing me not to kill this guy. All this stuff's irrelevant to me."

"Come on!" she says, excited. "Don't you find this all intriguing?"

I shake my head, slowly.

"Fascinating?"

Still shaking.

"A little odd?"

"Lady, I'm not a private investigator. I'm not interested in the plot."

"What are you interested in?"

"Wouldn't you like to know."

"Yeah, I would. So would you."

"What, you're my shrink now?" I say. "Y'know, right at the start of this conversation, I was supposed to be deciding whether to kill you. Now you're trying to psycho-analyse me."

"It's this stuff." She waves her hand over her new shot glasses. "It gives you powers. You can solve every single problem in the entire world if you drink enough of it."

"Every problem except your own," I say. She smiles and nods at that. Then she suddenly looks up at me like she's thought of a new game. "Twenty-four hours."

"What?" I'm more than a little bemused by her constant changes of direction.

"Don't do anything toward killing Geoffrey for twenty-four hours. Give me a head start of trying to find Jeremy. Okay, you don't care about the plot. Or the characters. Or whatever your metaphor was, now. But I do. I care about the plot, I care about the characters. Leave Geoff alone for twenty-four hours. Please?"

"Well…" I can't believe I'm even considering this.

"Thank you, thank you!" she suddenly yells and throws her arms around my neck from across the table. Funny, I thought I said the word 'well', not the word 'okay'.

But again, arguing with her seems like a really annoying exercise in futility.

"Fine…" I say. Technically it's not giving in if you never had the opportunity to make a stance. "But this time tomorrow, the clock starts ticking again, okay?"

She salutes me as she lifts cranberry vodka to her lips.

She drinks. She shivers. She slams the glass upside down. It looks like a ritual. A long standing one.

"That's a nice pendant," I say, inexplicably feeling the need to make small talk.

She rubs the front of the small, oval piece. "Yeah, sentimental value. Got it on a trip to Africa."

"I assume you are aware that supporting the ivory trade is hardly in keeping with your newfound altruism."

"Well, it's not really ivory," she shrugs, swirling a shot glass in small, quick circles. She doesn't say anything else but that's okay - I find I'm already bored of small talk. I've got to figure out if I still need to burn the car if I'm not going to kill anyone with it.

She looks back at me, suddenly. "Now, several minutes ago, you referred to me as your 'alcoholic friend'. I haven't forgotten, it stuck in my head."

I feel a little ashamed of myself. I don't even know her.

"Yeah, look, sorry about that, okay, it's just… y'know… all the vodka…" I stumble out. "But, hey, it's not for me to make any kind of -"

She screws her face up and makes a dismissive wave of the hand. "Oh, no, I'm definitely verging on being an alcoholic. I mean the 'friend' bit. Did you mean it?"

This woman is a bit crazy. And more than a bit drunk.

"Uh, sure, why not?"

Her face lights up. "Great! So I'm invited to the wedding?"

"Woah, I didn't-"

"It's okay, tell Emily you bumped into an old school friend of hers. It'll be cool, it'll be cool," she sounds like she's trying to sell me a second-hand car. I've only known her for – what, an hour? And I already know what she lacks in powers of persuasion, she makes up for in sheer persistence. Resistance, as they say, is futile.

"Look, I'll talk to her, see what I can -"

"Oh, thank you! It'll be a great day! I can feel it!"

Suddenly, the band start playing an Oasis track, can't remember which. But the strong guitar intro makes Sarah Jane raise both her arms, let out a 'whoo' and leap up from her seat.

I take it she's off to dance. I've no idea if or when she plans on coming back.

I really need to get back to Emily.

I sit back and watch.

Sarah Jane reminds me of those lost souls I was listening to on the radio not too long ago. Issues, man, she has issues. And they go a lot further than getting shot by her ex. I mean, she's got conflicts coming off her like steam clouds, clear as day. But unlike those other radio-losers, she'd never call into some show and whine about them. She's good at hiding her issues. She's not good at hiding the fact she's got issues, but she's good at hiding the issues themselves.

Even from herself.

She's an interesting one.

Yup, definitely interesting.

thirteen :
arcade

THERE ARE TWO things I need to talk to Emily about. One of the things, I don't really know how to raise so I don't know if I should even do it. So I've decided to start with the easier one. Well, it's not really that easy either. But it's easier than the other one.

Okay, just shut up and listen.

"Interesting?"

"Yeah," I answer. "Yeah, I think pretty interesting."

"How interesting?" Emily wants to know. "Interesting enough to distract me and make me lose all my lives and not get the high score?"

"Yeah."

"Interesting enough that I won't *mind* losing all my lives and not getting the high score?"

"Not sure," I say. "Depends how important getting the high score on Ms. Pacman is to you."

"Very important," she pulls the joystick around and dances her way past two ghosts and picks up some of the little dots on the screen. "But I'm intrigued. So go ahead. What's this interesting thing you have to tell me?"

I think this was a good idea. Em's been getting a little stressed over the prep for the wedding. Yesterday's trip into town didn't go so well, tablecloth aside. Tempers frayed, there might be court martials in the offing. So I thought I'd take advantage of a place I spotted while we were out yesterday. This morning, it'll just be me, Em and a whole bunch arcade machines. Oh yeah, and all the spotty geeks feeding in their pound coins.

There's one guy playing one of those shooting games; he's got a big, blue plastic gun pointed at the screen and he's blowing away all manner of pixellated terrorists.

His posture's all wrong.

"Okay," I say, "well, when I went to find my old buddy, I didn't find him. But I did find his roommate. A very pleasant lady called Sarah Jane Jackson."

Emily's pill-popping avatar makes a break for the last clutch of dots. "Still waiting for the interesting bit."

"Her maiden name's Wilson. She used to be in your class at school."

"Really?" now she is surprised, she even looks at me, wide-eyed for a moment. But she doesn't miss a beat on-screen. She mops up the last few pills and the machine tells her she's made it to level five.

"Something tells me you don't remember her," I say.

"No, I think I do, the name rings a bell – mousy brown hair?"

"That's the one."

The guy on the shooting game's really bad. He's lost all his lives so he's pumping more of his hard earned benefits into the machine and starting again.

"Yeah, I do remember her," Em starts her little yellow ball running around the screen again. "Quiet. Wouldn't say boo to a goose. Nice, I think, but a bit of a loner. She never had any friends. Apparently, her parents were away a lot."

"Well," I say, "she's certainly not quiet anymore."

Might still be a loner, though. Interesting.

"Well, well, small world. Congratulations, you were right. That was relatively interesting," Em says but she's still diverting most of her attention to her game. This has been her favourite since she was, like, zero years old, so she says. Her dad gave her a computer when she was a kid and it had a couple games on it. One of them was this. She used to whup her cousins at it, apparently. She's on target for getting the high score on this machine and having three letters of her name displayed for the rest of the day to any other sad geek who comes over and plays it.

I clear my throat. Then I say-

"Yeah, so anyway, I invited her to the wedding."

"*What?!*"

Now she turns to me fully, the game instantly forgotten.

"You invited her to the wedding?!" she appears not to have taken the news too well. "You can't just go around inviting random strangers to our wedding!"

"She's not a stranger, you were in the same class at school!"

"I don't remember her!"

"You just said you *do* remember her!"

"I don't remember her remember her, I just remember her!"

I love arguing with women. So easy to keep track of stuff.

"What..?"

"I mean, she wasn't a friend or anything! I barely spoke to her!"

The deep '*bong*' noise from the arcade machine momentarily draws Em's attention back to the screen. The first of her hard earned lives have just gone. When she turns back to me, she's even more annoyed than before.

Tough crowd.

"Well, look, this would be a great opportunity to get to know her better!" I argue. "Y'know, a lot of people who meet up with folks they didn't know that well at school, they end up becoming real good friends."

Man, I'm not even convincing myself.

Bong! There goes Em's second life.

"We've had to remove people I really wanted to invite to keep the numbers down and you're inviting some old nobody from a school that I, quite frankly, hated every minute of!"

"Okay, Em, I'm sorry, okay? I thought you'd like it, y'know, it'd be a cool surprise," considering the other thing I want to discuss with my fiancée, I can't believe I'm on the back foot here. Man, I ought to be using this as leverage.

Bong!

"There," she says after flashing a last look at the screen which now has the words 'GAME OVER' emblazoned triumphantly across it. "You've pissed me off *and* made me lose the game. Happy?"

She storms over to the drinks machine.

I walk slowly over to her, past the no-hoper on the shooting game. By the time I get to where she is, she's already shoved in her fifty pence, pulled out a diet coke, ripped open the top and started sucking it down.

"Why didn't you tell me?" I say softly.

She stops drinking and looks at me, still angry.

"What the hell are you going on about now?"

"About your dad."

"What…do you mean?"

She knows exactly what I mean.

"I overheard him on the phone taking receipt of a shitload of heroin. Why didn't you tell me?" I ask her again. "I would've -"

"We all have our secrets, Michael," she says suddenly. Then she just leaves.

I'm more than a little taken aback by this sudden attitude and even after I catch her up outside, she's not speaking to me at all. Following her through town, I realise she's heading back to the car and I figure, okay, that's us going home.

All the way out of town, along the Mapperley tops and into the north Nottinghamshire countryside, we drive without saying a word to each other. She's sat there in the passenger seat just staring out the window as big trees and fields full of pig crap and potatoes go flying by.

"I've never had anything to do with his business," she suddenly says out of nowhere. I look over at her for a moment. I'm surprised to see she looks like she's been crying 'cause I haven't heard her make a peep. I've got to admit, makes me feel pretty bad to think it was because of something I'd said to her – even though the topic of conversation is all about *her* lying to *me*.

"I've known about it since I was seven years old. I've done all I can to make sure I know as little about what goes on as possible. It's no excuse, I know, it's still… I'm still guilty of letting it happen…" she sniffs a little bit. "But what am I supposed to do? Turn my own father over to the police?"

I don't really know what to say to her.

"You know, I have to live with it over my head every day. I have to live with it coming out one day and ruining my career. Ruining my… my relationships…" she kind of glances toward me. "Most of all, though, I have to live with not turning him in."

She's looking at me now, sincerely, open and honest. "But he's my dad, Mike. I love him. It's wrong, but I'm never going to turn him in. Never."

This woman never stops surprising me.

She turns back to the window.

"That's all I have to say about it," she says. "Stay or go. It's up to you."

I drive along for a few more seconds. Then I pull the car over into a lay-by on the side of the road. Emily's expression is confusion mixed with … well, more confusion. Especially when I get out of the car, walk around to her side, open the door and kneel down in front of her.

I take her hand in mine.

"Miss Coleman, anywhere I go my whole life, you're going to be there, so just get used to it."

She smiles. Then she laughs and puts her arms around me. Holding her like this now, with no-one but the cows watching, I know I never want to let her go.

We pull apart and stare into each others eyes.

"Nothing's coming between us, Em. I'm serious. Nothing."

She sniffs again, but now it's happy crying.

"I love you, Michael Shepard."

It suddenly occurs to me now would be a really good time to tell her everything about my life.

I stroke her face and wipe the tears off her cheek. She kisses my hand.

"Come on," I say, "let's go home."

fourteen :
talking to nature

SEE, NOW THIS is exactly why I don't like listening to other people. I listen to myself, things go fine. I listen to other people, they start getting all messed up.

This is how it goes; I listen to myself and Geoff would have been dead yesterday.

I listen to someone else – in this case, a messed-up, drunk assassin turned private eye – and Geoff lives another twenty-four hours.

And a guy can cause a whole lot of trouble in twenty-four hours.

"Yes, dead. Of course I'm sure. Listen, do you handle assassinations or not? Okay, then, I need this person killing, can you handle that?"

Earlier, I made up a tale about overhearing Fraser taking receipt of a load of drugs. Funny how lies come back to haunt you.

After me and Em got back in, she went for a lie down. I needed to think things over so I decided to take a walk in what the Colemans laughingly refer to as their garden. Basically, it's a forest. Stretches down one side of the house and eventually leads to the shooting fields where I performed so admirably a couple days ago.

Anyway, I'm not the only one who decided they needed a little privacy. The man of the moment, Mr. Waterstone himself. Standing all alone but looking very secretive. Having a telephone conversation he obviously doesn't want anyone else to hear him having. As I hide behind a conveniently placed tree, I can tell why.

"No, I've never ordered an assassination before. Why?"

My blood's running a little cold, here.

"Well I heard you were supposed to be the best. I was referred by an associate. Apparently, the Agency are the ones to go to for the best results. So we hear."

Damn, the guy's talking to my bosses! Could this whole situation get any more screwed up?

"Look, I want Fraser Coleman to pay for what he's done to my son. He's not going to get away with this unscathed."

The guy is pissed off as pissed can be. It's all he can do to keep his voice down. No wonder he brought himself out here.

"No, I don't want to think about it. I just want you to -" he pauses while whoever's on the other end tells him something important. He sighs, resigned. "Okay, alright. Leave the – what did you call it? Abort option? Leave that on it if it makes you happy. I'm not going to call this off, not unless I see Jeremy physically standing in front of me, safe and unhurt, but if you want me to have the -"

More advice. You ask me, despite his reluctance to keep an abort option, he actually looks like the whole thing's leaving a bad taste in his mouth. He's not backing down, though.

"Yes, I'm fully aware of that. But he has to pay. It's my bloody *son* we're talking about, here. Okay?"

If my experience of these conversations is accurate – especially where my employers are concerned – it's about to move into the formalities stage.

"Okay, yes, the price is … no, that's fine… alright…" Geoff's rubbing his eyes, now. He looks drained. They usually are by the time they come round to talking about the price. Especially the first time callers. By the time they get to the point of feeling so strongly about something that they need to have someone killed, money's usually no longer any kind of issue.

He talks listlessly about bank accounts and fees and all the paraphernalia, all the boring stuff that has to be talked about before a hit can be penned into someone's calendar. Then, eventually, he hangs up. He stands there for a few seconds, looking up into the trees.

Then he throws up.

After a couple more minutes, he leaves. I keep myself hidden the whole time and eventually I'm there by myself. I sit on a tree trunk for a couple minutes, thinking things over. Then I pull out my cell and call the one person who, I think, fully deserves to know what's gone down because of her interfering little self.

"*No!* Really?!" Sarah Jane can't believe it.

"No," I say. "No, not really. I'm making it up. Yes, you little interfering harpy, it's really happened! Geoffrey Waterstone has taken out a hit on Fraser Coleman."

"Interfering harpy? That's harsh. I thought I was your alcoholic friend."

"Yeah, well, now you're an interfering harpy."

"Okay, I can see how you're blaming me because of that whole twenty-four hours thing…"

"So now, what are we supposed to do, huh?" I turn around and a fox is looking at me through the tall grass. Then he runs off. "This whole thing's getting more and more screwed up by the second."

There's a couple seconds of silence from the other end of the line while Sarah Jane turns her formidable talents (I'm being generous) to figuring out a way out of this mess.

"Well," she says, finally, "there is one way we can fix this. You said he left an abort option on the hit."

"Well, they pretty much made him."

"Whatever, it's there. Now, he's called in the hit on Fraser because of what Fraser's done to Jeremy. Or what he *thinks* Fraser's done to Jeremy. So the way out of this is that you help me find Jeremy. We bring the lad home and when Geoff sees his son's alright and that Fraser had nothing to do with it, he'll call off the hit. Then, just to top it off, you'll see how happy Geoff is that his son's alive and you'll suddenly develop a conscience and not kill him. Everyone's a winner, baby."

"Okay, just one flaw," I say, "well, actually, there's a couple, but let's hit the biggest one first. How do we know Jeremy's alive? And that Fraser *did* have nothing to do with him going missing?"

"My gut instinct," Sarah Jane says. "I don't know, something about this just doesn't feel right. I don't think Fraser's done anything to Jeremy. I think Jeremy's run away."

I'm quiet for a minute.

"There's another way."

"Oh?" Sarah Jane sounds intrigued, but also wary. She probably has a good idea what I'm going to say.

"I stick to my job. I kill Geoff. Then I camp myself on Fraser's shoulder and keep a lookout for signs of a hit being prepped. As soon as I so much as *smell* the hitman, I take him out."

"Okay..." she doesn't sound impressed with that idea. "That sounds a lot more risky than my plan. Also, the bit where you don't kill Geoff, your way doesn't cater for that so much."

"Listen, finding Jeremy, to me *that's* the long shot," I tell her. "What the hell do I know about tracking people down? What am I, a cop?"

"Damn it, get involved, Michael, you're a human being."

"I'm a *killer.*"

Silence from the other end.

"Look, let's not dress this up, okay?" I say eventually. "I'm a killer. I kill. It's what I am, it's what I do. I don't have any choice in the matter. Fraser's in danger, okay? Now, he may not like me and I may not like him ... but the woman I love loves him. So the only way I know to save his life is to stick to what I know. What I'm good at."

The silence from the other end of the phone goes on, longer still. Eventually, when Sarah Jane speaks again, she's not joking around, she's not teasing. I'm not sure, but I think she's disappointed.

"Fine. Go ahead. Be a killer. Just remember one thing," she says at last. "According to your rules, your laws? I'm a security risk. That means you should be seriously thinking about killing me, too."

Then she hangs up.

Well.

Sure glad I came for this walk to clear my head.

a MIKE SHEPARD film

a DENIAL STUDIOS production

starring
JAMIE PARSONS
TERENCE STAMP as 'UNCLE MAX'

INT. 'DOG RUN' DISCO STAGE SHOW BAR, SOHO, NEW YORK - NIGHT
It's dark. It's smoky. It's crowded. It's 1985. It's Disco! In drag!

Round tables fill the room, every one populated with drunk people. Gay, lesbian, straight and all the shades of pink in between. Scantily clad men and women with rabbit ears and bob tails move from table to table delivering drinks and storing tips in their thongs.

All the tables and all the people at them are pointed at a big stage which holds a man with two record decks, a stack of vinyl, a piano tie and a pair of headphones roughly the size of his white man's afro. It also holds one MISS RUBY LIPS. She is the sequined, undisputed queen of 'DOG RUN' - the sassiest drag dive in Soho. It's because of her the place is packed out every night from 7 till 3.

Right now, Ruby and her feather boa (Madge) are blowing the crowd away with their rendition of Soft Cell's 'Tainted Love'.

Everyone's loving it and showing their full volume appreciation. Including the only under-eighteen in the place; eleven year old MICHAEL. He's sat by himself at the best table in the house - front and centre, square on to the stage.

The show looks different to him than anyone else in the club. Everyone else sees Ruby Lips. Michael sees the man behind the woman. He sees Uncle Max.

A bunny girl saunters up to Michael's table with
a tray holding several glasses of beer and one
glass of milk. She puts the milk on the table
next to the fries and pizza he has spread out in
front of him.

>   CHARLOTTE
>   Hey, Mikey, here's your
>   milk. You make sure you
>   drink it all, now.

Michael takes time out from bobbing his head
to the music to mumble something through a
pizza-filled mouth that may well have been
'Thanks Charlotte'. The bunny girl takes it as
that, anyway; she ruffles his hair and goes on
about her business.

Michael continues to stare at his uncle up on
stage. He's seen this show a hundred times but
he never gets tired of watching. Eventually,
though, Miss Ruby Lips' set comes to an end. The
crowd cheers, she shows her appreciation then
she makes way for a bunch of ladies (some more
female than others) each dressed as the Statue
of Liberty.

Finally, Max, still in full regalia, joins his
nephew at his table. When Michael speaks, his
English accent is at odds with the rough New
York accents flying all around him, including
that of his uncle.

>   MICHAEL
>   That was wicked, Uncle
>   Max.

>   MAX
>   As long as you never
>   get tired of seein'
>   that same set, I'll
>   never get tired of
>   gettin' praise for it.

Max gestures at Michael's full glass of milk.

>   MAX (con't)
>   What's this?

                    MICHAEL
          Are you going to do
          that act with Lucy and
          Reggie tonight?

                    MAX
          Michael, what's this?

                    MICHAEL
          I'll drink it! I
          promise!

                    MAX
          You better — if I'm
          gonna raise you, I'll
          be damned if you're
          gonna grow up with
          calcium deficiencies..!

Michael's grin suddenly falters. Doesn't quite
disappear, but it's definitely not as broad as
it was. Max sees the pain in his nephew's eyes
and moves to change the subject.

                    MAX
          Hey, y'know, talkin'
          about that snake of
          Lucy's...

                    MICHAEL
          His name's Reggie.

                    MAX
          Yeah, whatever, talkin'
          about that snake?
          Lucy's goin' away this
          weekend. Needs someone
          to look after the
          thing. Y'know, feed it
          mice and like that. She
          thought, y'know, since
          you like the thing so
          much, you might want
          the job...

                    MICHAEL
          Oh, my God! I'll
          definitely, definitely
          do it!

                    MAX
          I kinda thought you
          might. She's expectin'
          you at her place first
          thing tomorrow, tell
          you what's what.

                    MICHAEL
          Wow... I can't believe
          it...!

Mike is getting more excited by the second.

                    MICHAEL
          Did you know he can
          crush a ten stone human
          to death in eight
          minutes?

                    MAX
          Well, I'm real jealous,
          Mikey. I wish I was the
          one cleanin' out the
          killer snake's cage.

Mike goes a little serious. He looks up at his
uncle appreciatively.

                    MICHAEL
          Uncle Max...

Max can see what Michael wants to say. And it
isn't necessary. He doesn't need or want
gratitude. He just wants Michael to start to
enjoy life again after all he's been through.

                    MAX
          Come on. I'm all done
          here for tonight. What
          say we get my friend
          down at the Empire to
          put us on a private
          showin' of 'Back to the
          Future'.

                    MIKE
              Uncle Max, <u>again</u>..?

EXT. 'DOG RUN' CAR PARK - NIGHT
Night time in mid-town New York – with all the
sights and sounds it offers. Michael and Max
emerge from the side-door of 'Dog Run'. Max is
now changed into jeans and a white t-shirt. He
is pulling on a brown bomber jacket. The pair
are engaged in a deep and meaningful discussion.

                    MICHAEL
              ...because he was the
              youngest! If his
              brother and sister were
              disappearing because
              their parents never got
              together, why didn't he
              vanish at the same
              time?

                    MAX
              'cause he was the one
              traveled back in time.
              It was down to him to
              fix things.

The pair are walking toward Max's beat-up
Chevrolet. As they get near it, the 'Dog Run'
side door bursts open again and Charlotte - the
bunny girl who gave Michael his milk - comes
running out. The pair don't notice her at first.

                    MICHAEL
              That makes no sense,
              Uncle Max, that's just
              unscientific. If he's
              the youngest of the
              three and their parents
              don't get together,
              then surely there's
              <u>less</u> chance of him
              existing than his
              brother and sister, not
              <u>more</u>.

Max opens the passenger door for Michael then he
walks around to the driver's side.

                    MAX
          Look, let's finish this
          philosophical debate
          over a disgustingly
          huge bucket of popcorn.

                    CHARLOTTE
          Max! Max!!

The pair turn to see Charlotte running toward
them. She looks pretty frantic. She finally
catches up to Max.

                    MAX
          Hey, Charlie, what's
          the-

                    CHARLOTTE
          It's Debs. Her
          boyfriend, Lyle, he
          made bail this morning.

                    MAX
          Is he coming to find
          her?

                    CHARLOTTE
          No, she's going to find
          him! Max, she's got a
          gun!

                    MAX
          You're shittin' me...

                    CHARLOTTE
          She's going to kill
          him, Max, she's not -
          she shouldn't...

                    MAX
          I know, I know. Look,
          calm down, alright?
                    (pause)
          Dammit, I told her he
          wasn't worth this...

                    MICHAEL
          Uncle Max? What's-?

                    MAX
          Mikey, you need to stay
          here. Charlie, do you
          know where Debs went?

                    CHARLOTTE
          Lyle's place, I think.
          He's still got that
          apartment in Queens...

                    MAX
          Okay, Mike, go with
          Charlie, get yourself a
          - Mike?

Michael has jumped into the passenger seat of
the Chevy and strapped himself in.

                    MAX
          What the hell do you
          think you're doin'?

                    MICHAEL
          I'm coming with you.

                    MAX
          Mike, get out of the
          car.

                    MICHAEL
          You might need me.

                    MAX
          I need you to stop
          talking nonsense and
          get the hell outta my
          car.

                    MICHAEL
          But-

                    MAX
          Now, Michael.

Michael can see his uncle has spoken his final
word. He gets out and stands next to Charlotte.

Max jumps in and talks to the pair out the open window.

                    MAX
          Charlie, take Mike
          inside, get him a hot
          chocolate.

Max releases the hand brake and guns the engine.

                    MAX(con't)
          I won't be long.

Max screeches out of the parking lot. Charlie and Michael are left standing in the empty lot looking at the rapidly receding tail lights. Charlie looks at Michael.

INT. KITCHEN, DOG RUN - NIGHT
The kitchen's a little messy but it's one of the places Michael has come to call home. But tonight, he seems to be finding no comfort in his previously reassuring surroundings.

Charlotte is trying to be upbeat and take Michael's mind (and her own) off things.

                    CHARLOTTE
          I hope it's not too
          milky. My mom always
          used to say that my
          hot chocolate always
          had too much-

                    MICHAEL
          Who's Lyle?

Charlotte stops in her tracks. She can see there's no point in pretending nothing's wrong. She can also see that this little British kid has more steel in him than he normally shows. She wouldn't be telling him anything he couldn't handle hearing.

                    CHARLOTTE
          Lyle's Debs'
          boyfriend. Well, ex.
          They broke up just

before he went to
prison.

          MICHAEL
Did they fall out?

          CHARLOTTE
You could say that.
Lyle beat up on Debs'
sister pretty bad.
Left her in a coma for
a year. She's got
pretty bad brain
damage now, can't walk
or eat properly.

          MICHAEL
Why did he do that?

          CHARLOTTE
It's a long story,
but...the story don't
matter. The point is
that Lyle put Debs'
sister into a coma. I
mean, the guy's a
total psycho.

          MICHAEL
Is that why he went to
prison?

          CHARLOTTE
Yeah. But, y'know, a
guy puttin' a woman
into a coma with his
bare hands - that's
not really that bad of
a crime and he said he
was sorry so they let
him out after three
years.

          MICHAEL
And now Debs wants to-

Michael can't quite bring himself to say the
words.

                    CHARLOTTE
          Yeah. And now, Debs
          wants to.

                    MICHAEL
          But why does Uncle Max
          have to get involved?
          It's not even got
          anything to do with
          him.

                    CHARLOTTE
          Haven't you noticed,
          Mikey? You've been
          here almost six
          months.

                    MICHAEL
          Noticed what?

                    CHARLOTTE
          Mikey, the guy's our
          protector. He looks
          after everyone here.

                    MICHAEL
          What, like,
          Superman?

                    CHARLOTTE
          Yeah, Mikey. Like
          Superman. No-one asked
          him to do it, he
          just...did it.

                    MICHAEL
          So...he beats people
          up for you?

                    CHARLOTTE
          Well, it's not that
          simple. He... it's
          like he knows what
          each of us can do,
          what we can handle. I
          mean, Bertha, you know
          Bertha, right?

                    MICHAEL
          You mean Brad?

                    CHARLOTTE
          Yeah. Well he's one
          big drag queen, right?
          Done time for assault.
          Now, when he decided
          he was gonna track
          down the punks that
          stole his car and
          break a couple bones,
          Max let him do it. If
          that'd been me? Or
          Debs? Or Kenny? He'd
          have stepped in,
          broken the bones
          himself. But Brad, he
          could handle the idea
          of breaking someone's
          bones. He's used to
          that kind of thinking,
          you know? Debs on the
          other hand...

Charlotte doesn't need to finish.

                    MICHAEL
          He's going to kill
          Lyle, isn't he? So
          Debs doesn't have to.

                    CHARLOTTE
          I... I don't know kid.
          I mean, he might
          just...

But Charlotte can't bring herself to lie to
Michael. They both know the score. They sit in
silence and wait for Max to come back.

END OF ACT 2

                    - 116 -

sixteen :

mrs. pepperpot

JUST SO YOU know, keeping someone alive is much, much harder than killing them. I mean, I have all new respect for Kevin Costner's character in 'The Bodyguard'. He just looked so constipated, the entire movie. Now I know what it was. Stress. The guy was stressed out. Always having to hang around a snotty, ungrateful yet beautiful client, trying to keep the wolf from the door. I just wish my 'client' was beautiful instead of just snotty and ungrateful.

Doesn't help when the guy doesn't even have the faintest clue that his life's in danger in the first place. Or that the son-in-law elect that he hates with a passion has been busting his ass trying to keep him alive since his business partner put the hit out on him yesterday.

"Michael," Fraser says my name in that kind of 'you again?' tone of voice. As well he might. He's just stepped out of the bathroom after having had some 'me' time sat on the porcelain throne with today's issue of 'Mean Old Bastards' newspaper. And I'm the first thing he sees.

Again.

"Hi," I try my hardest to be amiable. "Hey, uh, Mr. Coleman, I was wondering if you fancied a game of chess."

"Chess?" he raises a pseudo-aristocratic eyebrow.

"Yeah," I try to sell it. "Get down to the games room, lock the door, get out the scotch and have a few nice, quiet, uh – *safe*, games of chess."

A faint flicker of a smile passes across Fraser's features. It's not a nice smile, though. It's a kind of 'stop wasting my time you silly Yank' kind of a smile.

"Perhaps another time, Michael," and he starts to walk along the landing and towards the stairs.

"Uh – wait, one sec…" I run ahead of him and cast a quick, surreptitious glance down all the steps. Any of them slightly out of shape? The carpet moved on any of them? No. Okay.

"What is it?" Fraser is a little annoyed. Well, more than a little, I've been doing this all day – and it's only ten-thirty a.m.

"Nothing, just…" taking a flash-look at the window across the other side of the stairway, the one I identified earlier as the best place to hide if you wanted a clean headshot of someone descending the stairs, "…just making sure you can get down okay…"

"Thank you, Michael, I'm not a geriatric," he huffs as he turns and heads down the stairs.

We arrive in the living room. Emily's sat at the table with her mother, going over some big catalogue-looking thing. Seriously, they haven't bought everything yet? The wedding's in, like, two days. And it's not like they're in the States where they can nip out at any hour they fancy and buy whatever they want. They're in England. Once that clock hits 5 o clock, the only places left open to spend your money is pubs, bars, restaurants and take-outs. Which is fine if the only thing they have left to buy for the reception is three hundred fifty doner kebabs.

"See, Mr. Coleman, the thing is I was kind of hoping you could teach me."

He glances up at me as he rounds the banister at the foot of the stairs.

"The chess, I mean. I'm not that good and I've always wanted to learn. And Emily says you're the man when it comes to pushing horse."

"I *beg* your pardon?!"

"Horses! I mean horses. Pushing horses. Around a chess board. Y'know. Knights. Rooks. Bishops, all that good stuff."

Damn you, Sarah Jane. I could really do without the whole 'Fraser Coleman : international drug baron' thing bouncing around inside my head. It's kind of distracting.

"Michael," his tone tells me he wants to put this to bed, "leave me alone."

"Oh, come on, Dad," Em pipes up from the table, smiling. "I think it would be good for you two to have some Man time. Go and fire up some cigars or a Playstation or something."

Fraser, paper under his arm, wanders over to the table and kisses his daughter lightly on the top of her head. "Why don't you just kill me now?"

"I know what you can both do together," Mary's brain suddenly catches hold of something.

"Mary, you're not paying attention," Fraser says, trying not to glance in my direction. "I don't *want* to-"

"You can take your mother's dress over," Mary goes on, still clearly not paying attention. "You were supposed to do it last week. Take Michael over and introduce him to her. Tell her we've had to bring the hem up and she should try it on – *while you're there*, don't let her weadle out of it. And ask her again if she's having the meat or the fish, she keeps changing her mind. Oh, and see if you can pick up a card for Pat's birthday while you're out, it's on Sunday."

Just the sound of all that makes me want to chop my own face off.

"Hey, that sounds like a great idea!" I say.

"No," Fraser shakes his head, beginning to head off towards his favourite armchair, paper still in hand. "I'll go later. Alone."

"Fraser -"

"It's okay, Mary," I hold a hand up, and I smile my most amiable son-in-law smile. "I don't mind taking the dress over and introducing myself."

"Oh," Mary's squeak sounds more than a little surprised. "Well...that's good of you, Michael..."

I get a little smile of approval from Em, too.

"Not a problem, I've been wanting to meet the esteemed Mrs. Coleman." (In the same way I've been wanting to meet a drug-crazed, axe-wielding maniac.) "Just, I'm a little low on gas so if it's okay, I'll just take the Jag and-"

Twenty minutes later, Fraser pulls up the handbrake of his beloved Jaguar X-Type as we arrive at his mother's house.

"Right," he utters his first words since we got in, "come on, then."

Fraser gets out of the car and I turn in my seat to look at the sole occupant in back. "That was a pleasant drive. I think we're really starting to bond. The stony silence is a step up, right? He's starting to hate me less now, right?"

Em unbuckles herself and shuffles forward so she can put her hands around my face.

"My dear," she says, her lips all but brushing mine, "for all the effort you're putting in, you deserve the respect of the angels themselves. But I'm afraid all I've got to give you is this..."

She kisses me in a way that feels way too naughty to be doing within mere feet of not only her father but also her grandmother.

When she pulls away, she gives me a heartening smile. "I am proud of you, you know. All the time you're trying to spend with Dad. He'll come round, I know it."

I really wish I could tell her how much danger her father's in, tell her why it is I'm forcing myself to always be around the old buzzard. On the other hand, though, who wants that kind of knowledge? Especially when you can do precisely zip about it. So instead, I just say;

"Yeah. I know."

"Are you two coming?"

Em starts to scooch sideways. "His Lordship awaits."

I'm about to take a slow, calming breath when I suddenly realise I'm supposed to be sticking to Fraser's ass like fleas on a wino; I whip out of the car, round the hood and all but beat him to the front door.

"Allow me," I smile, a little out of breath as I knock on the old, wooden door. Fraser fixes me with yet another withering gaze as I make like I'm checking out the big, old house. Twitching curtains with tell-tale glints of metal peeking out from between them? Signs of the door rigged with explosives for that 'gas leak' touch? No and no.

"Nice neighbourhood," I say as we await the arrival of Mama Coleman.

"Haven't we come down to the Park before?" Em cocks an eyebrow.

"I think I'd remember," I tell her, looking around. The Park is right on the edge of town. Expensive. Exclusive. All the Ex'es. You got piles of cash and you want to live within earshot of the night-time police siren choir rather than the burbs or the countryside? You got two options; a high-rise, one-bedroomed bachelor pad or a big, old house in this little ring-fenced haven. Weird, though – I don't know if it's the gas-lamp streetlights (still can't believe someone gets paid to go round and light them all) or the hundred-year old houses but I swear I feel like Jack the Ripper's lurking round the corner, watching us with his beady eyes.

The sound of the bolts scraping tells us the door is about to open and I prepare myself to face the Mother of the Dragon.

"Morning, Mother."

"Oh, hello, Fraser! Ooh, visitors before eleven, how exciting! Come on in, I'll get some cakes out."

Well, I'll be -

- it's Mrs. Pepperpot.

"Come on in, then!"

"Hi Nan," Em gives her grandmother a peck on the cheek as she enters the house.

"Morning, dear. Oh, and this must be Michael? We meet at last!"

It's not until she looks at me that I remember the woman's blind. Has been for years, so Emily said. Probably smelled my aftershave or heard me wiping my feet or something.

I've got to say, I'm genuinely taken aback. She's the proverbial and original 'kindly little old lady'. Five foot nothing, white hair in a bun, multi-coloured cardigan and nice as all get out. All that's missing is the smell of apple pie drifting in from the kitchen. I wonder how something so sweet could have given rise to someone so bitter. But then, I guess it's no different to Darth Vader having that sweet Scandinavian mom.

"Good morning, Mrs. Coleman," I say, taking her tiny hand in mine, "pleased to meet you."

"Oh, Irene, dear, please," she says as she closes the door behind me. "Go on through, then, go on through."

We filter out of the narrow hallway and through into one of the front rooms.

The walls are all different shades of beige but there are pictures all over, all sizes. She must like the feeling of knowing all those people from times past are looking down at her, even if she can't see them anymore.

"You have a beautiful home, Mrs. Coleman – I mean, Irene."

"Ooh, such a lovely accent," she says patting my arm as she comes into the room. "Reminds me of a few naughty encounters during the war."

"*Mother* - " Fraser, pretty understandably, doesn't want that picture painting.

"How are you dear?" she pecks her son on the cheek.

"I'm fine," he holds out the plastic-draped outfit. "Mary wants you to try this on. While we're here."

Despite Fraser's abruptness (borne, if I'm honest, from me bugging him all morning) I can tell that I've just met the third (and probably final) person he has any affection for in the world. He truly loves his mother. Well, *duh*, you might say. But we're talking about Fraser Coleman here. Him loving his mother is genuinely news to me.

"Ooh, thanks, I'll make sure I do that," she takes the dress and drapes it across the nearest chair. Is it just me or does she have absolutely no intention of trying the dress on? In fact, I'm sure she takes pleasure out of suckering her way round people, just for a laugh. Play the little old lady thing to the hilt and see what she can get away with.

I think I like this gal.

"Right – tea? Cakes?"

"Just tea for me, thanks, Mother."

"Emily, I know you won't let me down."

"You know me so well, Nan," Em puts her hands on Irene's shoulders from behind. It doesn't surprise me at all to see how much she loves her grandmother. "Need a hand?"

"The two I've got will do me just fine, thank you," she pats Emily's hands before heading towards the door. She takes a hold of my forearm as she walks past me.

"What about you, GI Joe?"

Although my vocation necessitates me being a very good actor, some people make it easier for me to say the lines than others. Fraser, for instance, makes it difficult. Irene, on the other hand, is the kind of person that makes it easy to play the role I've created for myself as the likeable and polite yank.

"Real, authentic English tea and cakes will pretty much make this the best eleven o'clock I've ever had," I smile at her. She pats my arm again as she heads off to a kitchen that, no doubt, has never run out of tea, cakes or biscuits since rationing ended.

It suddenly occurs to me that she doesn't even use a white stick to get around. Guess she knows the layout of her own house.

"How are the preparations coming? For the wedding?" Irene calls from the kitchen as Fraser takes a seat in a big, high-backed dining chair, apparently testing it for firmness. Emily's pointing out various family photos to me.

"Okay, as far as I can tell," he calls back. "You know Mary, though. Never one to say enough's enough. Always trying to -"

"Oh, *bugger!*"

The kindly voice ringing through from the kitchen with such language makes Em and me look at each other with shocked and amused smiles.

"What is it?" Fraser calls out, not as amused as us.

"I forgot I've almost run out of milk." Irene pads back into the room. "It doesn't matter, though. The milkman'll be here soon."

A large bay window floods the room with bright, morning light. I wander over to it. To look out for the milkman? No, I don't think so. I reckon it's my Spidey-sense, tingling.

"Well, why don't I just pop out to the corner shop and get some?" Fraser suggests, getting out of his chair. I'm about to steel myself to suggest I should go with him – 'y'know, to keep you company' – when something makes me stand stock still.

"Oh, no, dear, don't do that; not with the milkman coming."

"No, I need some tobacco, anyway, it's okay."

I can see the milkman. He's on his way. Coming over to the house, milk bottles in hand. Something's not right, though.

"Do they sell cards at the shop? Birthday cards? If they do, Dad, you'd better get one for Aunty Pat."

"Yes, I think they do sell cards…" says Irene. "they're a bit hit and miss, though. You take your chances with what they've got in…"

"I'm not picking a card, Emily, you know how your mother is with cards. You'll have to do it. A woman's eye and all that."

Is it the way he's walking? His expression? Both, actually. Plus he's wearing a Bluetooth earpiece. Could be nothing. He's driving his milk cart, after all. He's only being responsible, using his cell phone hands-free.

So why's it making me jumpy?

"Dad, I can't just leave Michael to -"

"I'll be fine," I say, suddenly, startling everyone in the room. "You go and pick a card. Both of you. I can get to know Irene. It's fine."

"You heard the man, he'll be fine," Fraser says. He obviously doesn't want someone to suggest the logical thing of getting Em to pick the card *and* buy the milk. Doesn't want to be stuck here with me. Especially when going to the shop was his way of temporarily ditching me in the first place.

"Go on," I try not to sound as jumpy as I feel. "Take your time. Pick out a nice card."

"What do you care if Aunty Pat gets a nice card?" Emily smiles suspiciously at me as she takes my hands. "You've never even met the woman."

"Hey, your dad's right. You pick a bad card, your mom'll have *all* our asses." I kiss her. "See you soon."

Em flashes me a quick, slightly bemused smile as she follows her impatient father out of the room. I hear the front door go and I turn back to the milkman. I push the window open a little more and my hand goes to my jacket.

If that milkman deviates from his path by so much as a half-step in the direction of Fraser and Emily – if his hands move any differently than they are right now... well, the people of the Park are *all* going to have to start going to the corner shop for their milk.

Fraser and Emily get into the Jag and pull out the drive. The milkman doesn't even glance at them. He just walks straight by them and comes up to Irene's front door.

Something's really up. I know the big supermarkets are turning the milkman into an endangered species but I still don't think this guy should be sweating buckets and looking like he's constantly about to fill his drawers.

He knocks.

"That'll be the milkman now," says Irene. "I told them he'd be here soon."

Yeah, I'm thinking something bad's definitely about to go down because that bulge I can now see in the front of his apron is definitely a handgun plus silencer. Looks like the ads were right.

Your milkman really *does* do more than just milk.

seventeen :
full fat

"HE'LL BE WANTING his money, I expect," Irene magically produces a little red and gold beaded purse from nowhere in a flourish that's sure to make any future grandkids positively giddy with the thought of impending ice cream or candy or bread to feed the ducks.

Right now, though, the only thing threatening giddiness around here is the gun-toting milkman on the other side of the door.

"Hey, why don't I do that," I reach out and hold her hands in mine. "It's the least I can do when you're getting me tea and cake."

She smiles. "Oh, don't be silly, dear, you're not my skivvy."

"I am, too, your skivvy," the milkman knocks again. "I'll skivvy my little ass over to the door and pay the man; you go and get us some of that cake you promised before Emily and Fraser get back. Y'know Emily might be slim but she'll sweep through that cake like a swarm of locusts, I'm not kidding."

Irene laughs as she puts a ratty five pound note into my hand. "Okay, okay, I'll do the cake, you do the milkman."

"Sure," I say, turning to the front door while she shuffles off toward the kitchen, "if it comes to it."

I check through the peephole. The fish-eye lens makes the milkman look kind of round with a huge, comic nose. He definitely looks nervous – alarm bells are banging away in my head at that. If only I knew what they were trying to tell me. Still, the gun is still safely in his apron pocket so I'm not likely to get any immediate nasty lead-based surprises the second I open the door.

So I go for it.

"Cash do?" I say as I click the safety off and aim my Blackwell at his gut. The guy goes several shades whiter than the milk he's holding.

"Come on," I flick the gun. "Get in here."

He starts to shuffle in.

"Faster, faster," my tone more than my words encourage the guy to step it up. Well, my tone and the loaded pistol seconds away from giving him the last and worst stomach ache he'll ever have.

I glance up and down the street, quick as I can, before shutting the door and turning to our local bastion of independently farmed dairy products.

About a hundred different questions run through my mind. Who is this guy? Doesn't seem like your average assassin. Why's he here? Fraser? Then why let him go? Me? Irene? Far as anyone knows, we're both pure as driven snow. All these things and more race through my head at a hundred miles an hour but in the end, I settle for the easiest and fastest way of finding out what the hell's going on.

I raise my gun to point at his head and say, "Talk."

"Hel-hello... Michael..." the milkman's stuttering so bad, I think he's about to pass out from fear. "Nice to... meet you, at last... face to face... in a ... m-manner of speaking..."

Then it bites me on the ass, it's so obvious. Especially with the lilted way the guy's speaking, like he's being fed his lines off an auto-cue.

Or through a bluetooth earpiece.

"Where is he?" I all but press the barrel against milk boy's forehead.

"So...so rude..." the guy stumbles. "All I came to do...was t-talk..."

I feel a little sorry for this guy – caught between two psychos and all. But right now, his life is secondary, far as I'm concerned. Whoever has our boy dangling from this demented little string is nearby. I need to know where and I need to know now.

"St-stop stuttering or I'm...going to ... going to kill you when you come out..." the guy says, then his eyes suddenly widen as he looks at me in horror. He realises about the same time I do; that one was meant for him.

I suddenly think, this guy's no good to anyone nervous. If I keep threatening him, I'm just going to get him killed. Then I'll never find out where his puppeteer is. Besides, I need to keep things calm. There's Irene to think about – not to mention Emily and Fraser who could be back any minute.

I lower the gun and hold up my other hand, palm out.

"Okay, you want to talk? Go ahead, it's your dime."

The guy seems to visibly calm. His shoulders lower a little and some colour even comes back to his face.

"That's better..." he starts, "...isn't it nicer when we all just... get along?"

"Oh, yeah, I'm good at getting along – better when I know who I'm getting along *with*, though."

"How churlish of me – I haven't even introduced myself."

Well, I know one thing – our mastermind's definitely English. I mean, *churlish*? Who even says that?

"My name is...well, understandably secret," the milkman says, "but my profession is the same as yours, Michael. I'm an assassin. And I'm here to kill *you*."

I fight the urge to raise my weapon again. It won't do any good to kill this guy – unless he tries using that thing he's carrying in his apron. I need to find our puppet master and keeping his puppet from becoming a corpse is my best shot at that right now. But I can't take my eyes off him in case I get one in the back of the head.

Damn it – this guy's sick but he's good.

"Oh, hello, Malcolm – come inside for a rest have you?"

Hell, I didn't even hear Irene shuffling towards us, tray of cake in hand. I'm about to hide my gun when I realise she can't see it anyway.

How much did she just hear?

"Oh, hello, Mrs. Coleman – nice to see you," even though he's echoing His Master's Voice, Malcolm (seriously? Malcolm the Milkman?) regains a little more of his composure. He's obviously decided that even with his own neck on the block, keeping little old Irene safe is a priority. Bully for him.

"Yes, I just thought I'd come in to... say hello..."

"Oh, well that's nice of you," Irene says but her voice tells a different story. She spends all day listening to peoples' voices more intently than the rest of us and she can tell right away something's wrong with Malcolm. I can see her shrugging it off, though – it's none of her business. She's probably thinking his cat's died or he's having marriage troubles. The idea of him being manipulated by a hitman into having a conversation – and quite possibly a shootout – with another hitman is possibly not one that comes straight to her mind.

"I've just cut some cake, dear, would you like some?"

"Oh, no," says Malcolm, "not while I'm on duty... Don't want to lose control of a five mile an hour milk float..."

Irene laughs and heads into the living room. "Okay, dear – Michael yours is here when you're ready for it."

"Thanks, Irene, can't wait."

As Irene disappears round the corner and the milkman turns back to me, we're both visibly glad to have her out of the firing line. But then Malcolm's face falls as he says,

"Actually, now you mention it, I am a little peckish... so if the offer still stands...?"

"Of course," the little Mrs Pepperpot voice drifts round the corner. "Come on in, don't stand on ceremony here."

With a slightly despairing look, Malcolm walks into the living room and I follow. I'm not happy about being in here because – apart from the whole 'old lady getting gunned down in the crossfire' scenario, there's a great big window in here. If our invisible assassin is watching, he can now see us. And, looking out, I can barely see a damn thing what with all that morning sun and those lace curtains. Still, if he'd wanted to kill me outright, he'd have done it before now. This whole rigmarole screams of someone overflowing with demented extravagance. When he's ready to bring it all to a close and pop me in between the eyes, I'm sure I'll have plenty of warning.

It's up to me to make sure that, when that time comes, there's something I can do about it.

"Here you go, Malcolm," Irene holds out a tiny saucer with an extremely precisely cut piece of Battenberg cake on it. Malcolm takes it.

"It turns out we share a hobby, Michael and I. He was just telling me he's into dancing..." the milkman says as he takes a small bite, "...ballroom dancing."

Where's the sick bastard going now?

"Oh, really, Michael?" Irene seems interested as she hands me my own tiny saucer of cake.

I take the plate in my free hand. "Looks like."

"Well, we all have that in common, then..!" Irene takes her seat with her own cake. "Fancy."

"You dance?" Malcolm asks.

"I used to," she says. "You should have seen me back in my younger days. I know you wouldn't think it to look at me now, but I could really cut a rug back then."

"Hey, I can just see it now," I say. My voice has a smile. My eyes – fixed on Malcolm – don't.

"I have to admit, I do like the contests," Malcolm speaks again in that stiff voice. "You know – it's a challenge. You get given a brief and you have to fulfil it. Sometimes though…"

Malcolm's face fills with fear again. I don't like it.

"…sometimes…" he stammers a little, "…it's nice to freestyle…"

He puts his cake down slowly and finally takes his gun out of his apron. He points it at Irene's head at exactly the same time as I point mine at his.

"Oh, I know what you mean." Irene settles back in her chair with a faraway smile on her lips. "There's nothing like just flinging the instructions to one side and doing something completely wild."

"My thoughts exactly," Malcolm's barrel is inches from Irene's head.

"Oh, I don't know." My mind's racing. "There's a lot to be said for not making things more complicated than they need to be."

Why's this guy want to kill Irene? Simple. He doesn't. Well, not for its own sake. Otherwise he'd have just done it by now. What he's really trying to do is mess with me. And I know – just from the few words he's said so far – that he wouldn't hesitate to kill her just to see the look on my face.

"You shouldn't be such a stickler for procedure, Michael," Malcolm looks like he's going to throw up and I wonder if he'd actually be able to pull the trigger if commanded. Part of me doubts it very much – but self-preservation (the carrot apparently being dangled) is a pretty strong motivator. I've seen people do the most inhuman things just to hang onto a few more precious seconds of life.

So maybe it's a chance I can't take.

"If you just let rip and did what you wanted," the milkman goes on, "I'm sure you'd enjoy yourself a lot more. You certainly wouldn't find yourself stuck with a partner you didn't want."

"Who says I am?" I step towards Malcolm but he steps back – no doubt under orders not to let me get within bitch-slap range.

"Aren't you?" he says. "Big competition coming up and you're wondering how come you're even entering?"

"Oh, you can't go into these things if you're not sure, Michael." Irene creases a frown. I can see it reflected almost perfectly in Malcolm's silencer barrel. "You have to know what you're getting into. And you have to know you're going into it with the right woman by your side."

"Couldn't have said it better myself," says Malcolm. "Personally, I think the rigidity of that sort of dance is way too much of a bind for free spirits such as us. You really ought to do what I do and try dancing something a little more…impulsive."

Malcolm's gun, now, is almost kissing Irene's temple. She sips her tea.

I've re-evaluated. He's not trying to wind me up. He's a genuine nut job.

You can always tell a real psychopath. Not because they do such screwed up things but because they just don't get why everyone else gets so pissed when they do them.

"Hey, I made the same mistake you're planning on making, once upon a time," Malcolm says. "But I switched from the waltz to the allegro and, trust me, I'm much happier. Sure I step on some toes, now and then. But that's okay. I wear big boots."

Irene chuckles. "You are a card, Malcolm. Isn't he a card, Michael?"

Yeah, the joker.

"He sure is, Irene. Lovely cake, by the way. Listen, Malcolm, we really shouldn't keep you. You must be really busy."

"Yes, I really should be going," he says and, just like that, the gun disappears back into the apron pocket – the relief is writ large all over Malcolm's face. "I've got lots of dairy products that aren't getting any fresher."

And just like that, the curtain falls. Play over. The only person more relieved than me is Malcolm himself. He looks about ready to fall over with relief. Which just makes it look weird when he keeps on talking this other guy's words.

"It turns out, Irene, that Michael and I are both members of the same international dance organisation. We attend different branches but I actually have heard of him." He turns to me. "Yes, your reputation is a very good one. I just wanted to say that. You must pay respect where respect is due. Because you never know when the dance might come to an end. One tap on the shoulder and it's all over."

"Well, I hope you finish your rounds in good time," Irene says, about to get up. "I hope we didn't keep you too long."

Malcolm puts a hand on Irene's shoulder, tells her not to get up just for him. "I'll…see you again…" he says in his own words – hoping they're true.

I follow him out to the hall and he turns to me, one hand on the doorknob. "I'll let him live if you don't come out looking for me. I just wanted to come and pay my respects to a fellow professional before I killed you."

I try to read Malcolm's face, seeing if I can magically read from his expression how sincerely he believes those words are being spoken.

"Were you really going to kill her?" I ask.

"I was really thinking about it. But I remembered I was going to go and see a film this morning and I don't want to be late."

He's messing with me. No way he'd give out info like that – it'd be too easy for me to track him down.

"Enjoy the dance, Michael Shepard. The music's almost over."

He looks back at me but doesn't say anything more. He's probably thinking what I'm thinking, though. Is he going to live to see the end of his rounds? Well, our mystery hitman would almost certainly not have shown Malcolm his face – too much risk of things going wrong and Malc escaping with his description. That being the case, killing the guy shouldn't be too necessary. I'm sure he'll be told where to drop the gun, get back in his float and scurry off down the road before the hitman changes his mind.

Of course, there's always the little problem whereby Malcolm the Milkman knows I'm an assassin. Or at least that I go ballroom dancing with assassins. Not a good thing.

Without even another word, Malcolm shuffles out the front door.

"What a nice young man," Irene smiles as she finishes her tea. "Such manners."

"Yeah," I say absently, looking out the window as he gets back into his milk float and burns off down the road at five miles an hour.

"Scared out of his mind, though," she says. I look at her suddenly, surprised.

"About what, you think?" I ask.

"Oh, I don't know. It doesn't really matter." She dabs her mouth with her napkin. "One thing I've learned over all these decades I've been blind is that you can separate what's on the surface from what's underneath. I can't see what's on the surface – but then, none of us can, no matter what we believe. But what's underneath, that's what's really driving the world round. Take you, for instance."

I freeze.

"What about me?"

"Well, you don't have a very high opinion of yourself do you?"

"I don't?"

"No, dear, not at all! But you should, you really should. You're a good person, Michael. A really good person. You should remember that a little more often. Listen to that and you'll always make the right choices."

I'm a little stunned by Little Miss Yoda's reading. I mean people always reckon they can read other people. And old people in particular seem to like to believe everyone is a good person. But something in me's started ringing, I don't know what it is.

Oh, wait. It's the door.

"Ooh, there's Fraser and Emily with the milk. It's a shame they didn't wait and save themselves the trouble."

eighteen :
ask robin hood

I'M LAUGHING. EVEN though, right at this moment, I
don't feel like laughing. I feel like doing anything *but* laugh. Yet
here I am. Laughing my ass off.

I'll tell you why in a second.

After Fraser and Emily got back, we had cake and tea. We
chatted about the coming football season, about the local rugby
team, about twenty-four hour liquor licensing laws. Irene regaled
us with tales from the war years that I'm sure Fraser would rather
have not been regaled with (seriously, that girl was a *minx*). We
talked about the wedding and what was still left to do. Then Fraser
got his mother to try on her outfit so that he could report back to
Herr Commandant that all was well on the Russian front.

And I smiled the entire time.

Seriously, I could get an Oscar. I *should* get an Oscar. But
then, I'm well practiced. Been doing it my whole adult life. So,
yeah, a little tea and conversation doesn't really stretch the old
acting muscles.

"Did you two get on alright while we were gone?" Em had
asked me after we left, hoping I hadn't felt awkward alone in the
presence of someone I didn't know.

"No, everything was fine – the milkman almost killed your
gran but it's okay because I would have blown his brains out if he
had. She makes great cake, by the way."

The internal dialogue machine runs off all the lines required
to participate in the conversation and then – government
conspiracy style – puts the big, black marker over all the words not
fit for public consumption.

"No, everything was fine – she makes great cake, by the way."

"I know, doesn't it rock?"

Then we got home and I continued following Fraser around, offering to go shooting with him, do the gardening with him, hold the newspaper while he sat on the toilet, that kind of thing.

In other words, my day carried on as if a psychotic assassin hadn't told me he was going to kill me.

Of course, I tried to think about it. Tried to figure out what the hell was going on. But, actually, playing bodyguard for the rich and cantankerous was draining too much of my brain power and – in the end – patience.

Something just didn't feel right about the whole picture and things were moving a little too fast and a little too randomly for my liking. Usually, stuff's pretty straightforward. Even on the hard jobs. But right now – and for the last few days – I haven't been in control and now I'm getting milkmen wandering around knowing what I do for a living. It was all just getting too messy.

I needed to take a step back and re-evaluate everything that was going on from strained business relationships to missing children to slightly drunk private eyes to gun-toting milkmen. So I did something extremely unprofessional – not that I was being paid to shot-stop for Fraser – and I just downed-tools and left.

"Where are you going?" Emily was concerned that I seemed a little distant.

"I just want to get a little air."

"Do you want me to come with you?"

I gave her a kiss.

"I'll see you later. I've got my phone."

And I took the Beemer and went for a drive. All the isolated fields and stuff nearby were starting to stress me out, though. It was like, the anti-Manhattan. So I went into town where there were people and pollution and junk food. Then as soon as the car was safely tucked away someplace, accruing a nice hourly parking fee, I started wandering through the crowds (okay, not quite as densely packed and rude and loud as NY, but working hard at it) and I immediately felt calmer.

And, for the first time since Malcolm had shut the door, I had a good think. It went something like this;

Okay;

Fact – someone put a hit on Geoff.

Fact – someone kidnapped Jeremy.

Fact – Sarah Jane doesn't believe the kidnapper was Fraser but unfortunately, Geoff does so…

Fact – Geoff put a hit on Fraser.

Fact – Someone's now put a hit out on me.

Fact – Apparently, I'm a good person.

And you wonder why I never get involved with the human side of it all? It's enough to drive a person to drink. No wonder Sarah Jane's the way she is if she insists on trying to make sense of all that mess.

But my thoughts didn't seem to stick on that wall. For some reason, although there were all these pieces of an increasingly screwed-up puzzle that needed slotting together, the only thing I could think about was Granny Coleman's last words before Fraser and Emily came back from the shop.

I'm a good person.

As soon as I started thinking about that, I realised that it was this comment, this evaluation of me that was actually bugging me. Okay, all the other stuff was bugging me too, but this was sitting way, way at the top of the pile. Why?

Because I'm not a good person.

I'm not a bad person either. I'm just – nothing. I've known that for years. Ever since –

…well, I've known it for years. I have a purpose, I fill a role. People want to kill other people but they can't. They're not wired up for it. But I am. So I do it for them. To save them from the insanity that comes with going against your nature. I personally don't want to kill anyone. I have no feeling about them either way. I'm a… force of nature. Neither good nor bad.

So, why did Irene say she thought I was a good person? I mean, on the one hand, what the hell does she know? Blind old bat, living alone, thinking about randy GIs.

Except I don't think of her like that. She was a real intuitive old bird. She had that air that some people have – y'know, where you value their opinions because they can see stuff that most other people walk straight past.

So when she said that I was a good person, that really confused me. And now I can't get the image out of my head of me leaping in to save the day, guns blazing. *Don't worry! I'll kill them for you!* Shooting the rich on behalf of the…well, rich.

And that's when I looked up and realised I had walked right up to Nottingham Castle and was standing in front of the statue of Robin Hood.

And hence, the laughter.

Hey, I said I was laughing, I didn't say it was funny.

So I'm a good person. I'm Robin Hood. Yet I'm doing something that's not usually in the domain of good people. So how did you handle it, Robin? I look up at the statue of a guy in tights and a knitted baby-bonnet. How did you do all that robbery and assault and murder and stuff and still think of yourself as a good person?

Funnily enough, it isn't Kevin Costner (him again) that answers. It's Sarah Jane.

'Damn it, get involved, Michael, you're a human being.'

I realise I've got my hand on my phone. I pull it out of my pocket. I can barely believe I'm about to do what I'm about to do. But I do it.

I call up the dossier on Geoffrey Waterstone and for the first time ever, click on the link that says 'sponsor'.

Go on then. Tell me who. Tell me why.

I read the name of the person who took the hit out on Geoff and read why they did it. I read it all again, just to make sure I'm not imagining things. Then I shut down the dossier file and put the phone back in my pocket.

I feel a little weak. I have to sit down.

Well, I'll be damned.

Jeremy.

nineteen : the secret history of mike shepard : act 1

a MIKE SHEPARD film

a DENIAL STUDIOS production

starring
ASA BUTTERFIELD
SEAN BEAN as 'THOMAS SHEPARD'

EXT. SCARBOROUGH BEACH - DAY
It's a bright, sunny day. Scarborough beach is
filled with happy holidaymakers. The joyful
musical score swells as we pan in on a family
that seems more happy than the rest combined.
Their windbreaker is a little more ragged. The
children don't have as many seaside toys - in
fact, the two young boys share a single bucket
and no spade. Their packed lunch is certainly
more modest. But they are enjoying each others'
company and - consequently - are experiencing
the true joy to be had on the beach.

The family of four are THOMAS and ANGELA - the
parents. The two sons are MICHEAL and little
ADAM.

The scene dissolves into a montage of happy
times had by the family, looked over at all
times by the proud and protective Thomas. All
activities are modest and contrast with the
expensive pursuits being undertaken by others.
Yet the Shepards - whether all together, Father
and sons (one or both), Mother and sons or
Thomas and Angela alone - they always appreciate
the simple fact that the best things in life are
free. Their apparent material poverty doesn't
seem a problem at all.

EXT. FISH FACTORY - MORNING
A large fish packing factory on the coast.
Hundreds of men file in for work. Thomas is
among them, smiling as he jokes with a
colleague. They walk past two men in suits. The
men in suits are not smiling at all.

INT. FISH FACTORY, CLOCK-IN ROOM – MORNING
Men are getting changed, talking, laughing,
preparing to start another day's work. Thomas is
just zipping up his overalls as he scans the
ticket rack for his ticket. He frowns. Where is
it? Just then, a man in a short-sleeved shirt
and tie comes into the room. He looks around and
spots Thomas by the ticket rack.

> MR. TAYLOR
> Ah, Tom. Could I have a
> quick word?

EXT. FISH FACTORY – MORNING
Thomas' face fills the screen as he leaves the
factory with dozens of other men. He walks in
silence. Other men around him are more vocal,
more panicked. But Thomas' face is steely
resolve.

INT. SHEPARD HOUSE, KITCHEN – NIGHT
Thomas is sitting at the kitchen table, going
through the newspaper. Michael and Adam are
running about playing army soldiers. Angela is
cooking dinner.

Michael notices his father's frustrated
expression and, as Adam continues to play by
himself, the older brother goes and sits across
from his father at the table.

They sit in silence for a moment. Thomas
reading the paper. Michael looking at him.

> MICHAEL
> Any luck?

Thomas looks up from his paper and into the
eyes of his son. He looks over Michael's
shoulder and sees Adam still playing by
himself. Michael can literally see his father
deciding not to lie to him.

> THOMAS
> Not yet. Lots of jobs
> don't get advertised
> every week, though. You
> have to keep looking.

                    Don't worry, I'll get
                    something.

Michael nods. They sit in silence for a while
more as Thomas returns to the paper. Eventually;

                         MICHAEL
                    I'm not worried.

And he jumps down from the table and goes back
to playing with his little brother. Thomas
looks over at his sons. There is an
unmistakable measure of pride as he looks at
Michael, in particular. He starts a little as
Angela's hand comes to rest on his shoulder.

                         ANGELA
                    They've got faith in you.
                    So do I. You've always
                    been there for this
                    family.

                         THOMAS
                    I know we don't have any
                    savings to speak of. But
                    I'll not see us turfed
                    out onto the streets like
                    scum. I've worked all my
                    life to look after you
                    lot and I'm not stopping
                    now.

                         ANGELA
                    I'm like Michael. I'm not
                    worried. I'm actually
                    glad. It's times like
                    these the boys can really
                    learn from you. Michael
                    follows your example and
                    he'll learn things from
                    our troubles today
                    that'll stand him in good
                    stead for the rest of his
                    life.

Angela kisses her husband's forehead and
returns to the sink. Thomas takes one last
look at Michael and continues to plough
through the paper.

INT. REGENT CORPORATE HOUSE, RECEPTION - DAY
Thomas, looking as smart as a man like him
ever needs to look, walks up to the reception
desk. A young woman in a white blouse looks up
at him.

>   RECEPTIONIST
>   Good morning.

>   THOMAS
>   Morning. I'm here about
>   the security guard job
>   for Axa Systems on the
>   sixth floor. It was in
>   this morning's paper.

>   RECEPTIONIST
>   Oh, yes, I'm sorry, that
>   one's gone.

>   THOMAS
>   Gone? It was only in last
>   night's paper. I've got
>   down here as soon as
>   you've opened this
>   morning!

>   RECEPTIONIST
>   Yes, I think that
>   actually went as soon as
>   the ad went to the paper.
>   Apparently someone at the
>   paper knew someone who'd
>   got fired from the fish
>   factory. I think a lot of
>   jobs are going like that,
>   there's so many of those
>   fish blokes that got the
>   sack.
>   (smiles)
>   I'm probably not supposed
>   to be telling you that.

>   THOMAS
>   Right…

                    RECEPTIONIST
          Can I help with anything
          else?

Thomas shakes his head and walks away from the
desk. The receptionist answers a ringing
phone. Neither she nor Thomas notice a suited
man with a newspaper regard Thomas as he
leaves. The man folds up his paper, picks up
his briefcase and follows Thomas out of the
building.

EXT. REGENT CORPORATE HOUSE, RECEPTION – DAY
Thomas throws his newspaper in a nearby bin in
disgust and frustration. The suited man
appears behind him.

                    MR. WHITE
          Excuse me, Mr. Shepard?

Thomas spins round with some surprise. He
regards this man suspiciously.

                    MR. WHITE (cont'd)
          My name is Mr. White. I'm
          sorry - I didn't mean to
          startle you. It's just
          that you're on a list I
          have. I had to choose
          someone on the list to
          visit later today. You
          showing up here, though,
          where I happen to be
          waiting for a meeting -
          well, I'd say that
          providence has favoured
          you, Mr. Shepard.

                    THOMAS
          What do you want? What
          kind of list? Are you
          from the factory?

                    MR. WHITE
          No, not exactly. I work
          for the Campbells. I see
          from your expression that
          they're a family you have
          heard of. As I'm sure you

                    - 141 -

know, they make a lot of
money from all kinds of
criminal endeavours.

Thomas looks around at passers by, startled
that this man would be so blatant and open
about such matters. The man smiles at Thomas'
unease.

> MR. WHITE (cont'd)
> Oh, don't worry, Mr.
> Shepard. Nobody around us
> would be the least bit
> interested in our
> conversation even if they
> overheard me tell you I
> had the cure for cancer
> in my briefcase. And if
> you were to relate this
> to anyone, I would just
> deny it. My credentials
> are impeccable. Whereas
> you are simply an out of
> work fish packer. Now, to
> business; my meeting is
> in five minutes.

Thomas is a little stunned by the forthright
nature of this man yet finds himself listening
further.

> MR.WHITE (cont'd)
> The factory you have just
> been let go from - well,
> I say 'just', it's been
> over a month now, hasn't
> it? - well, anyway, that
> factory has some very
> expensive equipment in
> it. Obviously, it would
> struggle to run without
> said equipment but that
> isn't our concern. We
> want that machinery. And
> we will handsomely pay
> any former worker with
> knowledge of the security
> and layout of the
> required areas.

Thomas had an inkling something like this must have been coming as soon as the Campbells' name was mentioned. But upon actually hearing it, his expression immediately turns to one of disdain.

>   THOMAS
>   I'm sorry, Mr. White, but
>   you can tell your
>   employers to f-

>   MR. WHITE
>   Of course that would be
>   your initial reaction,
>   Mr. Shepard, we wouldn't
>   have expected anything
>   less. But I would hate
>   for you to miss out on
>   this opportunity because
>   of a small thing like the
>   law. And believe you me,
>   Mr. Shepard, it is a
>   small thing indeed.

Mr. White produces a card from his breast pocket.

>   MR. WHITE (cont'd)
>   Here, Mr. Shepard. When
>   your family has been
>   starving for long enough,
>   please get in touch.

To his surprise, Thomas finds himself gingerly taking the card from Mr. White's expensively gloved hand.

>   MR. WHITE (cont'd)
>   Don't forget, not a word.
>   Right, must go.

And without another word, Mr. White turns and re-enters the office building. Thomas is left looking at the business card.

Suddenly, he scrunches it up and throws it in the bin, after the newspaper. He's supposed to be protecting his family, not exposing them to this. He starts to walk off.

About two yards away, he stops and turns back to look at the bin.

INT. SHEPARD HOUSEHOLD, KITCHEN – NIGHT
Thomas is sitting at the kitchen table, his expression is unreadable. He appears to be staring into the middle-distance.

Suddenly, a clear plastic bag full of tied up rolls of £20 notes is dropped in front of him. There must be several hundred pounds in it. We pan round to see Mr. White sitting across from Thomas. They are evidently the only two awake in the house at this late hour.

>   MR. WHITE
>   You have our gratitude,
>   Mr. Shepard. My best
>   wishes in finding regular
>   employment.

INT. SUPERMARKET – DAY
Angela, the kids and Thomas are going food shopping. Even the kids appear excited about something that would normally be so boring. But this is the first time they've been able to do it properly for over a month and the boys are even allowed a little treat of a packet of chocolate biscuits.

Everyone looks happy – with the exception of Thomas, who has to force a smile when the boys show him their biscuits.

At one point, Angela catches Thomas' gaze. Her smile falters too. Clearly, Thomas has told her where the money has come from. But her smile re-appears when she turns back to the boys.

INT. SHEPARD HOUSEHOLD, KITCHEN – NIGHT
Angela and Thomas are having a heated conversation. But they are trying to keep their voices down so as not to wake the boys up.

ANGELA
But you said you
wouldn't… you said that
would be the only -

THOMAS
Angela, do you think I
want to do business with
these scum? Trust me, I
do *not*. But it's been
over three months. Three
months and not even an
interview! Right now,
working for the Campbells
is the only offer I've
got.

ANGELA
Thomas, you know there's
no such thing as
victimless crime. I mean,
you heard Bill. After the
factory lost that
equipment, it might have
to shut up shop for good!
What about all those
other men's families?

THOMAS
After you and the boys,
those other men and their
families were the first
thing that entered my
mind when Mr. White made
me that first offer. But…
Angela, my priority isn't
them. It's you. And
Michael. And Adam. That's
all I can allow myself to
focus on. I'm not
Superman, I can't protect
everyone. But I'll fight
till my last breath to
protect you lot.

Angela doesn't know what to say. The cupboard
doors behind her - thrown open earlier in the
argument - stand accusingly bare.

                    THOMAS (cont'd)
          Don't you get it, Ange?
          What happens to me
          because of how I choose
          to provide for this
          family – that's not
          important. The only thing
          that's important is that
          I get the job done. That
          you and the boys don't
          end up huddled under a
          blanket on the street,
          begging for pennies from
          people trying to ignore
          you!

Angela's shoulders slump. The fight seems to
have gone out of her as she resigns herself to
what's happening. She can't ignore the facts any
more than he can. They will be homeless within
weeks. Thomas takes her in an embrace.

                    ANGELA
          Just promise me, Tom, you
          going to work for those
          people. It's not going to
          change you.

                    THOMAS
          Nobody changes, Ange. You
          are who you are. All you
          can do is choose your
          actions. Then live or die
          by the consequences.

The camera pans back from the lit kitchen area
into the darkness of the hallway corridor.
Michael is hiding at the bottom of the stairs,
watching his parents.

MONTAGE SEQUENCE
Angela and the boys are shopping again, but this
time, they are able to get even more food.

Thomas is in a meeting with Mr. White and
others. He looks like he doesn't want to be
there. But he takes a deep breath – this is the
choice he made. He throws himself into it.

The boys and their mother are down at the beach.
Adam wants the biggest water pistol. His mother
smiles and can't resist letting him have these
things for once.

Thomas, meanwhile, is also handling a gun. He is
sat in his bedroom. A picture from Adam is next
to him on the bed. He puts his gun down next to
it. His expression is unreadable.

Thomas and a few other guys break into a house
where some other men are. Thomas and his
compatriots go to work beating the men up.

It's Christmas. Angela answers the door – Thomas
comes in with arms full of presents for the
boys. All the latest toys and even an Atari
games console. With Pac-Man! The boys are
excited, though Michael slightly less so. He
looks over to his mother and sees her worried
expression. Thomas gives her a ring with a huge
diamond on it and kisses her. Her expression
softens but doesn't disappear. When Thomas goes
to remove his coat, Angela's eyes glance in
Michael's direction. He smiles at her,
reassuringly and turns to help Adam set up the
Atari.

EXT. SHEPARD GARDEN – DAY
Michael and Adam are playing in the snow – it's
a bright, white day. They've built a snowman and
are now running around it, having a snowball
fight.

INT. CAMPBELL HOUSE, BACK ROOM – DAY
Thomas is sat at a table, looking at some
papers. Two men burst into the room. They say
something to Thomas, they're jabbering, excited,
frantic. Thomas' expression goes from perplexed
to concerned to downright fearsome. He rushes
from the room, nearly upending the table to get
home as fast as possible.

EXT. SHEPARD ROAD – DAY
Several metres down the road from the Shepards'
garden sits a car. Inside it are three men. One
of them has a beaten-up face. He is recognisable
as one of the men Thomas beat up in a previous
scene.

EXT. STREET – DAY
Thomas is in a car, racing. He stops for
nothing.

EXT. SHEPARD ROAD – DAY
The car looking at the boys playing in the
garden slowly moves towards them.

INT. SHEPARD HOUSE, KITCHEN – DAY
Angela is in the kitchen. She is calling to the
boys to come and get some food. They can't hear
her so she starts toward the front door.

EXT. STREET – DAY
Thomas screeches round a corner, snow flying
everywhere. Not far now.

EXT. SHEPARD GARDEN – DAY
The car rolls past the garden. The boys stop
what they're doing and look up. One of the
windows rolls down and a gun pokes out. The boys
are rooted to the spot.

INT. SHEPARD HOUSE – DAY
Angela opens the front door.

EXT. SHEPARD GARDEN – DAY
Thomas puts his foot down. Home straight. He
turns onto his road, skidding around in a wide
arc. He gets to his house and fishtails to a
screeching stop. He steps out of his car, his
eyes locked on the front of his house.

Angela is screaming. She stands at the front
door, eyes locked on the scene in front of her,
and can't stop screaming. The snowman is blown
in half and what's left is covered in blood. The
snow around the garden has also been daubed with
crimson splashes. Michael is half-sitting, half-
kneeling in the snow, blood stains his coat and
face. Adam is lying face down, still. A crimson
pool slowly radiates outward into the snow.

                    THOMAS
              No…no…

                    ANGELA (seeing
          Thomas)
          You! I told you this
          would happen!! I told
          you! But you wouldn't
          listen to me!!

Screaming and ranting, Angela races towards
Thomas and collides with him, beating his chest.
He remains on his feet but only just. He is
stunned beyond words at the heart-wrenching
scene before him. Michael looks up at the pair,
wide-eyed and equally speechless.

                    ANGELA (cont'd)
          I told you, I told you, I
          told you!

                    THOMAS
          I couldn't…I never
          wanted…

As Angela beats her husband's chest, something
falls from his pocket. Michael sees it first.
Then both Angela and Thomas see it. Thomas' gun,
lying in the snow. A dark, forbidding shape
surrounded by all that white – at first pure but
now splashed with blood.

Angela, already wound up, moves quickest. She
swoops the gun up and points it at Thomas.
Michael continues to stare, wordlessly, from his
position on the ground. The faces of alarmed
neighbours have started to appear in windows and
doorways.

                    THOMAS
          Angela…what are you…

                    ANGELA
          You killed him! You said
          you'd protect him! You
          said you'd protect all of
          us! But you killed us!

                    THOMAS
          Angela, no! Don't… don't
          do this! Lord knows I
          deserve it… but you'll

                            - 149 -

```
                    never forgive yourself!
                    Trust me, I know what
                    it's like… you'll never
                    sleep… you'll …

                         ANGELA
                    I don't care! You have to
                    pay for this! I don't
                    care if I never sleep
                    again… you have to…

Angela is suddenly taken by surprise as Michael
swoops in and scoops the gun out of her hands.
But to her and Thomas' surprise, he turns the
gun back on his father.

                         THOMAS
                    Michael…?

                         MICHAEL
                    I know you didn't mean
                    for this to happen. You…
                    you were just trying to …
                    just trying to protect
                    us…

Thomas looks into his son's eyes. Can he see
himself? If so, he already knows why Michael is
doing this before the boy speaks again.

                         MICHAEL (cont'd)
                    But Mum wants to kill you
                    for what happened to
                    Adam. I can't let her do
                    that… I can't let her…
                    she wouldn't… she didn't
                    even know to take the
                    safety off…

Michael can't continue but Thomas knows. Michael
is his father's son. And Thomas himself finds he
can't argue with his wife, distressed as she may
be. Maybe there was another way. Maybe this
could have been avoided. He spreads his arms out
and looks Michael in the eye and gives his
silent permission.

Michael straightens his gun arm but it's
trembling so much, he can't seem to pull the
```

trigger. As much as he tries, the moment won't
come. Before he knows it, he has let his arm
drop. The gun points harmlessly toward the snow.

                    ANGELA
          No!

Angela rushes forward and snaps the gun from
Michael's hand, points it at her husband and
pulls the trigger. Thomas' head flies apart. He
staggers then falls to the ground. He's on his
back, staring blankly into the white-grey dusky
sky.

Angela screams in grief and rage. She can't
believe what she's done. Michael stares at the
body of his father. He turns to say something –
he doesn't know what – to his mother; and sees
her with the gun to her own temple.

                    MICHAEL
          Mum, *no!*

But she has already pulled the trigger. Michael,
in silent shock and horror stands alone in the
crimson-stained snow of the front garden of his
childhood home, staring at the still, lifeless
bodies of his family.

END OF ACT 1

twenty :
fathers and sons

FOR SOME REASON, I'm not getting a whole lot of sleep tonight. I mean, the bed's warm, my fiancée's asleep beside me, the central heating's making that really quiet hissing sound that seems to annoy some people but sends me right off to sleep. So there's no reason I should be having trouble getting some shut-eye.

Oh yeah, apart from that whole 'watching my family shoot itself dead' thing.

For the last couple decades, I've managed to shut all that stuff out. Well, kind of. I made it unreal. Like a movie. It happened but not to me. Just to some made up people that don't really exist.

So it wasn't me who saw all the people I loved most in the world get blown away inside of five minutes. It wasn't me who went to live with my uncle – who I ended up getting to really like, only to see him get killed too. It wasn't me who ended up going through those early, painful days as a hired gun.

No, Mike Shepard – the *real* Mike Shepard, assassin extraordinaire – sprang fully formed from the universe's womb eighteen years ago. There was no heart-wrenching or hurtful decision-making process behind his birth. There were no long, sleepless nights obsessing over the nature of protection. Endlessly wondering what would have happened if I had pulled the trigger and killed my dad instead of letting my mom do it.

No, none of that. I just … popped into being. The most pain-free labour ever.

Well, until Emily came along, anyway.

See, it's all her fault. I've a mind to wake her up right now and tell her. 'Look, you,' I'd say, 'I was perfectly happy locking away all my emotions – then you had to come along and remind me I'm a regular human being. Next, I'll be crying at *Sleepless in Seattle*.' Of course, then I'd have to tell her about being an assassin.

Maybe I *should* tell her.

Not 'someday' but right now. Wake her up and tell her everything. See what happens.

I reach for my phone and dial a number I've only used once before. When the ringing stops and the weary, croaky voice on the other end answers, I speak.

"I'm coming over."

*   *   *

"This'd better be good. In fact, forget that. This'd better be huge. Massive. Like, bigger than when I found out who shot Phil Mitchell a week before anyone else. Is it that big? Bigger?"

"Jeremy," I say. "Jeremy hired me to kill his dad."

For once – and I wish I could take a picture – Sarah Jane is stunned into silence.

"Can I come in?" I ask. "I'm freezing my ass off out here."

I don't really wait for her to stand aside. I just walk in. By the time I hear her close the door, I'm already in the living room.

She comes in behind me, very fetchingly kitted out in paint-stained sweatpants, an old, nearly threadbare nightshirt and that small, ivory pendant.

Her living room's not a tidy place. Very her, though. Stuff everywhere but, still, you can just about see some kind of sense to it. Like her, the room needs serious help. But she can wait. I'm first in line.

"Jeremy?" she repeats as she wanders into the room. "You know, that actually makes sense."

"Really?"

"No. What the *hell's* going on?"

"Okay," I pick up an empty pizza box and glance at her. She nods at the two-seater sofa and I drop it on there, next to about fifty CDs all in piles of various heights. "So, Jeremy… I went and read the sponsor details."

"You did?" she somehow manages to combine surprise with smugness.

"Yes," I don't look at her. I look at the TV with a gang of beer bottles on the top.

She can't help herself anymore. "Finally caring about the plot, eh?"

"Can I finish?"

"Sorry. Please. Jeremy."

I'm sat forward. My elbows are on my knees and my hands are together. Like I'm praying, or something. I'm sure Sarah Jane the amateur psychologist can tell something more than Jeremy's involvement is bothering me. But if she can, she's wisely not pursuing it for now.

"Remember what you said about Geoff wanting to leave his half of Guardian Shipping to Jeremy?" I begin. "Well, turns out Jeremy's not so keen. Apparently, he's actually tried to get his dad to sell his half back to Fraser. Wants him to quit the crook game altogether. Turns out he doesn't want a crimelord for a dad."

I pick up an empty beer bottle off the floor. "He just wants a dad."

"But Geoff refused," Sarah Jane guesses.

"Apparently, he wants to provide for the kid and one day he'll understand," I exhale in what I think is a sour laugh. "But, Jeremy – far as I can tell – he can't take the whole thing anymore. Figures his dad's better off dead now. That way, him and his mom don't have to kill themselves with worry, waiting for the proverbial phone call in the middle of the night."

Sarah Jane puts her hands on top of her head and locks her fingers as she lets this new piece of information filter itself through the puzzle spaces in her brain. "Of course; then he runs away out of guilt – hence he wasn't thinking straight enough to take his wallet or anything. But if he's still not shown up, he must be getting help from somewhere. Assuming, of course, he's not dead. And if it's his first hit – and it sounds like it is – they'll have made him leave an abort option on. Chances are it'll just be a straight 'change of mind' one. So if I find him, I might be able to get him to call it in…"

Her voice trails off as she continues to think it all through but her eyes catch me sitting there still. Her hands come off her head and her expression changes - I can feel the next question before it even hits.

"Why did you read the sponsor details?"

"Because of Emily's gran."

"Come again?"

- 154 -

I take a deep breath. I pause. Then I leap in.

"My dad was a Protector. You know the type. They'll do anything to protect and provide for their own. But Protectors can get real caught up in their job. They can start providing things that weren't originally wanted. Protecting from things that weren't originally a threat.

"In the end, his chosen method of protection killed my kid brother. I tried to kill my dad. Not because I wanted to. On the contrary, I knew he was just doing his best. But I knew if I didn't kill him, my mom would. And I knew it'd tear her heart out to do it. But I couldn't pull the trigger. So, as predicted, my mom did it. And, as predicted, it killed her."

"What, she was torn up by grief?"

"No, by the bullet she immediately pushed through her brain."

Sarah Jane goes quiet again. She looks like I must have looked when she told me her tale of woe.

"The point is," I go on, "I can see both sides of Jeremy's problem. I've been the kid who just wanted his dad. But I also inherited my dad's bag; I can see how you would want to do terrible things to protect the ones you love. My dad did it. And now, so do I. Every job I take on. I'm not just fulfilling some cosmically-appointed role to protect random strangers from the act of killing. With every job I'm…with every job I'm…"

"Trying to save your mother."

My eyes are burning. I can't take them off the empty bottle my fingers are playing with.

Neither of us says anything for a long time. Eventually, I can't take the silence any more.

"God," I say, getting up. I thump the bottle down on top of the TV, next to its kin, "I had such great walls built up around me, y'know, around my feelings and all that. Made life real easy." I turn to Sarah Jane. "Y'know, between you, Emily and Jeremy, you've managed to wreck some mighty fine craftsmanship in a mighty short space of time."

She smiles. "I'm good at pulling stuff down, me. Not so good at building stuff, but good at pulling it down. I mean, I am working on my building skills – you can see the beer bottle tower I'm starting over there on the-"

I'm looking at her like she's some kind of crazy creature.

"Yes, anyway, that's not important," she goes on. "What's important is that you've remembered you're not some kind of elemental force or a mindless robot – you're actually a member of the human race. And when you're a person … well … life sucks. And it sucks for the exact same reason it's great. Because everything we do is up to us."

She sits down and tugs my arm so I sit back down next to her. For the first time since I came in here, she looks me straight in the eye.

"You kill people for a living, Michael. You kill people for money. You can't hide from that. If you're going to keep on doing it, you need to accept that you're doing it not because you were meant to or because it's how your father made you or any of that bullshit … you need to accept that you're doing it because you have *chosen* to do it. Then, whether you stop, like I did, or whether you carry on, at least you won't be lying to yourself anymore."

"As easy as that, huh?" I shrug. "Just…make a choice?"

"You have to. Hitman or married man. You can't have both. It just won't work."

I don't even pause. "I don't know that I'm ready to give up my job but I'm not calling off the wedding. No way. I love Emily. That's the one thing that hasn't wavered, hasn't even flickered this whole time. If I'm not sure about anything else, I'm sure about that."

Sarah Jane smiles a half smile. She's not happy I won't commit to quitting the hitman game. But then, this isn't about her. It's not her life gets changed beyond all recognition if I quit or if I don't.

There's another look in her eye, though, when I was talking about Emily. Something she's trying to hide.

"What?" I say, seeing the smile on her face, flicker.

"Nothing."

"Tell me."

"It's probably nothing."

"It's gone from 'nothing' to 'probably nothing' awful fast. Tell me."

"Well…" she's trying to figure out her editing process.

"Don't skimp," I warn her.

"Okay – it's just that I was talking to Geoff yesterday - since you told me he'd taken the hit out on Fraser. Y'know, trying to get the lay of the land, trying to get my hands on anything that might help me find Jeremy and put an end to this craziness. Anyway, from talking to him … I don't think he took a hit out on Fraser at all."

I shake my head. "I know what I heard…"

"Well, Geoff was talking about Fraser like he expected him to be around for some time yet. I mean, it's hard to mask that kind of loathing. Are you sure you heard absolutely right?"

I stand up, I need to stretch my legs. My head's throbbing, my mouth is dry. This is all coming at me a little too fast and from too many angles.

I definitely heard Geoff say Fraser had to pay. But if he didn't take the hit out against *Fraser*…

I suddenly go cold all over.

"Emily."

Sarah Jane's face suddenly takes on the kind of expression where everything starts making sense – except it's not the kind of sense you want.

"That's what I thought, too. Jeremy's got a hit out on his dad. His dad's got a hit out on your fiancée," Sarah Jane's shaking her head. "How many hitmen do we have running around Nottingham this week, anyway?"

"Well, maybe one more," I say and she looks at me, quizzically. "Someone's put a hit out on me, too."

Sarah Jane buries her head in her hands. "God… this is all getting a little too Guy Ritchie for me… Okay…"

She looks up and tries to get a grip on the situation. She's good at that – getting swamped in all kinds of mess but somehow taking control of it.

"Tell me."

So I tell her all about my antics with Malcolm the Milkman and crazy, lovely old Granny Coleman.

"She thinks you're a good person?"

I shrug.

Sarah Jane shakes her head. "Well, there's no accounting for taste. Anyway, we have three separate hits. But all interconnected. They've got to be. No co-incidence is this big. You want my guess on who took the hit out on you?"

"Oh, please, let me guess – the Easter Bunny? No, wait, Santa Claus."

Sarah Jane nods. "Okay, so we're agreed that one was probably Fraser. Wait a second..."

She roots around the clutter of her room and miraculously produces a sheet of paper and a pen. She writes three names down the left hand side and three down the right and draws lines between them; Jeremy to Geoff, Geoff to Emily, Fraser to me.

Sarah Jane's right – all we need now are two antique rifles, some gypsies and a big diamond and we'd have ourselves a movie.

She looks at me. "Thoughts?"

"Can we find out if Fraser used the Agency?" I start. "Because if he did, then dollars to donuts they've used the same guy for Emily and me. And I don't like the idea of that, because the guy that's after me is good. And also a total whacko."

"I can get right on that," she says, tapping out a message into a hurriedly produced cell phone. It goes unspoken between us that she has contacts, inroads and favours that allow her to potentially get info from the Agency that even I wouldn't be able to get.

As Sarah Jane taps away on her phone, my eyes scan the room, passing over some old bills addressed to Sarah Jackson – presumably her married name.

"Part of me just wants Geoff and Fraser to wipe each other out, pair of mean old bastards," I say partly to Sarah Jane and partly to myself. "But, boy, would that leave one hell of a mess. Apart from anything else, there'd be two kids whose worlds'd be blown apart. You don't care what your dad does, he's still your dad, y'know?"

My eyes continue to scan aimlessly around the room, not really seeing anything until they land on a yule-scene snow-globe (because, y'know, Christmas was only six months ago so it's totally understandable she hasn't gotten round to putting it away yet). I'm amused at first but then I suddenly see a little snowman kid standing in the middle of the blood red snow, a murdered snowman family scattered around him.

I find myself turning back to face Sarah Jane, a new resolve wrapping itself round me. "We've got to unravel this mess. I don't care if I've got to kill a thousand people, I'm not letting anything happen to Emily. Absolutely nothing."

Sarah Jane's sent her message and is sitting back on the sofa, the rusty cogs in her head cranking for all they're worth. "Well we know Geoff's got an abort and we're ninety-nine percent sure Jeremy's got one. So we've got a gap in this mess where we can jam our crowbar, so to speak."

I nod. "Find Jeremy, get him to call off his hit on his dad. Geoff has his son back, he calls off his hit on Emily. Hell freezes over, Fraser calls off his hit on me."

Sarah Jane shrugs, smiling. "Plan can't fail. All we've got to do is find Jeremy. And pray to God about the Hell thing."

I laugh a little. Somehow, I knew that coming here, thrashing things out with Sarah Jane, we'd work something out and I'd feel better. Everyone needs a slightly alcoholic friend – they're good at thinking outside the box.

"So I guess you get your wish," I say. "I help you find Jeremy after all."

"It wasn't for me I wished that," she says. "Well, okay, a little bit. But mainly it was for Jeremy. And for you."

I know what she means. Me looking for Jeremy shows that I'm at least starting to let the assassin thing slide a little. Accept there are other options to resolving a problem aside from killing somebody. Is that a good thing, though? The thought of loosening my grip on my gun handle, even a little bit, makes me feel strangely naked. Exposed. But then, the one person that makes all that not matter is lying asleep several miles away right now.

"I've got to tell her everything," I say, almost to myself, "and hope she still wants to marry me."

Sarah Jane shakes her head. "Absolutely not. Not until you've decided whether you're going to marry her or keep killing for a living."

"Hey, look," I don't want to berate her, she's being a big help, but *still...* "if there's a choice to be made, I'll make it – but in my own good time. When I'm ready. I'm getting married to Emily on Saturday, that's it. Okay?"

"Okay, fine," Sarah Jane says, a little annoyed. "But just think about the practicalities of telling her everything at this point. We need to concentrate on keeping her alive. We find Jeremy, then go ahead, sing like a bloody canary. 'Til then, though, I think it might just complicate things. What if she runs off to stay with a friend or something? You need to keep everybody where you can see them without having to turn your head."

I think about it for a moment, then nod slowly. "Okay, you're right. It's just that I don't know exactly how much practical use I'm going to be to you. I'm going to have to stick to Emily like glue to make sure that -"

Sarah Jane's phone beeps. Incoming message. She picks it up.

"Agency," she says.

"*Already?!*"

"I pulled in a big favour for this one, Mikey, and…" her face drops, "…oh my God…"

"What..?"

"You and Emily are sharing an assassin, like you thought. You'll never guess who it is."

I can't believe she got that info out of them!

"So, don't keep me in suspense…"

"Jack Winter."

Oh my God. Without wanting to sound overdramatic, he's pretty much the most feared assassin on the planet. And I was right in my earlier assessment – a complete whacko.

"What did I do to deserve that?" I wonder. "Run over the boss' cat or something?"

"I've got to admit," Sarah Jane says quietly, looking at her phone screen in case the words on it suddenly change to something more pleasant, "this is not good."

"Damn right it's not good," I still can't quite believe it. "The guy'd kill his own mom to get to his grandmother, you've heard the stories."

Suddenly, my encounter with the milkman seems to make so much more sense.

"Yes," she says, "and I also know he's going to kill you both in the church on your wedding day."

"How the hell do you know that?!"

She holds up the phone, so I can see the message. "Because he told the Agency he's going to kill you both in the church on your wedding day."

Numb, I read the message, taking in every word. It's true – once he was given the Emily job to be added to mine and saw he was now killing a betrothed pair, he told the Agency he was going to kill us both at the altar.

"Is this guy totally crazy?" I ask, somewhat redundantly.

"Crazy like a wolf."

"Fox."

"No," Sarah Jane says, "like a wolf. He's a predator, the kind you can't ever shake off. Once he gets his sights on you, it's just a matter of time. It doesn't matter if he tells you where, when and how he's going to get you, you can't do anything to stop it. Like a Terminator."

"So he's crazy like a Terminator."

"Do you remember the thing with Lars Henriksson?"

I nod, I remember it. I read about it in the paper and later found out from the Agency that it was one of Jack's.

The guy – billionaire businessman, mogul-type – knew a hit was out on him. Knew it was going to be before this big AGM where he was going to sign stuff that would put various other big corps straight out of business. So he surrounded himself with the best protection his huge fortune could buy – including some ex-assassins who knew what subtle things to look out for. Along comes the day of the AGM, old Lars thinks he's made it. Just as everyone sits down for the meeting, the boardroom lights go out. They come back on ten seconds later and Lars is nowhere to be seen. They find him two floors up in an empty boardroom. Hanging from the ceiling by his neck. Which was pretty impressive seeing as his head was nowhere to be found.

"Having said all that..." Sarah Jane looks thoughtful, "...this might really work for us." I'm sure I don't look convinced so she elaborates. "Nobody but nobody is invincible. Not even bogeyman Jack, I don't care what the stories say. If he wants to go throwing target sites around, he'll find you and me waiting for him."

I want to believe her but I keep seeing the headless body of Lars Henriksson being spirited past twenty bodyguards.

Come on, Michael. Faith. Otherwise, we might as well throw in the towel right now.

"Okay," I say, with a deep breath, "so we find Jeremy and thereby save Geoff and Emily. Then, somehow get the drop on Jack before he perforates my skull."

"Yup," Sarah Jane nods. "Also, not forgetting that if we manage to somehow survive all that, you then have to pull off the magical feat of convincing Fraser to call off his hit on you otherwise some other guy'll just get assigned. And it *does* have to be *after* the wedding – if Jack only has to kill Emily, he might not bother waiting 'till the big day and we'll lose our advantage. We won't know when he plans to get her until a bullet whizzes through her head."

"Well, that all seems easy enough," I say. "Hell, let's throw in bringing peace to the Middle East as well. Y'know, for a real challenge."

"You know you love it," I can't believe she's actually grinning. "Sit down, we've got a plan to draw up and a Jeremy to find."

"And I really do want to find him," I pull up a chair, "because I'm going to wring that damn kid's neck."

twenty one :
private investigations

THIS INDECISION'S KILLIN' me. *If you don't want me, set me free. Exactly who'm I s'posed to be? Don't you know which clothes even fit me? So come on and let me know – should I stay or should I go?"*

It's funny how that happens. Whatever your state of mind, your brain picks up the relevant things from the surrounding environment to echo it. Right now, I'm sitting in the Colemans' kitchen, eating my breakfast, trying to decide if I should carry on killing people for a living. And The Clash opt to join in on the debate from inside the radio.

I always planned on telling Emily about my job – but I never figured what I'd do if she wanted me to stop. My job is so deeply ingrained into who I am, would I even be the same person if I gave it up? Would I still like myself? Would Emily like me? Would I still get free subscription to 'Guns and Ammo'? So many questions.

It's not nice being indecisive about something. Not when life is usually so simple and decisions get made once and fast. Take the job or not. Use a gun or not. Have the eggs or not. I don't usually dwell on choices. But after thrashing things out with Sarah Jane last night, I know there's a lot more to why I'm doing this than I ever wanted to admit. So it's a decision that bears some 'dwelling'.

But, hey, let's wait until after the sociopath who wants to kill me and my bride at the alter has been stopped.

Like telling Em about my vocation, this decision can also be postponed until inclement weather has passed. And, hell, maybe a little longer after that.

The time will present itself. Why rush?

In the meantime, I need to just concentrate on looking after the woman that's the cause of and focus for all these unwelcome emotional conflicts.

Speaking of whom, here she comes. Bright sunshine of my day, light of my life, apple of my –

"Where the hell where you last night, you tosser?!"

Okay, she seems a little pissed right now…

"Morning, cupcake." I try to turn on the charm. "Would you like some honey crunchy cornflakes?"

Unsurprisingly, she ignores the honey crunchy cornflakes. "I wake up at two a.m. and you aren't home. Somewhat worried by how agitated you were earlier, I wait up for you for three hours until the matchsticks under my eyelids can't take it anymore and I fall back into an unsettled, fitful and altogether crap sleep. Then I get up two very unrested hours later and here you are merrily enjoying breakfast and listening to the bloody Clash! So, like I said, would you mind filling me in on where the hell you were last night, you tosser?"

I want to tell her everything, I really do. But Sarah Jane's right. The only way to save Em's life – not to mention mine and Geoff's – is to assume control over the situation. And it's going to be a lot easier to do that if all the pieces of that situation aren't bouncing around like Mexican jumping beans.

"I've been thinking about my parents."

"Oh," she suddenly turns the 'angry' dial down and the 'begrudgingly sheepish' dial up. "Sorry."

"It's okay," I turn back to my honey crunchy cornflakes.

"No, it's not okay," she says, coming round to my side of the breakfast bar. "I should have realised that's what's been getting at you. It's only natural to think about them at a time like this. It's just that… well… it's like, sometimes," she seems a bit embarrassed, "I forget they died because *you* seem to have forgotten."

"No, seriously, Em, it's okay," I turn to her. "You're absolutely right. I never mention them. Never talk about what happened. And I do want to tell you about it. But, to be honest, I'm not sure what I saw. I have to get it all straight in my head. And you're right, it has been this wedding that's making it all come out. But I'm dealing with it."

The fact that everything I just said is technically true doesn't make me feel any better for effectively spinning her a line. But I keep imagining her with a bullet hole in her head and I remind myself that whatever I have to do to keep this woman alive and safe, I'll do it.

She nods and looks for all the world like she wants to say something. Something that's been playing on her mind. But instead, she just says;

"You know, I wish your parents could have been here."

I suddenly feel all flush with emotion (that damn stuff again) as my mind races back to happier times, when dad was working and we were a family.

"You know what," I say, truthfully, "I reckon they would've really liked you."

Em smiles and I hold her in my arms. Whatever she wanted to say seems to be gone for now.

"I can never stay angry with you," she says. "Git."

The rest of the day seems to go pretty fast. While Emily and her mother are making yet more changes to the seating plan, I get a crash course in being a P.I.

In lots of ways, it's no different to what I'm used to. When I line up a hit and figure out my window, there's a lot of deduction and character assessment goes on. Generally, the more I can figure out from watching afar, the less I have to show my face by going in to verify things in person.

Then there's digging up info on other people in the target's circle of movement. Friends, relatives, whatever. Studying the target's interaction with others can give valuable insight into the target itself. It's this activity that seems to yield our first lead of the day.

"Gillian Gasforth," Sarah Jane says. "Jeremy's favourite aunt, apparently. Well, she's not really related at all, just a friend of the family. That's why it's taken me so long to track her down."

We're sat in a coffee shop on the outskirts of the city centre. It's kind of studenty so we shouldn't be spotted by any of Emily's friends or anything. I told her I was going to Scarborough today to visit my parents' graves. I think I actually would quite like to do that, if I should live so long.

It's daytime, so the 'Keane' track coming out the jukebox is at a low, hangover-friendly volume. There's a few people dotted around, mostly reading. A few chatting. I can hear something about skipping a lecture and getting the notes off someone called 'Dodge'.

There's something different about Sarah Jane today but I can't put my finger on what. In the end, I settle for a new hairstyle. But I don't say anything in case I'm wrong. I figure – right or wrong – that it's better to miss the fact she's done her hair than to compliment her when she hasn't done anything to it. If I need to revise that tactic, I'm sure married life'll set me straight before too long.

I look at the info Sarah Jane's scribbled down on Gillian Gasforth.

"How come you had to 'track her down'?" I ask. "Didn't Geoff give you this?"

"He's been frustratingly reticent in giving me family details."

"What?! Does he want his son back or not?"

Sarah Jane shakes her head. "Don't forget, he's convinced Fraser's done something to Jeremy. As far as he's concerned, he's hired me to dig into Fraser's comings and goings. He considers any attempts to look at Jeremy running away as a waste of time."

"You're sure it's *not* a waste of time?" I can feel the passage of time pretty keenly at the moment.

"He's definitely run away. I can feel it," Sarah Jane says, sipping her coffee. I'm tempted to ask her if the coffee's neat. "And hopefully Ms. Gasforth here'll be able to give us something solid to go on. You planning on eating that?"

I push the remainder of my toast toward her. "You know, there's a guy at my work you'd get on with."

"He an assassin?"

"Insurance salesman. So, we're going now? To see this Gasforth woman?"

I really want to get this show on the road.

"Let me just finish my coffee and your toast," Sarah Jane lifts her cup and lets my glare slide off her. "I'll be five minutes. I just need to try and revel in being one hundred per cent sober for a couple of minutes every few days."

That's when I realise what's different about her today. She's different than I've seen her before. She seems calm. Relaxed. Not running her mouth off.

Like she says, she's enjoying her moment of clarity. Or trying to. I've seen drunks and I've seen drunks and I know when they're itching to get some alcohol into their system. They genuinely enjoy *not* drinking and you can see them literally fighting the urge to leap over the bar and sink a bottle of whatever they can get their hands on. Holding the darkness at bay, so to speak. And I can see Sarah Jane doing it now.

It's really a very sad thing to watch.

What's really sad – and I am feeling a bit of a rat about it – is that I don't want to dig any of her issues up with her. She's clearly got things that need dealing with and she seems to have been successfully ignoring them since way before I showed up. As much as I don't need Emily jumpy right now, I *really* don't need Sarah Jane jumpy.

"What are you thinking?" she says, still looking out the window at the early shoppers.

"I'm thinking it shouldn't take so long to eat some damn toast, come on already."

"You know," she suddenly smiles a smile so sad, it breaks my heart to see it, "for an assassin, you're a rubbish liar."

"Yeah, I skipped those classes," I sit back in my chair and look around a little before going back to her. "Okay, I was thinking about your drinking."

"And what exactly were you thinking about my drinking?" she seems amused by the fact the sentence rhymes. Even still, I swear she seems like she's about to cry or something.

"Well…" I stumble, "I just think there's something you're not telling me."

"About what?"

"Your ex-husband. The one you killed."

"I didn't kill him."

"What?" I stop, puzzled.

"That's what I'm not telling you. There you are, you were right. God, you're good at this game. What shall we play next?"

"You didn't kill him?" I repeat, a little surprised. "So why tell me-"

"Oh, why do you think, Michael?" this is the first time I've seen her actually annoyed. "Because that's what I *wish* happened."

"Oh..." I say, stupidly.

"Yeah. Oh." She smiles bitterly to herself. "I mean, I shot him. Definitely shot him. Probably clipped his leg or something. But blowing his brains out? I wish."

All of a sudden, like some kind of load-bearing brick, that one piece of information lets loads of others all slot into place.

"He's still out there, isn't he?" I say. "Killing people."

She nods, mute.

"And you're here, trying to find people. Lost people. To... what? Balance the people he's taking away out there? Because you didn't kill him?"

She nods again, still staring out the window. All of a sudden, she can't look at me.

"And you haven't just tracked him down and killed him because...?"

"I can't find him," she says, trying to hold her voice steady. "I just can't find him."

The crushing reality of the situation she's built up for herself suddenly comes clear.

"So you can't stop finding people. You've got to keep going. For... what... forever?"

She slow claps me. "Well done, give the man a gold star."

Man. Between her burning for revenge, feeling all his kills are on her conscience and chasing an impossible, eternal task, it's no wonder she drinks. Hell, it's a wonder she doesn't drink *more*.

But there's more. I don't know why, but her words don't ring true as being the be all and end all of her emotional problems. I don't know what she's not telling me – but, hey, I reckon it's none of my business. Hell, we hardly know each other, really. It'd be rude to keep on pressing.

Yeah, yeah, whatever rationale flies your plane, Mikey. Truth is, I don't want her messed up. I need her on her game, Emily's life depends on it.

Am I being selfish? Well, when it comes to Emily not ending up with a bullet in her head, hell yes I am.

We sit in silence for a couple minutes. She just carries on sipping her tea and eating my toast.

On the other side of the shop, a girl's annoying ring tone goes off and she starts talking too loud into her phone. The girl next to her sits back in her chair now her chat-buddy is otherwise engaged. She starts to text some essay on her own phone.

Keane finishes and Kaiser Chiefs comes on.

"Come on," Sarah Jane is suddenly back from outer space, that cover-all yet engaging smile back on her face. "Let's go and see Gillian Gasforth."

twenty two :
house call

ANTI-CLIMAX. THAT'S the only word that can describe my first foray into the world of the private investigator. Here I was, all primed and ready to pump this Gasforth woman for answers, trying to decide whether I should be good cop or bad cop and...

She's not in.

"Let me try," I step forward and bang hard on the door.

"Good idea," Sarah Jane says. "If you hit it hard enough, she might suddenly be in."

I step back at stare at the door, like I'm expecting it to do something.

Frustration. That's another word. Some other words are starting to form now, too, but they aren't nearly so polite.

"Okay, plan B," Sarah Jane says. She takes a furtive look around then sets off down the side of the house. I follow her and we soon end up round back.

It's a fairly large place which is pretty burglar friendly – it has loads of really high trees and bushes to give people in the garden privacy from the neighbours. Also, it faces a church rather than another house so there's no-one looking at the front to notice any odd behaviour. Well, y'know, except God.

I watch, mightily impressed, as Sarah Jane jimmies the back door lock and pops it within about eight seconds. She shakes her head and smiles triumphantly as the door swings meekly open.

"Multiple choice question," she says with an insufferable grin. "I'm 'A' – Brilliant, 'B' – Brilliant or 'C' – Brilliant."

I flash a little salute to her greatness and she strolls into the kitchen, her pain from this morning apparently forgotten.

"Wait a minute," I freeze, suddenly. "What about an alarm?"

"I've got one, thanks," she's already started opening drawers.

"No, I mean-"

"She hasn't armed it," she says going from drawer to drawer. "The little box on the front of the house? It's an Artek, very old model. They have relatively complicated arming processes – made before technology was supposed to be easy to use for regular people. Most alarmed houses that get robbed have got unarmed Artek alarms fitted. Gillian's in her fifties. Chances are she *never* arms it."

"You were so confident of that before you came in, were you?"

She looks up from her latest open drawer with a crooked smile. "Do you *hear* an alarm going off?"

I shake my head. The woman never ceases to amaze me. When I'm prepping a hit, I'm a dot the I's, cross the T's sort of guy. This woman blows through on a wing and a prayer. Or maybe the speed that she sizes people up, sometimes without even meeting them, just makes it look that way.

Either way, I have to admit to being impressed.

"So, what are we looking for?" I might as well help rather than sit around with my thumb up my ass.

"Not 'looking'," she says with yet another air of triumph. "Found."

She pulls a drawer right out and places it on the counter top.

"Receipts," I nod, approvingly. "I like your thinking."

"If Jeremy's been in touch and hit her up for any cash," Sarah Jane rifles through the slush pile, "we just might find...ah ha!"

She holds it aloft, checking it over, making sure it is what it appears to be. Satisfied, she turns it round so I can see it, yet another grin of triumph spread across her face.

An ATM receipt for two hundred and fifty pounds.

"Check out the date," Sarah Jane says. "The day Jeremy goes missing."

I nod. "Not cast iron proof but pretty good for starters."

"Now I know what kind of telltale reactions to look for when I start questioning her," she says, putting the receipt and the draw back.

- 171 -

"He must have told her why he's run away," I think aloud, "for her not to have told Geoff she's been in contact with him."

Sarah Jane nods as she slides the drawer home. "Either that or he's convinced her he'll go home or contact his parents soon. When he's sorted his head out or whatever."

"Okay, so what now – we go back outside and wait for her to show?"

"Well, actually, I need to leave her a note – a-ha!" Sarah Jane finds a pad of blank paper next to a pen on a string.

"What?! You're going to break in and leave a note?" I can't quite believe it. "You going to wash the dishes too?"

My PI mentor doesn't answer me – she just scribbles something down about needing to talk to her about Jeremy. She leaves her cell number. Then, she wanders out to the hall, right to the front door, folds the note in half and drops it on the mat.

She comes back down the hall, toward the kitchen and smiles at my bemused stare.

"There's no point in going outside to put a note through the letterbox when I'm already in the house," she says like this situation is the most normal thing in the world. "Where's the logic in that?"

"You don't think she'll notice the paper's from a pad inside her own house?"

Sarah Jane shakes her head. "Plain paper, standard size? Not a chance."

I raise an eyebrow as she walks past me. "You sure about that?"

She doesn't even turn to look at me.

"Do you *hear* an alarm going off?"

twenty three :
progress

GILLIAN GASFORTH HASN'T called back and it's
almost four pm. Which is worrying on the one hand and just plain
frustrating on the other. She's almost certainly been in touch with
Jeremy since his disappearance and I need to know what she
knows.

The fact she lives on a street where no-one knows the first
thing about their next door neighbours didn't help us track her
down. Has she gone for a day out shopping? Has she gone on a
swingers' holiday to Bermuda for three weeks? Who the heck
knows?

Chances are, if she's been in touch with Jeremy, she won't
have gone anywhere for long – she'll want to continue being there
for him. But if we don't speak to her and track that damn kid
down before Saturday morning when I head down that aisle, it
won't matter *what* she knows.

So how have we been spending the rest of our day, Sarah
Jane and me? Why, doing the glamorous job of a private detective,
of course.

"Excuse me, have you seen this kid?"

"No, sorry."

That's one of the polite ones.

"Excuse me, have you seen this kid?"

"No."

That's one of the psychic ones who can say 'no' without
even looking at you or the photo.

"Excuse me, have you seen this kid?"

"Get a job."

That's one of the ones that are so behind their conviction, they say it over their shoulder as they walk away.

After four hours of this, I turn to Sarah Jane, a single word summing up everything I'm feeling about this activity.

"Seriously?"

"What, you didn't think I spent my whole time in car chases and fist fights?" she smiles that crooked smile.

"Well, not your *whole* time," I admit, "but I did think your job would be slightly more productive than showing the kid's picture to a bunch of disinterested strangers."

I look around me at Mansfield town centre. Like Doncaster, it's another historic town with mining roots but even closer to Nottingham. Sarah Jane figures this would be the perfect place for Jeremy to have gone to ground; not too far away but far enough that he's nowhere near the scene of his guilt.

But having no idea whereabouts in Mansfield he might be – or if he's even here in the first place – we're reduced to this most basic, mind-numbingly dull and (most crucially) excruciatingly ineffective method of searching.

I'm sure if getting the police involved wasn't a no-no, Sarah Jane would have us hanging a banner across the market with 'Jeremy come home, your dinner's getting cold' scrawled across it in giant red letters.

"Look," she says, rubbing her hands together against the unseasonal cold, "when you've got no leads, no clues and your quarry isn't listed in the top five search results on Google, then you hit the streets. A lot of this job is throwing darts blindly at a dartboard and seeing if any of them stick in."

"And what if one of your darts sticks in the ass of one of the big, beefy skinhead guys playing pool over in the corner?"

"Then I've probably pulled."

My cell beeps. At first I ignore it in case it's another request for a progress report from the Agency about my job on Geoff. There's only so many non-committal messages you can send in order to avoid saying 'I'm actually trying to save his life now'. But in the end, I reckon I'd better check in case it's Emily wanting to know how I made out in Scarborough.

I feel a twinge of guilt about lying to her. And an even bigger twinge of loss, that I'm not spending these last few days before the wedding with her. She's probably getting all kinds of stressed and I haven't noticed because I've been busy trying to kill her dad's business partner...before moving onto saving his life, her life and – if at all possible – my life.

Even so, I'd really like to be with her right now.

But the message isn't from the Agency or from Emily.

'Just hired our car. Did u know there's a funny stick in t middle wth numbers on it? What's wth that?'

It's from Jody.

"Hey, hey, the gang's all here!" I find myself saying out loud. I'm actually surprised at how glad I am the bunch of reprobates have arrived.

"Who's that?"

"The guys from the office."

"Oh, the ones with the fake pretend jobs that they think are real?"

"No..." I start to tap out a response, "the jobs are real it's their boss who's fake pretend."

Sarah Jane clicks her finger and puts it to her temple like, *'yeah, got it'*. Then sighs and says;

"Okay, look, you'd better go. I'm going to start hitting the main B&Bs in the area and maybe try one or two other things. I'll probably move faster on my own, anyway."

"I'll try not to be too offended," I stuff the picture of Jeremy in my jacket pocket, "but keep me updated, okay? I'm going to try and maybe figure some stuff out, too."

"Okay," she says, turning away. "Catch you later, Robin."

I let Batwoman wander off and watch her wave Jeremy's picture under a few more uncaring noses.

Even though none of the shoppers-on-their-way-home seem to recognise the kid, I feel a strange sense of positivity. I say strange because, so far, we've hit zip. Nothing. No clue, no help, barely any lead. And yet, for some crazy reason, I feel like Sarah Jane and me, we're going to come up with the goods, somehow. We'll dig up what we need to dig up and put the brakes on bogeyman Jack's plans. Maybe it's that strange woman's never-say-die attitude mixed with a generous helping of denial, but she certainly does inspire confidence. Y'know, once you get to know her.

The feeling stays with me all the way to the Gateway Hotel back in Nottingham where I meet up with the Shepard Insurance

Crew. I get there just ahead of them and watch Scooby Doo's mystery machine pull into the hotel parking lot before jolting to a stop about an inch away from some businessman's shiny, brand new Mercedes.

I watch Jody, Whilce, Bud and Lianne all spill out the side door and once again I feel internally surprised at how happy I am to see them. Am I turning into a woman, or something? Well, anyway, whatever it is, I listen with genuine interest at their multiple tales of travel woe – including but not limited to a nearly missed flight, a big, fat, sweaty man sitting next to Lianne on the plane, an over-enthusiastic drug-sniffing police dog and multiple near-death experiences on the motorway in the Mystery Machine.

"Bud and Lianne didn' want their food on the 'plane," Whilce reports when we're all chilling in Jody's room, "so I had to eat theirs as well as mine. Didn' want them going to waste or nothin', eh?"

"They didn't want their food because you told them the chicken was from Mexico and it was really rat," Jody's already checking to see if the mini-fridge has tiny bottles of alcohol in it.

"Hey, s'wat I heard, man."

"And you didn't believe him?" I ask my office manager.

"I didn't care," she says. "You any idea how hungry I was by that point? Hell, rat sounded good."

They tell me they're looking forward to the stag night (although Jody and Lianne are not supposed to come, being girls and all, I decided what the hell – they know me more than Emily, and she'll already have, like, a hundred girls going out with her while I'll have pretty much no-one). They're also looking forward to sight-seeing tomorrow daytime when I'm at the wedding rehearsal and (as Whilce puts it) preparing for my new life as Emily's bitch.

When I finally leave them after almost an hour (with Bud having thoroughly annoyed everyone by continually shouting *'London, baby!'*) and head back to the Colemans' through the rush-hour traffic, my previous feeling of confidence has been topped up with a good dose of happiness (yeah, you heard me). I mean, I've always liked all those guys - but today, they were different. More vibrant. More... *real.*

But I know it's not them that's changed. It's me. It feels kind of like I'm losing some of 'Mike the Assassin' and getting a little of

'Mike the Regular Guy Who Doesn't Kill People For a Living'. But despite what I might have thought just twenty-four hours ago, it actually feels like a *good* thing. And Karma's got to give me a thumbs up, right? After all, if you decide to put a little less emphasis on collecting paychecks for pushing strangers out of windows and put more emphasis on... well... *not* pushing strangers out of windows... the universe has got to cut you a break...

...right?

twenty four :
on the other hand…

"STOP LOOKING FOR Jeremy or I'll kill him and hang the corpse of your blushing bride over the doorway of the church to greet you when you arrive. Ta ta."

I just now got back to the Colemans' and this is a note pinned to their front door. Recent enough so that I'd be the only one who'd find it. He's watching me. He's been watching me and Sarah Jane all day. And he's standing by ready and waiting to feed us our own asses.

Karma sucks.

twenty five :
dry run

I'M NERVOUS. VERY nervous. Even more nervous than that time in Honduras with the pig market conference and all those soldiers and that accountant with the bomb in his pocket. Until today, that was in the number one spot.

We're at St. Margaret's, a little church out in the village of Bilsthorpe, a bunch of miles past Mansfield. We're not in the new part of the village where all the houses built for the coal miners are – we're in the old part. The picturesque part. One main road, one duck pond, one church.

Two assassins.

I know he's here somewhere. Jack. After the message he left on the door last night, I know he's following me. I mean, he could be following Sarah Jane to make sure she isn't still trying to find Jeremy. But he isn't. I know he isn't. He's here in Bilsthorpe watching me rehearse my wedding.

Having said that, I don't know where he could be hiding. It's not exactly a bustling metropolis out here. Maybe he's dressed as a frickin' cow or something.

"Look, Michael, you're behaving like a hysterical woman, now calm down before I put this phone down, come round there and bitch-slap you."

These were Sarah Jane's sympathetic words last night when I found the note.

She was as disturbed as I was to find that such a creature was stalking her every move, unseen. So, in case he was somehow listening in to our phone conversation, she just said to me that she would 'probably' stop looking for Jeremy. The unspoken plan was, of course, that as soon as we hung up, she'd go back to looking for the kid – just, maybe a little quieter.

So I didn't push it. After my initial shocked (and, okay, slightly and uncharacteristically hysterical) rant, we spoke briefly and then hung up. We didn't need to discuss too much about it all because it was mostly self-evident; he knows what we're doing, he really wants to kill me and Emily together in church, he's a complete and utter psychopath.

Yeah, I think that about covers the things we didn't talk about. In fact, all we did end up saying was 'keep your eyes open'.

So that's what I'm doing now. Pretending to get married. And keeping my eyes open.

"Okay, are we all ready?" says Reverend Mann. Seems like a nice old guy. Kindly face. Disarming smile. Could he be an assassin in disguise? Could he hide a tiny knife in that dog collar? I know he could hide two M-16 assault rifles in his cassock (yes, from experience...) – but is he our man?

I've checked out available info on the Rev so I know he is who he says he is. Definitely not an imposter and unlikely to be a part-time assassin.

Okay, let's discount Rev Mann. For now.

The only other people inside the small church are myself, Emily, Fraser, Mary, Emily's bridesmaids (Claire and Amanda, childhood girlfriends, they check out) and that's it. *What, no best man?*, I hear you cry. Well, I don't know anyone well enough to bestow that honour.

And it's only over the last twenty-four hours that I've become the least bit bothered about that.

Okay, so locations; Mary and me are sat up front, row one. She's on the left, I'm over here on the groom's side. She doesn't do a whole lot over this entire process except practice sitting there with an unfeasibly floral hat.

Rev Mann's standing front and centre, facing the imaginary congregation. Fraser, Emily and the bridesmaids are back by the door – they 'haven't arrived yet'.

And Jack? Who knows? Floating around with his anti-gravity, invisibility belt on.

"Okay, Michael," says Rev Mann in movie director mode, "you stay sitting down there just for now. Then when the car arrives, one of the ushers will give a nod to our organist-"

And everyone jumps out of their skin as the main door creaks open and a man in an ill-fitting grey suit shuffles in.

"Oh, Bert, speak of the devil!" says the Rev. "Everyone, this is Albert, our organist. Albert, I didn't think you were coming. How's Carol?"

The man mumbles something amiably to Emily and the group by the door and walks quickly but humbly up the aisle toward us. His suit looks old and comfortable for all its lack of girth around his gut. He pads quietly up the carpeted aisle in tartan slippers (also old and comfortable) and mumbles something to myself and Mary as he passes. I think it was 'hello'. He smells of chips. In a nice way.

He mumbles something to the Rev.

"Oh, I see," says Rev Mann, clearly fluent in this particular dialect of English, "and is she going to be okay?"

More mumbling. I think I catch 'stairs' and 'hairdryer'. And 'crutches'.

The pair share a brief, friendly chuckle and Bert bows and scrapes his way toward the organ.

"Well, we can have a full rehearsal now," Rev Mann says to us all, obviously pleased, "complete with organ music!"

"Oh, splendid!" says Mary, smiling at the Rev and Bert in turn. Well done, Mary, you can now practice sitting still to music.

While everyone else throws a little mini-party that Bert the organist has made a surprise appearance, I put a temporary hold on the balloons and mini-sausages. Does this guy look like a hitman?

Stupid question, of course. Hitmen don't have a look. They look like anything. Most look like nothing. Plain, dull, boring – but not too boring. They're not movie stars, they benefit from people not looking at them twice. They don't tend to have black, slick-backed hair with a scar across one pupil-less eye and a gold tooth. The ones that do don't tend to last too long.

So, Bert the hitman organist?

Well, the Rev checks out and he recognizes Albert so he can't be an imposter. That being the case, next question; is he actually Jack? Well, he's not pinging my radar. Doesn't feel like a secret hitman. Not because of his appearance. Actually, his appearance is perfect. Nobody'd suspect him. But just…I don't detect anything, y'know? Body language is wrong. Apparent physical fitness doesn't look anywhere near good enough. So for now, back seat.

"Okay," Rev Mann brings me back to the room, "the bride has arrived and the usher has given us the nod…" he nods at Bert.

Then two things happen at once.

'Here comes the bride' (or whatever it's really called) hammers out of the pipe organ. The instrument is only a little thing, like Bert himself. But when the two of them get together, they produce this powerful, breathtaking sound that you'd have never thought possible when looking at them as individuals.

The second thing that happens is my cellphone vibrates.

I've got a message.

Even though Emily, Fraser, Amanda and Claire are slowly walking up the aisle toward me and I really should practice looking wowed by Emily's radiance, I pull my phone from my pocket.

Ignoring the disapproving look I get from the Rev, I check out the message because I know in my gut who its from.

Should I shoot her now?

My whole body goes cold and I put the phone straight back in my pocket.

"Michael?" Rev Mann can see my face and his disapproval's turned into concern. "Are you alright?"

Well, I'm just about managing to keep myself from running around the room shouting 'everyone duck, there's an assassin in the church!'. Apart from that, I'm fine.

"Just nerves," I manage. "Ignore me."

By this time, Emily and Fraser have pulled up next to me. I smile but Em can see something's not quite right. But she doesn't say anything.

"Dearly beloved," the Rev starts, "we are gathered here today…" and on he goes. But I don't really hear him. I'm glancing around as subtle as I can. And thinking. Thinking real fast. Where can he be? There's only so many places but I don't see him. Neither the Rev nor Bert moved their hands when the message was sent. So unless it's Amanda or Claire, I don't think Jack's hiding in plain view.

My mind's racing, though. Might he actually just do it here, today? Why wait for the real day? Despite what he said on the note, he might have gone ahead and changed his plans anyway, not trusting we'd leave Jeremy alone.

Is Emily about to die? Am I?

"Michael?" the Rev, once again, brings me back to the room. I realise he's looking at me. Everyone's looking at me. Then, his words filter through from my subconscious to the surface of my brain. I suddenly remember his last few words.

I fumble in my pocket and bring out the ring. Rev Mann takes it and puts it on his little tray with the one Fraser's just given him.

My phone vibrates again.

"Sorry," I apologise to everyone as I pull the cell out again. "Real important, from New York, got to read this…"

This time, Emily can't keep the annoyed look off her face.

Maybe now. Let rings fall 2 the ground at same time u both do. Tragic image. I may cry.

I stuff the phone back into my pocket. Everyone is still looking at me.

"Lawyer's going through some stuff of mine back home. Important but boring, you know?" I say. "Sorry."

"At five in the morning?" Fraser says, somehow managing to exude annoyance and triumph all in one go.

"They're eager," is the best I can manage.

"Can we get on, then?" Em says. She's using that voice that says 'keep this crap up and your life won't be worth living'. That's fine. Our lives are potentially coming to an end in a few seconds anyway.

Except, maybe not.

My radar's quiet. Going by my brief encounter with him at Granny Coleman's house, I think he's toying with me again. Showing me how close he can get. Demonstrating how his finger's sitting right on the button. I'd be reassured that his overconfidence was a weakness to be exploited if not for the fact that I really do believe he actually could kill us whenever he wants.

But I'm convinced that 'whenever he wants' is not now.

I take Em's hand. "Sorry. Let's move on."

Rev Mann, as nice and understanding as can be, simply smiles and carries on.

My phone vibrates again.

I ignore it. I'm not letting him get to me. He's going to come for us tomorrow. I know it. This is just him trying to rattle me.

Trying to convince me to take him seriously when he tells us not to look for Jeremy. Well, screw you, Jack. I've got a rehearsal to –

About eight feet away, a small glass candle holder suddenly shatters. Everyone jumps at the tinkling sound.

"Oh, what was that?" Mary says from her spot in the pews.

The Rev shuffles over to the metal tray with the fallen candle and the shattered holder.

"Hm, how odd," he's examining the glass fragments like he was Columbo. Then he turns to us, a smile of reassuring contentment on his face. "Must have been the heat from the candle. It got too much for the holder and made it shatter."

Amanda makes some kind of joke about a poltergeist not wanting Emily to marry me. Everyone but Fraser laughs.

The fact that the candle's been burning inside that holder for God knows how many years with no problem seems not to bother anyone. I know what that was, though.

I take out my phone while people are still chuckling.

I'm going to get a coke. U want one?

The man is beyond psychopathic.

"Well, if it's okay with the poltergeists, shall we continue?" Rev Mann smiles as he takes mine and Emily hands. The group gets back on-mission and we go on.

We speed right through with no more interruptions. Jack has almost certainly actually gone to get a coke. He obviously feels he deserves one. After all, I'm not the only one running through a rehearsal today.

Before long, Bert and his little pipes are banging out a rousing round of exit music as Emily and me walk down the aisle, imagining we are looking at all the smiling, clapping relatives.

I don't bother looking around for Jack. He's not here anymore. He's not interested now. Far as he's concerned, we won't be doing this bit.

And I know for a fact, unless I can come up with something, he's absolutely right. We won't be walking out, we'll be carried out.

"Okay, come back!" Rev Mann calls and the music stops. We dutifully return to the front and the Rev runs through our exit from the church (don't use rice, use proper confetti because it's bio-degradable) and the photos (have a pre-prepared list of photos, it'll cut out the confusion). He asks if we have any questions. Em has a couple. Mary has one. I smile and shake my head.

Eventually, after more smalltalk about previous marriages in the church, Rev Mann says he's looking forward to seeing us tomorrow and we all get our coats together and prepare to leave.

"Well, I must say, I can't wait for tomorrow," Mary comments to anyone within earshot, "it's going to be so exciting."

Sister, you have no idea.

I hear Fraser and the Rev chatting but my mind is spinning round its own problems. Namely, trying to figure out what colour Kryptonite I'm going to need to stop Jack.

As we all leave the church through the front doors, Rev Mann tuts. He bends down to pick up something that's been left on the ground right in the middle of the main doorway.

"Honestly, some people just don't think. What a place to leave this. I could have broken my neck. It hasn't even been opened, does anybody want it?" I'm stood closest to him so he holds it out to me. "Michael?"

It's a can of coke.

twenty six :
free speech

I DON'T KNOW how come I forgot this – but I've got to do a speech tomorrow. I mean, I've got to get up in front of a whole bunch of people I wouldn't know if I stepped on them and I've got to talk about … stuff. And it's got to be funny. I've got to relate anecdotes from my life. Michael Shepard Before Emily. Like maybe the time I killed that embezzling businessman only to be mistaken for him as I left the office and told 'my' lottery ticket had just won two million dollars. That's going in, that's definitely going in.

Man, I am so screwed.

"Can't I just rip something off the internet?"

"No." Emily doesn't look up from her Cosmo, not even a little. "You cannot rip anything off the internet. I'll know. In fact, everyone will know. Those internet speeches are more well known than - well, you know…"

"Stuff that's well known."

"Stuff that's well known."

It's mid-afternoon and I haven't left Em's side since this morning. Well, since last night. Since that note. But I'm going to have to leave her soon. She's going on her hen-night in a couple hours. And I've got my stag night (woo-hoo). I've been given my last task before the big day and it's one I was quietly praying everyone would just have forgotten about. Seriously, like I don't have enough to be concentrating on right now.

"Can you give me some hints?" I'm drowning here. "What do grooms normally talk about at these things?"

"You've never been to a wedding?" she cocks an eyebrow at me over the top of her magazine.

I think for a moment. "Does watching 'My Best Friend's Wedding' count?"

She puts the magazine down. "You've watched 'My Best Friend's Wedding'?"

"Does it count?"

"No."

"Then I've never been to a wedding."

"You've watched 'My Best Friend's Wedding'?"

I shrug and look back down at my blank piece of paper. "It was on, I was in the room, I didn't have the energy to find the remote and turn over, you know how it is…"

Em shakes her head and goes back to her Cosmo, smiling. "Well, well – the things I don't know about you, Michael Shepard."

Hm. Indeed.

I start tapping both ends of my pen alternately onto the table top. It's really annoying. I'm hoping it's so annoying, Emily will put down her magazine and help me out.

Suddenly, she puts down her magazine. Score.

"So, anyway," she says, "what's happening with you?"

No score.

"Sorry?"

"Well," she says, "you know. How are you feeling? About tomorrow?"

"Well…I…"

"Because, y'know, we haven't really had a chance to talk properly over the last few days."

"Yeah…there's been…"

"What with you being so busy."

I find that I'm rolling my pen back and forth across my blank page. I stop doing that.

"There's been…stuff I have to take care of," I say and then tap my head, "in here."

"I know," Emily says. I can feel her warmth, her sympathy because she knows I'm talking about my parents. It makes me feel sick with guilt. "I just wondered how you were feeling about all that," she says. She draws one foot up onto her chair and rests her chin on her knee.

"Well, now I've had a chance to think through some stuff, I'm feeling great," I lie through my teeth. "I actually can't wait."

"So, you've…you've had a long think and stuff…"

I nod.

"…and…you feel great," Em says. She seems to be saying it like that's not a good thing.

"Yeah," I say again. I nod as well, just to get across how great I'm feeling.

"So, nothing you want to…I don't know…" Em shrugs, "…nothing you want to talk to me about?"

I make like I'm thinking but can't find anything. I shake my head.

"Nothing at all?" she says and I'm getting a little confused.

"Like what?"

"Well," she sounds a little more annoyed, now, "like anything. Like, are you nervous? Like, am I nervous? Like, do you think we rushed into this? Y'know, stuff other nearly-married couples talk about!"

"Oh, yeah, okay," I think I'm finally tuning into what's bothering her. "Sorry – I know we haven't spent much time together the last few days…"

"I know - you were thinking," Em sounds real bitter as she sits back in her chair and picks her Cosmo back up.

"Um, yeah…" now I'm not so sure I'm tuned into what's bothering her.

"And now you're feeling great," she's buried her head back into the magazine.

"…kind of…"

And we go back to how we were five minutes ago; her reading her magazine and me staring at my blank page. Except now, somehow, she's mad at me.

Preview : Married Life.

I try to clear my confused mind and go back to my speech.

I wonder if I could tell them about the time I killed that Brazilian sex slave trafficker but pass it off as, like, some kind of fictional morality tale.

So, so screwed.

the wedding morning
sarah-jane and the dead end

"A WEDDING?"

"Yeah, an old school friend I bumped into. Want to come?"

"Sarah, I've got to go to work."

"Nobody *has* to do anything. Come on! We can play that game where you try and guess how long the marriage will last. It'll be fun!"

"I'm already late."

"Excellent reason to call in sick. You've clearly been throwing up all morning and despite your best efforts to make it into work, your bus journey was cut short by an encore performance of 'The Exorcist' so you turned around and came back home. Then you donned your glad rags and came to a wedding with me."

"I don't really like weddings."

"Trust me. This one, as the yanks say, will be a blast."

"How come?"

"That'd be telling. Come on, Liz, I think we'd have a really good time. We haven't done anything together in ages."

"That's because you're always chasing crooks and adulterous husbands. I don't know, Sarah, I've never pulled a sickie before."

"The best reason to do something is because you've never done it before."

"Fortune cookie?"

"Cereal packet. Come on…what do you say? Please? For me?"

"…okay, okay, what time is it starting…?"

"You won't regret this, we are going to get *so* pissed!"

"That's it, I'm going to work."

"Joking! I'm joking! Ten o'clock."

"Church?"

"Of course."

"Okay, I'm going to go and use the phone in my room because I won't be able to act sick with you prancing around in the background putting me off. You didn't answer your phone."

"That's why God invented voice mail. Is this the note?"

"Is it my shopping list?"

"No."

"Then it's the note."

"You should have been a doctor, your handwriting's terrible. What's this name?"

"Give it here. Look, it's easy, that's a 'G'."

"It looks like a 'B'."

"It's a 'G'. Gasforth. Gillian Gasforth."

"No. Way."

"What?"

"When did she call?"

"Last night, late. Apparently, you left her a note?"

"I've got to go."

"Wait, you convince me to pull a sickie then you dump me?"

"I won't be long, honestly, I've got to go and see this woman. It's a matter of life and death."

"Whose?"

"That's the big question. I'll be back, soon as I can, then we'll party. I promise. Oh, by the way, I wrote out a card earlier on for the happy couple. It's in my coat pocket, already sealed. Can you bring it to the church for me? In case I end up having to meet you there. Cheers, chick."

*   *   *

"Mike, it's Sarah. Look, about last night…"

"…"

"I know. But, Mike, it was as much my fault as yours. I really need to show a bit of restraint sometimes, you know? Unfortunately, restraint isn't really part of my character."

"…"

"Prioritise, Michael! Blew up how?"

"…"

"What?! No way…"

"…"

"So…you are you still…?"

"…"

"So, it's going to be…?"

"…"

"Wow. I'm, uh, impressed at everyone's…composure…"

"…"

"What?"

"…"

"And, Geoff? They're not going to -"

"…"

"So everyone's lives rest on me finding Jeremy. Lovely. Let's hope I'm one of those people that can handle pressure without breaking down and turning into a complete psycho."

"…"

"You'll never guess."

"…"

"That wasn't actually a hard thing to guess, was it?"

"…"

"Anyway, yes, it's Gillian. I got a phone message from her this morning."

"…"

"Let's hope so. If not, we've officially run out of time. Jack's got our privates in a vice and he's spinning that handle."

"…"

"*What!?*"

"…"

"D'you see his face?"

"…"

"Okay, okay…geez, man, that's serious. He's totally playing games with us. Well, look, we better bring back the goods. We need to nail this psycho, Mike."

"…"

"Okay, I'll let you know how I get on with the elusive Ms. Gasforth. With any luck, I'll hit jackpot very soon - and it sounds like you're going to need every scrap of luck you can lay your hands on. How's the nerves?"

"…"

"Heartless, you mean."

"…"

"Don't worry, I'll be there. Oh, I'm bringing a friend to the church, is that okay?"

"…"

"You're a doll. I'll call you after I've - HEY! Get off the road, you blind bastard! Sorry, about that."

"…"

"Yeah, we don't want that. Talk to you later – enjoy your salmon and eggs."

*   *   *

"Ms. Gasforth?"

"Yes? Are you Sarah Jackson?"

"I am, can I come in? Standing out here makes me feel like a Jehovah's Witness."

"Have you got a card or something?"

"I have but do you know what a registered private investigator's card looks like? I could have just bashed it together on my computer for all you know."

"I'd just like to see it please?"

"Okay - here you go."

"It says Sarah Wilson here."

"That's my maiden name. My card's the one thing I've changed since my divorce. I did it on the computer."

"Well, I suppose you'd better come in."

"Thanks. My Watchtowers are all getting wet."

"Excuse me?"

"Nothing."

"Would you like a cup of tea?"

"With all due respect, Ms. Gasforth, I'm kind of running against the clock. I need to find Jeremy as soon as possible."

"Well, I don't actually know where Jeremy is at the moment. I'm actually quite worried because he was supposed to get here last night. He decided he was going to come and stay with me for a while. You know, to hide out. Lay low together and all that. I was always his favourite aunt, you know, even from when he was a child. Anyway, he never arrived and I got worried. So when I saw your note, I thought I'd better call you straight away."

"When did you last speak to him?"

"Last night, on the phone. It was about … eight thirty, yes, eight thirty. I remember because he was going to catch the nine o' clock bus. I'm sorry, would you like a cup of tea?"

"You already asked me, no thank you."

"Oh, yes, of course I did. Sometimes I forget things. The doctors said I would, you know, after the fall and everything."

"Well, you're doing very well so far, Ms. Gasforth, but I need you to think very hard about the conversation you had with Jeremy. I need you to remember every detail."

"It wasn't a very long conversation, really. I kept having to ask him to repeat things, I think I was getting on his nerves a bit. Well, he's all jangled isn't he? Being on the run and everything, he's bound to be a bit irritable."

"Why did you have to ask him to keep repeating things? Was there a lot of background noise?"

"Not really, it was the line, it wasn't very good. It kept, you know, clicking."

"Clicking?"

"I expect it was a crossed line or something. I've been getting it a lot lately. And, you know, they have the effrontery to cold call me and try to convince me to purchase a more expensive package!"

"This clicking, was it irregular?"

"Irregular?"

"Yes, you know, kind of … well, irregular sounding."

"Um … well, yes, I suppose it was…"

"Ms. Gasforth, can I take a look at your phone, please?"

"Of course, but why's that -"

"Do you mind if I just -"

"Oh my! I hope you're going to replace that handset! Look, there are bits all over the floor!"

"Yeah, one bit in particular that doesn't belong. Arse. Arse, arse, arse."

"I'm sorry?"

"Ms. Gasforth, this bit here, it's a bug."

"A bug? Like in the movies?"

"Like in the movies. It means someone's been listening in to your telephone conversations."

"Someone? Who?"

"I'm sorry to have to tell you this, Ms. Gasforth, but your nephew … Jeremy … I'm pretty sure he's dead."

the wedding morning
sarah-jane and the prostitute's jacket

"MIKE? GOOD NEWS, bad news. Good news; Jeremy may still be alive. Bad news; he so isn't."

"…"

"No, I haven't seen the body. But I'm pretty sure Jack's caught up with him. And if he has, then Jeremy is deader than disco."

"…"

"No, don't worry. I haven't given up yet. It's like when football teams are about to get relegated and the managers talk about keeping going until it's mathematically impossible to stay up. Well, I'm going to keep going until it's mathematically impossible for us to stay up."

"…"

"Actually I hated maths. Gillian gave me a lead. She didn't know where Jeremy was holed up but she did remember he mentioned that he was only round the corner from the bus station."

"…"

"Well, pretty useless except for the fact he'd also told her he'd be coming to see her on the 141 bus. Put those two facts together and I am, as they say, weapons hot. He was staying in a B&B in Mansfield. I've narrowed it to one of five. I'm on my way now."

"…"

"I know but don't kiss my arse just yet. All I'll probably find is a corpse that's really pissed off at his dad. But if he is still alive, I'll get him to the church on time. See? I'm looking out for you,

Mikey-boy, don't worry. Happy endings are my stock in trade, okay? Just keep your head down 'till I get there."

"…"

"Or your eyes peeled, whichever you prefer. I'll see you with Jeremy or not at all."

"…"

"Yup. 'till it's mathematically impossible."

*   *   *

"Good morning. Listen, I don't have time to be polite. You're the fifth bed and breakfast I've run into in the last eight minutes and you're the last one in this area, so if you're not the answer to my prayers, I'm going to have to start actually praying, okay? Now, have you had a young lad stay here in the last couple of days; seventeen, blonde hair, blue eyes, probably pretty jittery? Please say yes."

"What does that sign say?"

"Please don't ask for credit as a smack in the mouth often offends."

"The other sign."

"Rooms available by the hour."

"No the - wait a minute. Oh, sorry. Fell over. What does this sign say?"

"I'm deaf. Please speak slowly so I can lip read. Oh. Did you just get everything I-"

"Slower."

"Did you … just get … everything-"

"Slower."

"Did."

"Yeah."

"You."

"Yeah."

"Just."

"Okay, now you're just takin' the piss."

"Look, I really don't have time for this, I'm trying to save one or two people's lives here."

"Alright, just don't run all your words into one long string of noises. Enunciate. Y'know; talk proper."

"I'm looking for a young lad."

"Blonde. Seventeen. Jittery."

"So you actually understood me."

"Yeah."

"So why were you pissing me about?"

"Do you know how bored I get sittin' here all day?"

"Please don't force me to shoot you. Did you see this lad or not?"

"If I did, what makes you think I can tell you? You're a complete stranger."

"A stranger with money."

"You can't bribe me, duck. I'm incorruptible."

"Look, here's fifty quid. Is he here or not?"

"Bit stingey, but alright. Room 101."

"What?"

"He's in room 101. Right now."

"Right. Okay. Not what I expected. But, okay. And where is that?"

"Top of the stairs. Turn right. Last door on the left before the fire extinguisher."

"Thanks, enjoy the money."

"We don't take fifty notes, duck, you got change?"

*   *   *

"Who is it?"

"A friend. Open the door."

"What friend?"

"One you badly need right now. Seriously, open the door. I don't want to have to kick it down. I couldn't afford to replace it."

"Hello, hello. What are you? A prossie?"

"You're not Jeremy."

"Look, it's a bit early on a Sat'day morning to be bringing your business round here but - well, okay, since you're fit..."

"Who are you?"

"Who am I? *You* came to *my* room! Who were you expecting, like?"

"I'm after Jerem – wait a minute, why did you think I was a prostitute?"

"Dunno, the jacket, I s'pose. Wait, so are you saying you're *not* a prossie?"

"Look, I think someone's been taking bribes off more than just me today. Have a nice life. What am I saying? You think I dress like a prostitute. Have a shit life. Bye."

"Wait a sec, sweetheart, you can't just come to a bloke's room, tease him and then just swan off."

"Advice; if you ever want to scratch yourself with that hand again, I suggest you remove it from my arm right now."

"Why what are you going to -"

"SHIT!"

"Oi! Come back!"

*   *   *

"Mike, Jack's here."

"..."

"I just saw him. Well, his silhouette, but who else could it be? He was on the roof across from the B&B where Jeremy was staying. Except Jeremy isn't here anymore. I think the lad bribed the landlord to send anyone looking for him on a wild goose chase. Our psycho friend was on the roof of the next building along. He was about to ventilate Jeremy's cranium. When he realised it wasn't Jeremy and also that I'd seen him, he scarpered. This is all good; Jeremy may still be alive. MOVE!"

"..."

"A couple of old dears just stood on the bloody stairs, nattering. I mean, who just-"

"..."

"Don't get cute with me, Michael. I'm trying to get outside before Jack gets out of that building."

"..."

"He's been bugging Gillian Gasforth. Heard that Jeremy was coming to stay with her. He was probably going to wait for him to show up last night but when he didn't and I did this morning, he obviously decided to follow me to him instead - YOU! I'm coming back for you later!"

"Didn't catch a word of that, duck."

"..."

"The bloody landlord. Money grabbing bast- oh, crap..."

"..."

"Mike, I'm going to have to call you back. There's a car screeching off up the road and my tires have all been slit. I'm not thinking co-incidence."

*   *   *

"Ooh, you looked pissed off, duck. Look, nothin' personal, it were just business. If people want to chuck money at me, that's their - HOLY F-"

"What does this say?"

"W-Walther..."

"Further along."

"PPK."

"Further along."

"Nine millimetre..."

"Further along."

"Safety...on and off..."

"And which one is the little switch pointing at?"

"...off..."

"Read my bloody lips. Jeremy. Now."

twenty seven :
staggered

"DRINK UP, BOSS, we've got alleyways to puke in, walls to piss against and bars to get thrown out of."

I look at my office manager and wonder how I ever doubted that the women would be able to hold their own on this screwed up stag do. I mean, Lianne, sweet, naïve Lianne, she's already three bars ahead of us. Kind of like a drunk advance scout, making sure the territory we're about to move into is suitably stocked up with alcohol. And women.

As for us, we're in our second bar of the evening. Well, this isn't a bar – we're in a pub. I forget the name. But it's old. Like, medieval old. Obviously, people back in Robin Hood days were a lot shorter than they are now because some of the ceilings and doorways get you doing the limbo. Yet despite its olde worlde charm, the place is thumping with unfeasibly loud rock music.

"Whilce back from the bathroom yet?" I ask, putting down my half-finished bottle of orange juice.

"Right here, boss," he appears out of nowhere and turns my half-finished bottle of orange juice into a finished bottle of orange juice.

"We ready to roll?" Bud claps his hands. He's finished his twelfth beer of the night and he's raring to put Lianne's last advance report through its paces. Beer and girls pretty much has him in the only heaven he'll ever need.

By the way, the observant among you will have noticed that I was able to tell you exactly how many beers Bud has had. And that's because – yep – I'm a long way from drunk.

I know. My own stag night. Stone cold sober. Tragic.

But, y'know, assassin trying to kill me and everything.

"Okay," I say, mustering all the enthusiasm I can, "let's hit the bricks."

Whilce and Bud bounce up from their seats, all grins and enthusiasm, and head for the door. I get up, all pretend grins and enthusiasm and make to do the same. Until Jodie puts her hand on my arm.

"Hey, boss," she says.

"Are you guys going to do that all night?"

"What?"

"Keep calling me boss. It's annoying. Call me Michael. Or Mike. No, Michael. It won't be weird, I promise."

"Okay," Jodie shrugs. "Listen, Michael –"

"Actually no, I was wrong – it is weird. Just call me boss."

"Listen," Jodie's fighting back a little impatience, "boss man, Mike, sir, glorious leader – I wanted to ask you something serious for a second."

I know; why do you think I was trying to distract you?

"Sure," I say. "What?"

"Well, I just wanted to ask if you're okay."

"Okay?"

"Yeah, you don't seem your usual effervescent self."

"I'm usually effervescent?"

"Effervescent-ish."

A rocker-guy, clearly pushing fifty with long blonde hair and a jet-black beard emerges from the bathroom. He looks how I feel being here tonight. i.e. wrong.

"Well, now you mention it, I do feel a little bit under the weather, y'know, like I've got a bug or something," I lie. "So I won't be drinking much tonight. Plus, I want to keep my wits about me because I know Whilce and Bud would gladly risk their jobs in order to handcuff me naked to a lamppost in Aberdeen."

Jodie laughs and nods. "Aberdeen is on their list of potentials, yeah," then she looks at me with the kind of look only friends give each other. Which is strange since I didn't think I had any of those.

"As long as you're okay," she says. "Y'know, about tomorrow. But if you need anything just – I don't know – just give me a yell."

To my surprise, I smile the first smile of the night that I didn't have to force out. "Thanks. Seriously, Jodie, thanks a lot."

"Come on then, Mikey," she says now, "those alleyways aren't going to puke on themselves."

We leave the medieval sweat-box behind and step out into the bitingly cold wind of an unusually brisk July evening. Still, summer in England means nothing. Sun, rain, snow, it's all game.

We're about two steps into catching Bud and Whilce when my cell goes. I glance at the caller ID then give Jodie a nod and she goes on ahead to the boys. I flip the phone open.

"Hey. Any closer?"

"A little," comes the reply. "Pretty much got to wait until morning before I can move forward, though."

"Well," I say, "I guess you better come out where I can see you, then."

Sarah Jane steps out around the corner of the curry house in front of me looking like a schoolgirl caught smoking behind the bikesheds.

She's shaking her head. "How did you -?"

"Elementary my dear Wilson." I put my phone back in my pocket. "I could hear the same cop car siren over your phone that I could hear with my own ears."

"Well," she says, "I'll have to work harder on getting the drop on you."

"Clearly. So, seriously – no closer?"

"I said a little."

"But -" I already don't like where this conversation is heading, "you're here talking to me instead of somewhere else talking to Jeremy. So, that 'little' is a little too 'little' for my liking."

"I'm nearly there," Sarah Jane's suddenly miffed. "Managed to get hold of a family friend of Gillian Gasforth's. She's out but he doesn't know where she's gone. Or when she'll be back."

"Doesn't she have a cellphone?"

Sarah Jane shifts to her other foot as she goes from miffed to annoyed. "No answer, I left a message; look, I wasn't aware you knew so much about my job that you could start telling me how to do it."

I'm about to lose my temper. "Sorry, I wasn't aware that you were the one stuck on a stupid stag night for a wedding that's going to end in a double murder."

"Well," she shoots back, enmity literally dripping from her voice, "what did you expect? You're never going to quit being an assassin in a million years – I knew you and her were doomed from the second you told me about her."

I'm a little shocked and speechless, I've got to say. She's thought that all along?

"Boss? Problems?" Jodie, Bud and Whilce have appeared from nowhere. Forgot about them.

"Uh, hey," I try to think fast but my brain's gone numb. "Guys, this is an old school friend of Emily's. We're – uh – planning something for her. For Emily. Y'know, for the wedding."

The awkwardness of the moment completely flies past Bud and Whilce who are totally checking out Sarah Jane's ass.

The awkwardness of the moment doesn't fly past Jodie.

"It's kind of a surprise, though," I say, "so why don't I meet you at… where we headed..?"

"The casino bar," Jodie says.

"Right, I'll meet you there."

"Emily's friend coming?" Whilce's eyes are about to pop out of his sockets or something. Jodie, ever the pillar of tact and diplomacy, grabs the boys' arms.

"Come on - you boys can protect me from all those ravenous Brit fellas. Stop me from becoming the next conquered territory of the British Empire."

The three of them head up towards the casino. I turn back to Sarah Jane. But she speaks first.

"Hey, look, mate, I'm sorry, I didn't mean it, it's just-"

"We're doomed?"

"I didn't -"

"Where did that come from?"

"Look, I'm sorry, I just -"

Something in her eyes suddenly catches my attention.

"Are you…" I can't quite believe it, "…have you been drinking?"

She makes that look again, like she's been caught red handed. But this time, it's not a cheeky look. There's nothing amused about it at all. If nothing else, at least she's got the decorum to actually be ashamed about this.

"Oh, well, that's just *great!*" That's it, I can't keep my temper anymore. In fact, at this moment, I find I don't care which passing night-time merrymakers look our way or overhear whatever it is we're about to say.

"Hey, look, it's not like that," she tries to defend herself.

"It's not like what?" I want to know. "Not like what? Not like my fiancée is going to get shot tomorrow but instead of doing something about it, you've decided to get hammered? Is that what it's not like?"

Agitated, she opens her mouth to say something, but nothing comes out.

"Sarah, you told me to come out on this bastard stag night because you could handle things better on your own! Me coming out tonight was the best way to keep everyone calm while you found Jeremy. Instead you're here, well on your way to waking up in a gutter!"

"Hey!" Her anger rises to match mine, like she has the damn right. "Who the hell do you think you are, you little shit! Standing there like some -"

"Don't turn this around on me, you're the drunk bitch who's meant to -"

"- holier-than-thou lecturing me on right and wrong -"

"I mean, what the hell were you thinking?!"

"- you're just as bad as me; you know what, I *did* mean it. You *are* stupid for trying to get married."

"Oh, please," I almost spit my anger in her face, "just because your marriage ended with your husband putting a bullet in your heart and turning you into a self-absorbed drunk, don't put your shit onto me-"

"*Fuck* you!"

Followed by the hardest slap I've ever taken to the face.

Yeah, and as the red mist starts to recede, I reckon I really, really deserved it.

"You can …" she's trying to talk but I've never seen her look so hurt, I mean, she's crying and I swear she'd shoot me if she was packing - "…you can just… I can't believe you don't even…"

And she turns and storms off down the road. She doesn't go far. She heads into the pub we just came out of. I try to make myself go after her but I'm still too mad. I can see now, she's not going to be any help. How wrong can a guy be.

Screw it, to hell with her.

I'll do it the hard way. And I'll do it by myself. It's how I should have done it from the sta-

Phone beeps. Text message.

Tut, tut. Pissing off your only ally? Not smart. Think I'll see how your intended is getting on. Maybe ask for a dance.

twenty eight :
big red L

"WHAT DO YOU mean, where are am I?"

"Which bar are you at right now?" I try to sound as casual as possible. "I want to drop by."

I'm walking really fast but I don't know where to. I've already sent a text to Jodie telling her I'll catch up with them later, I've got things to do. I need to find Emily.

Before *he* does.

"You know, it's bad luck to see me on the night bef-"

"Damn it, Emily, just tell me where you are," I lose my composure for a second. "Please."

There's a silence from the other end of the phone and for a second, I'm afraid of what it means. Then she speaks.

"Alright, I'll be at the waterfront. At one of the tables outside. You'll see me from a distance, I've got a helium balloon with a big, red 'L' on it floating above my head."

"Okay, see you in five."

And I hang up and run.

twenty nine :
to cave or not to cave

EMILY WAS RIGHT. Spotting her is easy when she's got a big, heart-shaped balloon bobbing above her head like some target marker in a video game. Having said that, given the current situation, having a target marker point out your position so clearly is possibly not the best thing in the world.

"Hey," is all I can muster at first, despite the joy of seeing her alive.

Em smiles when she sees me, jumps up and drops a big, drunken kiss on me. Which is definitely better than being greeted by her gunshot-riddled body.

"Hey, you," she says, arms around me, breathing, like, six kinds of alcohol into my face. Why is it the women in my life are all drunk tonight? Still, it says more about me that it's my stag night and I'm *not* drunk.

"How's your night been so far?" I ask.

"Great!" Emily's in that place where you're not yet slurring your words but you're definitely having to put a lot of concentration into pronouncing them. And she's right – in terms of being drunk, that usually means you're still having a great time.

"We've been to that seventies bar in Upper Parliament Street, and the eighties bar, then we came down to the waterfront then we're going over to Hockley to one of those late opening bar/nightclub type things."

"Sounds cultural," I smile. "Any strippers yet?"

She grins and winks. "I've been positively promised."

I look about, briefly, but I can't see anything or anyone out of place. The tables around us are all empty seeing as it's relatively cold out. The cold, silent, dark water of the canal is in front of us and muted, thumping music blasts out of the assortment of bars behind us. There are merrymakers coming in and out of the them, mostly drunk, mostly in pairs or more. Girls in unfeasibly short skirts and tiny tops (and some with those fluffy cowboy hats) hugging their handbags to keep warm, guys in shirts burying their hands in their pants pockets.

Any one of them could be our guy.

"You don't call me out of my hen do," Em turns my head back to her with a single finger to my chin, "and then hold me in your arms while checking out all the totty walking past."

"Trust me, that is *not* what I'm doing."

"Then to what do I owe this pleasure, my big Easter bunny?" she smiles and I literally go all fuzzy inside. She hasn't called me that since, like, our third date or something. I hold her a little tighter.

"I just wanted to see you," I say. "Make sure you were - y'know -"

Alive

"- having a good time."

Still smiling, she shakes her head slowly. "You're such a bad liar."

I frown. "I am not!"

Of course, not usually the kind of thing you should defend.

"I mean…uh…really? Am I?"

She nods.

"You came to tell me something," she says, conspiratorially. "Didn't you?"

I crease my brow, puzzled. "Like what?"

"Well, you tell me," she shrugs.

"I…uh…" I'm genuinely clueless as to what the hell she thinks I'm here to tell her. I shake my head; I don't know what else to say.

The smile vanishes from her face.

"I've had enough of this," and she says it like the words have suddenly sobered her up. I mean, they haven't – she's still drunk. But sometimes drunk people suddenly get so mean, so serious, that they seem sober. In fact, more than that, they actually get scary. You don't want to mess with a drunk person who gets so suddenly serious, you just don't.

"You've got one chance to save this marriage, Michael Shepard," she says with a fierce determination you only get from alcohol and it scares the crap out of me because she means it, big time. "Just one. Tell me something. Anything you like. But make it the right thing. Or, so help me, from God's mouth to your ear, the wedding is *off*."

I'm totally stunned. What is she saying? What is it that she could possibly want me to say? I have no idea. And she's talking about –

"Em, you can't be serious, listen, you're drunk, just take a sea-"

She throws my hands off her shoulders and steps back. "Tell me now, Michael. This is your last chance."

Of course, there is one thing that pops into my head, but it can't be that. There's no way in the *world* it could be that.

"Em, you got to believe me – there's absolutely nothing I've got to tell you."

"Oh, really?" the drink has reasserted itself over her emotions – she's lost that scary, steely edge but now she's more manic, louder.

More hurt.

"You've got nothing for me, then," she says, on the edge of tears. "You don't want to tell me you've forgotten to take your vitamins for the last few days? Or that you're worried we haven't ordered enough drinks for everyone at the reception? No? What about the little thing that since, pretty much puberty, you've been killing people for money? What about that?"

I can't move. I physically can't move. How did she know about that? How long has she known? What the –

"No? Alright, well, since you've got nothing to say for yourself, let *me* say something -"

She literally rips the engagement ring off her finger and stabs it into my hand, me looking at her like the dumb son of a bitch I am.

"Bye."

And wends her way off into one of the bars.

And, still, I can't move. Or think. It's all collapsed around me. In one lousy night, it's all gone sou –

"…where the…" my head's absolutely throbbing and it's dark and I don't know where I am and I feel so, so groggy and I'm waking up, I recognize the sensation, I was unconscious and now I'm waking up and what the hell happened, what was I doing, oh yeah, Em just called off the –

Stop.

Breathe.

Okay, better.

It's dark. I'm sat up against something hard.

Someone knocked me out. Right after Emily walked off. And now I'm waking up in a … cave?

Shit, there's a girl in front of me. Early twenties. Dressed for a night out.

Dead.

No, don't jump to conclusions. Wake *up* dammit!

Fighting the throbbing at the back of my head – damn, it's about to split open, what the hell did I get hit with – I crawl over to the unmoving figure. Check the pulse.

Okay. Still there. Just.

There's a small bottle of clear liquid next to her head.

And a note pinned to her blouse.

She's been poisoned. Give her the antidote, or she'll die within the next two minutes. I'm right outside but I'm not waiting. If you chase me, I'll run. But if you catch me, you're safe. What's it going to be?

My head immediately snaps up and I realise there's a shaft of orange light streaming in; it's still nighttime outside and the orange streetlamps are just a few yards away.

And so is Jack.

I get up and actually take a step toward the cave mouth when I realise what the hell I'm doing. I turn, get back down and unscrew the cap off the small bottle. Holding the girl's head, I slowly pour the clear liquid into her open mouth – praying, incidentally, that the sick son of a bitch isn't fooling me into poisoning her myself.

I throw the empty bottle to one side and check the girl's eyes. Not a flicker. Check her pulse. No change. I glance at the cave mouth. Right out there. If I go now, I might still –

The sudden screaming and vomiting makes me jump out of my skin.

"Okay, okay, calm down – shit…" I try and control her as she fits and screams and vomits, all seemingly at once. Shit, is she dying? What the hell have I –

And all at once, she stops and she's just crying, confused as hell and scared out of her mind – but alive.

"Alright, alright," I say as calm as I can, in a faultless east London accent, holding her in my arms, "it's alright, girl, you're gonna be fine…"

It takes nearly ten minutes to calm her down and then to convince her I'm not some drugging, kidnapping rapist. The darkness of the tunnel means we can't make out each other's faces properly – hence the accent to make sure she can't ID me to the cops. I tell her I saw some guy drag her in here but I chased him off. Then I convince her to just stay sat down to recover from whatever it was he gave her and I'll be right back.

I scramble out of the cave but I know he'll be gone.

But he did leave another note.

Making that choice proves you will never be good enough to stop me. Now, stop messing around – fix things with Emily. Get her to walk down that aisle tomorrow or I'll get you both soon enough. And trust me, she'll be a long time dying. And I'll leave you alive just long enough to imagine all the places I might have hidden her head. Ta ta.

The blood drains from my body. But, still, I'm relieved that the ball's been dropped – albeit temporarily – in my court.

I can tell straight away where we are – the courtyard right outside the caves, beneath Nottingham Castle. So, not far from the waterfront. I check my watch. A shade shy of half an hour since I was with Emily. Man, that sick bastard works fast. Especially as the caves are all gated and chained shut. He would've have had to break one open to get us in there.

I call the cops to come and take care of the girl – then call in to her and tell her she'll be okay and stay put and the police'll be here soon to take her home.

Then I get the hell out of there. Not just to avoid the cops but to find Emily, fast as I can.

I've got some talking to do.

thirty :
and nothing but the truth

I'VE NEVER DRIVEN toward the Coleman homestead at such velocity. Usually, the nearer I get to The Bastille, my vehicle mysteriously *loses* speed. No idea why. Tonight, though, everything's different.

I went back to the waterfront bars but all I found were Claire, Amanda and the rest of Em's hen crew. They said she'd gone home upset after talking to me. Ignoring the Gloria Gaynor, all-women-together-against-the-evil-bastard-men glares, I lit out of there, got the BMW out of the car park and headed out to the Colemans', foot down.

The whole time, my brain's spinning.

She knows.

How the hell does she know? How long has she known? Does this mean we're over? Stupid, of course it does.

But my head keeps coming back to the same thing – how did she find out? Did I give myself up somehow? Or was it Sarah Jane? Did she tell her after I pissed her off? But that doesn't gel. Emily's mood was all wrong for that.

Then, how?

Coleman Manor looms large in my headlights. Well, looks like I'm going to find out soon enough.

I get out of the car, don't bother locking it, crunch straight across the gravel driveway and head inside the house. At first, I don't see anyone, all the lights are off. But as I head quietly through the living room, I jump a little bit when I see Fraser standing, silhouetted and looking at me, in the doorway to his study.

He doesn't say anything, he just looks at me. Then he turns and goes back into the room. I follow him in, palms sweating. For the first time in a long time, I'm actually afraid. I'm in a situation where I'm controlling *nothing*.

I expected to see Emily in here, but it's just me and the old lord. He's over at his drinks cabinet, pouring out a glass of whiskey. It's the good stuff, too. I've been around enough people with expensive liquor to know you only drink the good stuff when you're either in a really good mood or a really, really foul mood.

Glass poured, and still with his back turned to me, Fraser quietly, slowly and deliberately screws the cap back on the bottle. He still hasn't said anything and even though I'm desperate to talk to Emily, I don't say anything either. I know she's around. I can tell from his manner. So I know that to get to her, I'm going to have to get through him first.

Finally, he turns to me, glass in hand.

"So," his voice is low and threatening. "An assassin, eh?"

I kind of half shrug, half nod. No point in defending myself to him. It's not going to be that kind of conversation. Then the man does something that almost knocks me right off my feet.

The corner of his mouth turns up in a teeny, tiny hint of a smile. And he holds out the glass to me.

"Scotch?"

I should have known. A man involved in the kind of stuff he's involved in. Of course, he's going to have more time for someone in my line of work. Man, forget keeping it secret - it should have been my opening line.

"Thanks," I say as I take the glass from his outstretched hand. I don't smile, though. Kodak moment or no Kodak moment – I'm here to straighten things out with Emily, not him.

Fraser motions to a big, high-backed leather chair a couple feet away. "Please."

Wordlessly, I go and take a seat. He sits in a similar chair right across from me. He isn't smiling now. But that scowl he always wears, the one that promises he wouldn't piss on me if I was on fire, that's gone. Now, his face is merely serious. Which, for our relationship, is a big step up.

"So," he says again. "Talk."

"Well…", what is it with this family – they want you to talk but won't say about what, "…I've been an assassin for eighteen years. I work for a company called the Agency, I'm one of their top ranked killers. My specialty is any kind of sniper rifle, though I can instantly kill a man with my bare hands in over a dozen distinct ways."

"I see," Fraser takes a sip out of his own glass of scotch. "And into which part of that charming diorama of images does my only daughter fit?"

I shrug, there's no hesitation. "I love her."

It doesn't sound like much. But it's, quite literally, everything.

And, strange as it may seem, I think Fraser actually gets it.

He puts his glass down and sits forward, his eyes locking mine. I feel like I'm being pinned down like a bug on a museum display board.

"Michael," he says my name for the first time like he doesn't want to add the words 'piss off' on the end, "I know you're fully aware of my … vocation. So the fact I have no problem with *your* vocation should make sense to you. However, the fact that I only started liking you since I found out what you do for a living must leave you thinking this is a screwed up state of affairs."

I opt for a deferential shrug instead of saying 'yup, no shit'.

"The thing is," he goes on, "you actually make sense to me now. Your manner. Your foppish nonsense. It was your Clarke Kent bit. I get it. When I add that to your job, I can then ascertain that you're actually a good bloke. Killing aside. Just like I'm a good father."

"Drug dealing aside."

"Exactly. I can see you love my daughter and that you'll protect her."

When he says the 'P' word, it sends a cold chill down my back, but I stay silent.

"It's all any father could ask for, really. All any father wants. Someone to love his daughter. Someone to protect her. So, for what it's worth, I suppose, what I'm saying is you have my blessing to marry Emily."

"Well, Fraser, I don't want to sound ungrateful but…"

"I know – Emily's called off the wedding. Well, it's up to you to convince her she's made a mistake. Because I think she has made a mistake. However…"

I know we're now getting to the point of what he wants to say.

"...at the end of the day, what she says goes. She's my only daughter and I love her. And if she says she wants you out of the house and she never wants to see you again, then you leave. Tonight."

I nod. I get it. He isn't explaining the situation. He's issuing me with a command.

Apparently satisfied, Fraser gets up and heads out of the room. When he gets to the door, he stops and turns back.

"I can't guarantee she'll want to see you."

I nod again, and he leaves. I feel numb, thinking that I may not even see Emily again. Never have the chance to put my side forward. But what is my side? *Yeah, sorry about that – I was going to tell you at some point, honest.* Hell, I wouldn't want to see me again eith-

"Hey," she says.

I look up and there she is. My heart breaks to see she's clearly been crying. A lot.

"Hey," I say back. There's only one thing that I can say next – though it's as hollow sounding as it is genuine.

"I'm sorry."

"I know you are, Michael," she says. Her words might sound like I've got a chance, but her tone says otherwise.

"So..." I take a deep breath, "...how long have you known?"

"Remember my work Christmas do? You were dressed as a giant rabbit. Well, that night."

"The night we met?!" I can't believe this. "You've known since our first -"

"I believe you were trying to get me drunk on punch," she says to no-one in particular.

I stand up, then sit down then stand up again, I don't know what to -

"You've known for the last eighteen months and you haven't said anything?!"

"Or more to the point," Em looks at me, anger etched around her red eyes, "*you* haven't said anything."

She's right. That *is* more to the point.

I look around. Turns out I'm standing up at the moment, so might as well stay that way for the minute.

"And, how did you -"

"Your bosses told me," she says flatly. Now, I really am stunned.

"The Agency told you that I was an assassin?"

"A woman came to visit me, that night I got back home after the party," Em's talking in measured tones which means she's probably been practicing this speech for months. "She said she was here on behalf of the Agency, then she told me what the Agency was. I didn't believe her at first, then she started talking about you. Told me things that…"

She catches herself, losing control for a second. I take a step toward her, to comfort her, but she steps back. She takes a deep breath then goes on.

"…she told me things about you, your past, your job, just…everything. Everything I was hoping to find out about you over the coming months, she told me in twenty minutes. I still didn't believe her, of course, but then she brought out the photos…"

I feel cold and I'm pretty sure the blood just ran out of my face because I know just what photos she's talking about.

As part of the whole thing of making sure they have loyal employees, the Agency send a photographer on your first mission to capture you doing your thing. You never see them, they're real, real good at staying out of sight. It's just a little something for their files (no, how rude of you to imply it's for blackmail purposes).

My first job was a Texas oil baron, big guy, bad hair. My photos show me setting up my rifle, taking up my position, taking the shots then clearing up again before leaving the room. They sent me a copy afterwards. Y'know, for my mantelpiece and whatnot.

"Then she said to me," Em goes on in her measured but strained voice, "it was up to me whether I saw you again."

She shrugs. "Then she left."

Stunned. No, stunned isn't the word. I don't know what is the word. I'm not even sure they've come up with the word for what I'm feeling right now.

"Why would they do that…?" I murmur, not even sure I've spoken out loud.

"I've been thinking about that for eighteen months," Emily says. "And especially hard that night. I didn't sleep for thinking about it. And you know what I came up with?"

I look up at her.

"I think they were testing you," she says. "Well, me too, but mostly you."

"I don't follow…" my mind is still a few clicks behind hers right now.

"I think it was their view that, one day, you would stop being an assassin. You'd realise it was wrong, realise you wanted the simple life of a regular person and jack it in. Because from all those tests they gave you when you joined, they saw something you didn't know. You were, actually, not a mindless killing machine. You were a good person."

I hear Granny Coleman's words come back to me yet again.

"But since you were not yet aware of that," she goes on, "and since you were so proficient, they knew you'd be good for service for a number of years in the meantime."

She sits down in Fraser's chair now, apparently – and understandably – exhausted. A little numbly, I sit down too. She's mentioned me being a good person but once again, her tone gives me no hope she's about to change her mind.

She picks up Fraser's discarded glass and takes a sip. I know how hard this must be for her – she hates scotch.

"So, anyway, eventually, I come along and you give me your number and such and they think 'ey up, this might be the one'…"

Something about the way she says 'the one' gouges at my heart – like she thought of herself as the one but now realises she was stupid for thinking that.

"…so they send someone over to me and tell me all about you. Then they wait and see what I do. Luckily for me, I'm sure, my first instinct wasn't to call the cops."

I nod in agreement – she would've been dead before her fingers touched the dial.

"No, I stick with you, we get on, we get engaged and all the time, they're watching and watching and watching," she talks really matter-of-factly. I don't think I'm feeling the same nonchalance about the Agency's eye in the sky. I know they like to do it from time to time but the thought of them having a notebook somewhere with the amount of times we've had sex or whatever…

well, if I wasn't still so shocked, I'd be pretty damn angry right now.

"They're watching because they know one of two things is going to happen." Emily counts on her fingers. "One – you're going to marry me or two – you'll back out. If you back out, then they're happy. You get to carry on being their pet killer. But if you don't back out, if you go ahead and marry me…"

The words stick in her throat considering how the night has turned out. I complete the sentence.

"…they kill us both."

Emily looks at me like I really don't get what's going on. "No…! They wish you well, let you go and let you live happily ever after."

I mentally slap my head. Of course. If they didn't want me to get close or marry her, they'd have killed her right at the start. This is them cutting their losses. Letting me go happy means I'm less likely to ever blab about them to anyone. I mean, blabbing would obviously get me and Em killed real fast but still, I'm sure the Agency would prefer it didn't come to that.

I look at Emily and I'm overwhelmed at how she's figured it all out. She didn't panic or do any of the things that would have gotten her killed. She just dealt with it.

"That explains them," I say, hesitantly, "but what about you? Why *did* you stay with me? Why deal with all that? You could have just walked away that night. They'd have been content with that. Why put up with it all?"

Even as I ask the question, I know the answer.

"Because I loved you," she says.

Like even Fraser had to acknowledge, it's all that matters. But it was kind of hard to miss the past tense on that sentence.

"I knew you were only a killer on the surface. Your past had moulded you into that. Deep down, you were this great, sweet, charming guy. And you didn't even know it," she smiles briefly at that, but only briefly. "And I knew you loved me. And respected me. In fact, I knew you were going to come clean to me before we got married. I knew you wouldn't think so little of me as to start our married life with that kind of secret hanging over our heads. I knew you'd face me with it before we made the biggest commitment of our lives. Because you knew that if you didn't, everything we did and said would just be a big, cruel, farcical *lie*."

If it's possible for me to feel as bad as a person can feel, well, I'm feeling it.

"But," she sighs, "it looks like I was wrong. You do think all those things. That's why I don't love you anymore. Because you're not the man I fell in love with. He obviously only ever existed in my mind. Him, I still love. But you…I've never met you before. You never took off that rabbit mask. I only thought you had."

My mind races backward and forward, all over the place, looking to gather arguments to tell her how wrong she is. To tell her how much I really do respect her, how much I love her.

Only, it comes back empty.

At first, I'm puzzled. Where are all my sentiments, my speeches about how Emily has been the most important thing in my life since I met her?

But then the horrible realisation starts to filter through. Right from the start, I could feel like this wasn't going to work – but I ignored it. Sarah Jane told me it wouldn't work if I didn't come clean – and I ignored her, too. Then when she told me I'd never come clean, I lashed out at her. I kept telling myself I just needed to adjust. Kept repeating to myself that Emily was the most important thing in my life. But the facts speak for themselves. They draw me to the only conclusion it's possible to make. The reason I didn't tell her about my job is because I was more willing to risk messing up my life with her than I was willing to risk messing up my life as an assassin.

In short, I value being an assassin more than I value settling down with Emily.

I can't quite believe it – it doesn't feel right. But the facts are there. They speak for themselves. I was going to marry her without telling her about me. It doesn't matter what justification I use – needing to concentrate on catching Jack or whatever. They're just excuses. If I really wanted to tell her, nothing would have stopped me.

Basically, no matter how much I think I love Emily, I don't love her enough to stop doing this job. Period.

I sit back, slowly, and stare at my no-longer fiancée through dead eyes.

"You're right," I say, my voice feeling more devoid of emotion with every word that comes out. "You saved me from making a big mistake. But more importantly, you saved yourself from making one."

Her face falls. Although she had already called everything off, there was probably still a tiny part of her, deep down, that wanted to be talked out of it. That wanted to be wrong. But it doesn't get its wish – because she isn't wrong.

Emily and me are over.

"But," I say, "we still have to get married."

Her eyes had dropped off me for a moment but they're back on me now, confused, angry.

"*What?*"

"We still have to go through with the wedding. I'm sorry, but things have gotten pretty complicated over the last week. It's all to do with Geoff and Jeremy. And your dad, we're going to have to get him back in here."

"Michael, what the hell are you talking about? Jeremy… what the hell…?" she's trying to make sense of this new twist to our lovely relationship. "What in the world makes you think I'm going to walk down that aisle with you?"

"If you don't, people are going to die," I say, flatly. "Starting with you."

Okay, now I have her attention.

thirty one :
i'm getting shot at in the morning

RING, CHECK. BUTTONHOLE flower, check. Beretta .45 with silencer, check. Unfeasibly shiny shoes, check. Well, I'm ready for the most memorable day of my life.

I look out the window of my motel room. Gloriously sunny. Just to really piss me off.

My jacket's lying flat and neat on the bed, looking for all the world like someone had been lying there and evaporated and left it behind. It's the only thing left to put on. I wrestled with the cravat for nearly fifteen minutes but it finally cried uncle. 'Course, if I'd had a best man, he'd have done all that for me. No best man for me, though. Well, strictly speaking, no wedding either.

My cell rings.

"Hello?"

"Mike, it's Sarah. Look, about last night…"

"Forget it. I was being a dick."

"I know. But, Mike, it was as much my fault as yours. I really need to show a bit of restraint sometimes, you know? Unfortunately, restraint isn't really part of my character."

"No shit. Listen, it all blew up with Emily last night," I frown. "What's that noise - are you in the car?"

"Prioritise, Michael! Blew up how?"

"She knows everything. I mean, she already knew."

"What?! No way…"

"Way. Then I told her everything that's kicked off this week. About us, Jeremy, Geoff, everything."

"So…are you still…?"

"She agreed to go ahead with the wedding. I told her this was our best chance of getting Jack. We miss this opportunity, he'll pick us off at will some other time. And she wants to save Jeremy and Geoff."

"So, it's going to be, what…fake?"

"We'll get it annulled later, if we live so long."

"Wow. I'm, uh, impressed at everyone's…composure…"

"She wasn't happy with her dad about hiring a hitman for her fiancé, I can tell you that. That was a fun conversation to participate in. But, you know what that mean old bastard did?"

"What?"

"He only refused to cancel the hit on me until I can prove Emily's safe! Says, if she dies, I die. Can you believe it? And this is the guy says he likes me, now!"

"And, Geoff? They're not going to -"

"I explained it all to them. How it's out of Geoff's hands, how only Jeremy's appearance is going to save Emily completely. Confronting Geoff's just going to make things needlessly messy. I just hope Fraser keeps his cool, though. Man, you should have seen him, the guy was *crazy* mad…"

"So everyone's lives rest on me finding Jeremy. Lovely. Let's hope I'm one of those people that can handle pressure without breaking down and turning into a complete psycho."

"Anyway, look, back on mission – where you going in the car?"

"You'll never guess."

"Gillian Gasforth?"

"That wasn't actually such a hard thing to guess, was it?"

"Not really."

"Anyway, yes it's Gillian. I got a phone message from her this morning."

"Reckon she'll actually be able to help after all this?"

"Let's hope so. If not, we've officially run out of time. Jack's got our privates in a vice and he's spinning that handle."

"Oh, yeah, I had a run in with him last night, too."

"*What!?*"

"Yeah, made me choose between catching him and saving this girl."

"D'you see his face?"

"I didn't go after him, Sarah! I saved the girl."

"Okay, okay...geez, man, that's serious. He's totally playing games with us. Well, look, we better bring back the goods. We need to nail this psycho, Mike."

"You don't have to tell me."

"Okay, I'll let you know how I get on with the elusive Ms. Gasforth. With any luck, I'll hit jackpot very soon - and it sounds like you're going to need every scrap of luck you can lay your hands on. How's the nerves?"

"Don't worry about me, I'm fearless."

"Heartless, you mean."

"Well I'm about to fortify myself with salmon and scrambled eggs. Man deserves a last meal, right? Anyway, my nerves and my heart'll do a lot better if you show up with Jeremy before the service starts."

"Don't worry, I'll be there. Oh, I'm bringing a friend to the church, is that okay?"

"What? Sure, whatever. Can't be much of a friend, you're bringing her to this car crash."

"You're a doll. I'll call you after I've - HEY! Get off the road, you blind bastard! Sorry, about that."

"Geez, don't get yourself killed now lady, that'd just about finish me off altogether."

"Yeah, we don't want that. Talk to you later – enjoy your salmon and eggs."

And she hangs up.

It's amazing how fast and easy it is for me to make up with her. I mean, it was no playground tiff last night – we really went for each others' jugulars. But in the cold light of day, a few well chosen words and it's cool. Not forgotten, not forgiven. But cool.

It's because we have a connection. An understanding. Before you get excited, I'm not going down that whole 'she understands me better than my fiancée does – let's jump into bed together' route. That's not what I'm talking about at all. I just mean we each have a worldview that only people in our profession have. It may come in different flavours, but the core of it's the same. It's the same for any two assassins - we look at each other and we see ourselves. We like to think we're completely private and invisible creatures, but we forget that there are these odd moments when we can literally see through each other like glass.

I talk to Sarah Jane two more times before I check out of the motel.

The first time, she tells me Jeremy's unlikely to still be alive. Apparently he has been in contact with his lovely aunt Gillian but her phone's been bugged. Almost certainly by Jack. So Sarah Jane's convinced he's tracked down the wayward kid by now and stuffed the proverbial apple in his mouth.

The second time's to tell me he probably is still alive after all. While she was there, she saw Jack but Jack's going after Jeremy and she's going after Jack. Then she finds her tyres have been slashed and Jack's got away, chasing Jeremy.

I'm really having to push my keep-it-cool dial right to the limit. Here I am sitting in a motel room in my wedding clothes like some kind of modern day, pre-non-wedding Mr. Haversham while Sarah Jane's out there chasing down the bad guy. It's like an old world war two movie I saw once where the big beat down between the Nazis and the allies is in full flow but the soldier can't get there - he's stuck getting some local's truck out of the mud or whatever the hell it was. He knew the battle that was going to decide everything was going down and here he was getting earache from some old Dutch dude.

Still, he and I have something in common – the battle eventually made its way to his front door. He soon started giving and taking licks in a big beat down of his own. I know I'll be getting my gun-hand warm soon, one way or another. And, you know what? When that time comes, I'll be the happiest man on earth.

There's a knock at my door and a spotty student-type brings in my salmon and eggs. Since I'm in England, I resist the urge to tip him (at least enough to buy some damn anti-bacterial facewash) and he disappears, leaving me to my breakfast.

I wheel the table over to the foot of my bed so I can look out the window at the rolling countryside as I eat my wedding breakfast alone. As I tuck in, I reflect on my feeling that I will actually start to feel more comfortable once the bullets start flying around St. Margaret's.

Sarah Jane spent a lot of time trying to convince me that killing was not the way to solve problems. Well, it happens that I agree with her – if folks can do so without coming to people like me. Because by the time it comes to *my* door, there's no going back. You make the call, you send us on our way, and there's only one way the situation comes to it's end – and that's by someone dying.

It's what I've been trained for, what I've done my entire adult life. And what the universe intended for me ever since that snowy afternoon all those years ago.

The events that are going to unfold this morning are out of my hands. They were initiated by other people and, as always, I'm part of the solution, not the problem. Whatever happens today, however it ends, I'll just be part of the equation fulfilling itself out to its logical conclusion.

And that's just as things should be.

I'm indebted to Emily. I loved her? Sure, possibly. I'm capable of that true, deep love of another human being that would stop me from being an assassin?

Nope. Never.

If I'd have suffered my little break in protocol (yep, aka 'fell in love') with anyone else, someone not so strong or clever, I might have actually gone through with the wedding. But she was a one-in-a-million find; she shone a light on the lie that I was blinding myself to and she forced me to snap out of my delusion. And even Sarah Jane had to eventually admit that there could have been no other conclusion – especially considering her own long and successful marriage.

So, for saving me – and therefore also saving countless others in the future from having to kill someone themselves – and for the feelings I do still have for her, I owe Emily big. I'll do everything I can to save her today. Everyone else, though? Let the chips fall where they may.

Well, either I got a kiddy portion of eggs and salmon or else I was really hungry, 'cause it's all but gone. I scoop up the last of what was a mighty tasty breakfast – I mean, smoked salmon just rocks – and wonder absently how Emily and Sarah Jane will take it when the situation's resolved only for me to turn around and shoot Geoff in the head (assuming Jeremy doesn't call in his abort). Yeah, I imagine they'll be pretty pissed.

Still, Sarah Jane's a big girl. She'll sink some vodka shots and get over it. And Manhattan's a pretty big place. I'll bet me and Emily never see each other again. And that can only be a good thing for both of us.

Well – I wipe my lips with my napkin, put my cutlery straight, pull on my jacket and slip my Berretta into an inside pocket.

Better go get married.

thirty two :
the assassin's wedding

"YOU KNOW WHAT, Michael," the Rev says to me as we stand at the front of the crowded church, listening to the pipe-organ quietly play Moonlight Sonata, waiting for my bride to arrive. "I don't believe I actually know what it is you do for a living."

"I'm an insurance salesman. Life, Equity, mostly. Mainly, I sell into corporates, blue chips. Premiere services. High premiums but big payoffs, you know? APRs to die for."

The Rev's eyes start to glaze over the same way everybody's do when I start with the insurance salesman routine. That's why I do it. Stops people asking questions. They move onto another topic, they don't get bored, I don't have to kill them...win, win, win.

"Ready for the off?" Rev Mann asks. Topic changed. Mission successful.

"Certainly am," I say, scanning the congregation. A woman in a broad-rimmed hat smiles at me. I nod back. "I can't wait to become George to someone's Mildred."

"Well, Emily and her father should be pulling up any minute now," he smiles that kindly smile that all elderly, Anglican Reverends must go on some kind of course to learn. "You've only got about eight minutes to relish being young, free and single." He pats my shoulder and wanders off to go and memorise his lines or whatever.

Eight minutes. Not a long time. I mentally pat the loaded Beretta .45 with silencer that's snuggled in my inside jacket pocket, a couple inches behind my pastel yellow buttonhole flower.

Eight minutes to figure out which upstanding member of this congregation I have to kill.

And once that unpleasant business is out of the way, perhaps I can finally concentrate on getting married.

I force a thin smile and shake my head as Whilce gives me two thumbs up from the third row. Bud and Lianne think he's hilarious. Jodie's trying to look happy but she can tell something's wrong. Hell, the way things have gone over the last couple days, I'll probably find out she works for the Agency. Along with Emily, her parents and that dog that sometimes comes into the Colemans' garden to poop.

I scan the congregation, my baddieometer cranked up to full. Nothing. I mean, it's not like I recognise everyone here. I did as much as I could to see pictures of all the church guests – made every effort to look through family albums and all that. Well, I'd said, I wanted to be able to recognise people at my own wedding. No good. Not everyone on the guest list has been privileged enough to make their way into the Coleman family albums.

This is bad. No Sarah Jane. No Jeremy.

No chance.

My cell vibrates in my pocket.

I quickly check it, hoping for a late reprieve from Sarah Jane but my heart sinks when I recognise the dark intent hidden behind those two words.

Batter up.

"The car's here," Rev Mann whispers to me. "It's time."

My brain's cranking overtime. Damn it, I've got to figure what to –

What the hell?

There's a murmur from the congregation and I look up. Fraser's stood by the door. Alone. The look on his face has me instantly running down the aisle to meet him. When I get closer, I realize he has a slight bruise next to his left eye – like he's fallen against something. Or been pushed.

He only says two words and when he says them, they're quiet and angry. But they also hide something I've never heard in the old lord's voice before. Total and absolute fear.

"She's gone."

thirty three :
the brideless car

I SEE THE sleek, gunmetal grey wedding car sitting there like something out of James Bond. I see the ribbons tied along the hood and the flowers down the side. I see the chauffeur standing by the car, holding a bloodied hankie to the back of his head. And I see Fraser, slightly bruised eye, fighting hard to keep his self-control.

What I don't see is Emily.

"What the hell do you mean 'gone'?" I've got to fight to keep *my* self-control. It's the only thing that's going to get me and Emily into tomorrow still breathing.

"We were just coming down the road into the village," Fraser says, trying hard not to talk too fast, "and there was a car in the middle of the road, parked sideways. Just sitting there, blocking the way. So we stopped and I got out to take a look. That's the last thing I remember. When I woke up, the driver had a bloody head and the car was gone. So was Emily."

I hold back my urge to grab the stupid bastard by the shoulders and shake him. He knew what the score was today, what was going down. Why the hell would you get out and check something like that? Just spin the car round and get the hell out of there!

I pull my phone out again but there haven't been any more texts from Psycho Jack. He wants me and Emily both so he should be telling me where to find my fiancée any time now. So far, nothing.

"Come on," I say to Fraser as I start towards the wedding car, "take me to where you were when -"

I'm interrupted by a car screeching onto the small lane leading up to the church. My hand moves towards the inside of my jacket until, half a second later, I realise I recognise the car.

Sarah Jane skids to a halt feet from me and Fraser and leaps out of her old, battered red Fiesta. My heart leaps for a second - until I realise she's on her own. No Jeremy.

She sees my expression and pre-empts my question. "I lost Jack. I don't know if he caught up with Jeremy. I thought I'd better get back here to help you out when he finally shows...up...here..."

She trails off as her eyes and brain finally catch up with her mouth and she sees Fraser, the driver and the brideless car.

"Let me guess...festivities have already started..."

I turn back to Fraser. "Just as you were about to enter Bilsthorpe?"

A couple seconds and he clicks into what I'm saying. "Yes, right before you get to the first few houses and the duck pond. But, Michael, you're not leaving me here, I'm com-"

"Fraser," I look at him for the first time with more authority than he's looking at me, "right now, you're one of the few people at this wedding who *isn't* supposed to be getting killed. Enjoy it," I hold up a finger to his face so he knows how seriously he has to take my next three words. "You stay here."

And I turn and head towards Sarah Jane's car, looking at nobody and nothing else, seeing only Emily. "Come on. I'm driving."

I strap myself in, Sarah Jane jumps in beside me and hands me the keys. Within seconds, I'm reversing back down the church lane, fast. I hit the main road, screech to a halt, throw it into first and screech off up the road as fast as the little 1.1 engine'll shift.

"I take it Jack's made his move."

I nod.

"So where are we going? Scene of the crime?"

I nod again. "Clue hunting."

Damn it! This thing's trudging like a snail through treacle – I've driven plenty of 1.1s and they all shifted faster than this. Sarah Jane needs to look after this thing more. Jack will have had Emily sliced and diced by the time we get anywhere near him.

I snap my head round as Sarah Jane's phone rings. She picks it out of her pocket and shows me the screen, briefly, with an apologetic smile. Someone called Catherine.

"Hey, girl," she takes the call.

I focus on the road. We shoot past the Chinese takeaway, past the newsagents, past the duck pond.

"Sorry, I know, I've been all over the place this morning. I was going to call you."

My mind's racing. What kind of clues am I going to look for? What if Jack doesn't call? I need to calm down. Focus.

"No, definitely still come over. Just go straight to the reception. The address is on the slip I left on the fridge."

I need to think.

"Don't forget my card! Make sure you put it in your…okay, okay, I'm just saying…"

Actually, I need to *stop* thinking. My usual approach of dotting the I's and crossing the T's just ain't cutting it on this crazy ride. Not this time. I need to take a leaf out of Sarah Jane's book, how she handles tough situations. Gut feelings. Intuition.

"Okay – look, don't call me for the next little while, okay? I'm kind of busy. Yes, important stuff. Okay, see you later. Ta ta."

Instinct.

Sarah Jane closes her phone at the same time I stop the car at the point in the road where Emily was taken.

"Sorry about that. My best friend."

Looking away from the entrance to the village, there's nothing but farmland and grazing pigs as far as the eye can see. Nearer to, I can see the displaced grass and bushes from where the car that was blocking the road eventually made its getaway.

"Actually, my only friend. This the place?"

I nod, looking around us.

And I take my Beretta from my inside jacket pocket.

"Ideas already?" Sarah Jane asks with a smirk, nodding at the gun.

I nod. "Just one."

I point the Beretta at Sarah Jane's stomach and pull the trigger.

A deafening bang reverberates around the inside of the car and buckets of blood and flesh splatter the inside of the passenger door. Sarah Jane screams a scream that would curdle my blood if I hadn't heard screams just like it a thousand times before. Then she rattles off a long string of obscenities through blood-stained teeth as the barrel of my gun is now pressed hard against her temple, pushing her head against the passenger window.

"Emily," I say. "Now."

thirty four :
buckaroo

OKAY, SO NOW you're thinking I've totally lost it, right? Don't be shy, you can say it. You think this whole adventure's finally made me snap. So much for the cool as ice yank assassin. One kidnapped bride and he goes Rambo.

Look, I've got evidence, okay? Well, okay, not evidence exactly. Bits and pieces. If you wanted to be cynical, you'd call them scraps.

You'd say I just shot my only ally and almost-friend, just shot her and given her the most cripplingly painful stomach injury you can imagine – over scraps.

If you were being cynical.

You ever played buckaroo? Sure, you have. You've got that scrawny-looking donkey, that ass. You laden him with all kinds of bags and ropes and tools, one by one. Each time, the donkey doesn't move. Not even a little. Like it doesn't even notice anything's going on. Then one time, a time like any other, you put something on its back and *blam* – it bucks its hind legs in the air and sends all those bits and pieces flying.

That one, last, crucial piece made the difference – but only when combined with all the other pieces.

Well, like that donkey, I'm also an ass. And I also had lots of bits and pieces that I didn't even notice were weighing me down.

Like when she first told me she used to be an assassin over a glass of flavoured vodka. She sounded a little too proud about it.

Or when Malcolm the Milkman told me not to get involved with things I shouldn't – I'm a killer. Almost a word-perfect counterpoint to Sarah Jane's constant admonishment to me to *get* involved with things because I'm *not* just a killer.

Then just now, when she took the call from her friend. A little too casual. A little too in control. I know that's how she handles pressure situations – but still…

Then there was the buckaroo moment. The way she finished her call. *Ta ta.*

Jack's favourite message sign off.

None of those is proof. Hell, they're barely even clues. But my subconscious says different. And right now, my subconscious is the only thing giving me any help whatsoever in this catastrophic day of celebration. So, until further notice, what my subconscious says, goes.

I push the Berretta hard against Sarah Jane's skull again, hard against the blood-splattered glass of the passenger window. She lets out an angry cry of pain.

"I'm sure you can tell," I say, "that the gut shot I just gave you won't kill you for some hours yet. But it's about the most pain you can feel aside from having your kneecaps blown off. You going to tell me where Emily is or do you want to test what I just said?"

Sarah Jane's eyes fight their way across and look at me. She's taking me in; the controlled anger, the poise, the apparent lack of inhibitions. She's wondering who the hell I am. She's never met me before. She's genuinely taken aback. Shocked. Stunned that I could do something like this to her.

When I see that look, I go cold all over. Oh, shit. Shit, shit, shit – I've got this wrong. She isn't Jack. How could she be?! What the hell have I -

"You…didn't have to…shoot me…" she rasps. "I was going to…take you to her anyway… we'd better…hurry, though…" and she grins a bloody grin that scares me enough into wanting to forget the whole thing, "…she'll be dead in…fifteen minutes."

thirty five :
pigs n' hay

I'VE DRIVEN PAST here a number of times over the past few days, what with wedding rehearsals and what not. Funny how places you never usually take any notice of can suddenly become the location for the most important events in your life.

We've driven out, away from Bilsthorpe, down the A617, across the roundabout, headed briefly for Rainworth and Mansfield but then quickly dropped off the road and onto a farm overlooking said roundabout. About one hundred and twenty seconds drive, the speed I was going. That's used up two of Emily's allotted fifteen minutes left on this Earth.

I'm assuming, of course, that I'll be able to do anything to affect the outcome of the all-powerful killing machine sat bleeding to death beside me. Okay, so I've got her holding her stomach together with blood-covered hands while I keep her head pinned to the passenger window with my gun. But if even one tenth of what I've heard about Jack is true, all that means absolutely diddly-squat.

"Stop…here…" Sarah Jane rasps. I stop the car.

In front of us are three barns, one much bigger than the other two. It kind of looks a little bit like one of those high streets in a Western. Y'know with the bar and whorehouse, the undertaker's next door, the frontier supply shop across the way and so on. Then, right in the middle, the road where no end of cowboys and sharp shooters have met their end duelling the Frisco Kid, scourge of all the sharp-shooters. The one who has them pissing their bed at night at the thought of facing him. But then, one game of cards, one bad hand, a hidden Ace of Spades up a sleeve and, suddenly, before they know it, here they are. The Frisco Kid, grinning at them through blood-stained teeth, and them wondering if the Indians are right – and today really is a good day to die.

"Okay," I fix my gaze on her bloodied face and press the Beretta hard into her temple, "here's how it's going to work."

Somehow, I don't know how, she manages to kick me in my gut, then in my head - then she twists the gun out my grasp and kicks me in the chest and I fly backwards out of the car, and all of a sudden, I'm lying on the ground, spitting pig shit out my mouth. Apparently, *that's* how it's going to work.

I look up in time to see a boot head for my face and that's all she wrote.

When I wake up, my gun's next to my face in the mud. A pig's sniffing my ear and I groggily shove it away. I quickly check what's what with the Beretta. One bullet left. She's ditched the rest, or kept them for herself.

My head's clearing fast, now, as I remember the magnitude of the situation and I stand up, single-shot pistol in my hand. My cell beeps. Message.

First one to shoot loses.

I look up and see muddy footprints leading into the middle barn. The biggest one. Huge place. Looks like an aircraft hangar. Two floors. Probably lots and lots of hay. And somewhere in there, Emily. She can't have long left, now. Fifteen minutes, Sarah Jane had said. I don't feel like I was out long – couple minutes, maybe. By my reckoning, she's got maybe just less than ten minutes left.

And what's this message about? First one to shoot loses.

Then it hits me. I bet she's only got one bullet, too. She's playing with me. Some kind of sick, shooter game. Nerves against nerves. Aim against aim. With Emily as both the stack of cans and the fluffy teddy bear prize.

Guess that makes me the coconut.

I run over to the open doorway and stare cautiously into the darkness. So it all comes down to a this. Half her guts hanging out and she's still playing games. Stringing me along like a sucker for a whole week, that wasn't playing enough.

She's either stupid or good. I'm hoping for the first. But I know I'm wrong.

I take a deep breath and step into the darkness.

thirty six :
till death us do part

I WAS ONCE on a job up in Manchester. A major drug
dealer on the Malach Estate, a big-ass collection of high-rise
concrete flats. Six of them. Place was a frickin' nightmare. Like hell
on earth, all the scum living in that place. I had to tippy-toe
through one of the buildings at night, looking for my man. Now,
I've been from drug dens in South America to rebel outposts in
Africa to mafia bases in the far east and I have never been more on
edge, more agitated than sneaking my way through that council
estate. The closest I've ever been to actual fear, I reckon. Course, it
didn't help when the building I was in suddenly caught fire and
burned to the ground. Some disgruntled local, apparently.

My point is, I usually don't get into the whole 'sneaking
through the enemy compound' thing. Too risky, too close to the
wire. Each step can be your last. An assassin needs control over a
situation and in those instances, you've got nothing.

That visit to Manchester – up to and including being
engulfed in flames – always sticks in my mind as one of the best
examples of why those 'Bruce Willis' situations are best avoided.

This barn in the middle of the picturesque countryside of
northern Nottinghamshire, though, has already just about topped
it.

The bright sunlight of what was meant to be my wedding
day shines behind me and I look around, trying to get my eyes
accustomed to the dark, trying to spot my bride, trying to pick out
one of the most feared assassins in the world.

I could do with a drink.

So, what do we got? Lots of hay in bales. Lots of plastic
containers of who knows what. Some machinery parts. Various

pieces of equipment. And a bride hanging by her arms by a rope from the ceiling.

My heart skips and I take an involuntary step towards her. Then stop.

Sarah Jane, I *don't* see. But you can bet she's lying around here somewhere, a sniper rifle trained on Emily. And all I've got to do to get her to let off a shot is go towards my suspended fiancée.

Okay, stop for a second. Go back to assassin school 101. Assess the surroundings.

Emily's hanging above one of the gangplanks on the second floor. The second floor's kind of suspended. There's various rickety metal stairways dotted about the place where I could get up there. There are some dangling ropes and pulleys around the place, too. For pulling bales of hay up and down, I guess, I don't know.

There are bales and crates all over the place. A hundred excellent hiding places.

I step into the shadows, gun pointed at the floor, both hands on the grip – and I start to move. Slowly. Silently. Looking for any telltale sign of Sarah Jane's presence.

Internally, I shake my head. I still can't believe she had me, hook, line and sinker. All week. Damn, she must have been peeing in her pants from laughing so hard.

Except – that doesn't really sound like her. I know she's played me like a harp, but I can't really accept the image of the stereotypical villain, twirling her moustache and laughing maniacally every time my back was turned. I get a good feel for people – and her, I saw genuine sides of. She's a sad woman. Hurt. Vulnerable. That's really her, it's not an act.

I step silently past a half shredded tyre. I look up at the floor above me, peering for any shifts in light coming from the cracks between the floorboards. Nothing, she's not there. Okay. Move on. But faster.

My brain brings me back to her text message from before.

First shot loses.

What's that about?

Well, my first shot – if I get one – is going to be at her. So, for me, that's good. Unless…unless Sarah Jane dying is bad news for Emily.

Poison. Like the girl in the cave. Hence the ticking clock on Em's expiry date. Sarah Jane's got the antidote, or knows where it is. So I shoot her, I lose.

But what about if *she* shoots? What'll *she* lose?

I freeze – I think I've spotted her, a few feet ahead, up on a suspended gantry. I move slowly toward the person-shaped mass above me, Beretta pointed up, now.

It's a frickin' sack.

I resist the urge to swear out loud. I can't stop. Got to keep going. Got to find her before she spots me. Seems like a million years ago when she said I was good at staying hidden, but she was good at finding people who were good at staying hidden.

Guess we get to find out just how good we both are.

As I move even further into the darkness, punctuated as it is by intermittent beams of bright sunlight, my mind drags me back to something so annoyingly irrelevant, I feel like banging my head on the nearest column just to get it back onto the business at hand.

Sarah Jane's ivory pendant.

The damn thing just kept drawing my eye to it. Kept picking at my brain, all along. Even now, when I've got more important things to concentrate on. Why, though? What's been annoying me about it so damn much?

'Well, it's not really ivory…'

Her words, that night. And, suddenly, it lands on me – it's been right in front of me all along, only I was too distracted…

"That pendant around your neck," I suddenly find myself calling out. "It's human bone, isn't it?"

Silence.

"It's a part of your husband," I call out, "…right?"

Silence again.

I send my spidey-sense shooting out in all directions, trying to pinpoint her location – she didn't answer like I'd hoped but maybe, if I've hit a nerve, she might make some involuntary movement, creak a floorboard or something.

Not a peep.

I quickly change position, just in case she manages to zero in on me.

But – I can feel I was right. It just seems to make sense all of a sudden. She did kill him, just like she said over all those vodkas. She killed him on the day he shot her.

"You lost your husband and child in one instant," I call out loud as I continue to move about, sweeping my eyes back and forth, "but Jack...he was *born* in that instant, wasn't he?"

Still, silence.

She's not biting. Not at all. But I know Sarah Jane, deception notwithstanding. I'm sure I'm right. And if I am, she's in turmoil right now, listening to me peel her heart bare, layer by layer.

Still can't pinpoint her location, but the more we go on, the less I think finding her is the answer to all this.

I shake my head, I'm sure I'm on the right track. She creates this alter-ego after surviving the thing with her hubbie. Like – I don't know – like a defence mechanism or something. And he's, like, the ultimate assassin. Total badass. The 'Scourge of the Assassin World'. But she's still Sarah Jane, too. And she knows all the things 'Jack' does, all the people 'he' kills – it's totally, utterly wrong. His actions need to be balanced out. Hence the private eye gig. But she was right the other morning – she can never balance it out. Because Jack will never go away. Not as long as she's alive.

I suddenly realise that, yes, this is a game. But not the twisted 'Psycho Jack' game I'd assumed. Right this second, Jack may be holding the gun, but Sarah Jane's pulling the strings. At least for now. At least long enough to give me a chance. But a chance to do what? What is she after?

First shot loses.

What would *she* lose by killing me? What do I represent to her?

All she's ever done is badger me about rising above my killer nature. Half the time, she's telling me to stop being a killer, to get involved, to care about the plot. The rest of the time, she's telling me I'm doomed to be a killer forever.

Then it hits me and it's so obvious, so damn obvious.

She wants me to make a choice. It's what she's wanted from me all along. Am I a killer or not?

So, I stay a killer, utilise a killer's thinking to try and resolve this mess – that means I shoot Sarah Jane and lose Emily to the poison. Or else, I shoot at Sarah Jane, miss, and get my head blown off. Either way, I lose.

Or I stop being a killer – and think of some other way out of this.

But she's not just doing this for my benefit – it's also about her. Her and Jack, duking it out.

And suddenly, her battle becomes my battle.

The layers of caked-on lies and justifications, built up over the decades, are scraped away and this simple but fundamental conflict shows itself. For me, Sarah Jane and who knows how many others in our profession, it's the single most important question we will ever ask ourselves.

Are we normal human beings who made a choice to become killers – and hence can make a choice to stop...

...or are we killers, natural and born, never to be anything else?

What I do next can't be faked, just to get out of this situation. I have to figure out who I am. What I am. Then act accordingly, right or wrong, live or die.

But, what's the answer?

> ANGELA
> Just promise me, Tom, you
> going to work for those
> people. It's not going to
> change you.

> THOMAS
> Nobody changes, Ange. You
> are who you are. All you
> can do is choose your
> actions. Then live or die
> by the consequences.

Turns out I've known the answer all along.

I stick my Beretta back into my jacket pocket, then, keeping to the shadows, I turn and run like hell back to the doorway and out of the barn.

My eyes feel like they're about to burn out of their sockets, the sudden glare I get from the sun as I burst outside. I sprint toward Sarah Jane's Fiesta. I can almost feel Granny Coleman smiling with satisfaction at my choice. But it'll all be for nothing if my sudden inspiration about why the car was so slow and heavy earlier turns out to be completely wrong.

I reach inside the still-open driver's door and pull the trunk release, then run round the back of the car, hoping all the time that

Sarah Jane isn't about to come running out of the barn after me. I rip open the trunk and look down...

...right into Jeremy's unconscious face.

Fresh bruises. She must have got him today. This morning, when she was giving me the bullshit about Jack chasing him. Well, I guess it wasn't really bullshit at all. It was him she spotted spying on the room, not Jack. She obviously caught up with him even after he slashed her tyres.

I just hope she hasn't poisoned him.

I pull out my cell and call Geoff's number.

Come on, come on...pick up, pick –

"Hello?"

"Geoff!" I've never been so glad to hear the guy's voice. "Geoff, it's Michael."

"Oh, hello, Michael, what's -"

"Shut up. I've got Jeremy with me. He's okay. You've got to call off the hit on Emily."

Silence. I can almost hear his thoughts. He doesn't know what to respond to first - the 'Jeremy' thing or the 'you hired a hitman for your business partner's innocent daughter' thing.

"Jeremy's..."

"Geoff, call off the hit. Now!"

Defiance, suddenly in his voice. "Prove it."

I reach down to Jeremy with my free hand, pull him up to a seating position and start shaking.

"Jeremy! Kid, wake up! Jeremy!"

You can guess how it goes for about the next twenty seconds. There may be one or two bitch slaps in there, too.

He starts to groan.

I switch my phone's video recorder on and film him.

"Jeremy – talk to your dad!"

The kid's pretty groggy and has no idea where the hell he is.

All I can see is the hourglass of Emily's life and the sand is almost all gone.

"Jeremy, talk to your frickin' dad, right now!"

"...dad...where am I?"

That'll do. Send.

"You got that?"

"Wait...wait..." Excitement. Nervousness. Fear. All those and more, I can hear in Geoff's voice. Then I hear something else.

Sobbing.

"…thank you…my son…thank you…"

"Geoff, Emily's got maybe a minute to live – call off the hit, right *now*!"

"…okay…okay…just give me a…"

And the line goes dead. My battery runs out.

You do not want to know the deluge of foul language that issues from my mouth.

"Who are…" Jeremy's looking at me in total confusion.

"Wait here, don't move," I say without really looking at him and I sprint back to the barn.

I run right inside, right into the open space in the middle, directly below Emily's suspended body.

"Geoff's called the hit off! Emily can leave! Please, let me wake her up. Then you can have me!" I shout. No reply.

"Did you hear me? Emily's off the menu!"

Nothing.

I'm really hoping Geoff got through. You could say I'm banking on it. Banking on him calling the hit off. Banking on the Agency sending a message to Sarah Jane. Banking on her having signal enough to receive it. Banking on her giving a shit…

A small, clear bottle suddenly flies out of the shadows above me and lands at my feet.

I don't stop to thank God, Allah and Buddha, I just scoop the thing up and sprint up the nearest set of stairs. I run across to where Emily's hanging and, quickly figuring out the winch, I lower her to the ground. Then, holding her head, I rip the top off the bottle with my teeth and pour the contents down her throat.

Then wait.

I can't hear anything apart from my ragged breathing and the blood rushing through my ears.

Still, nothing's happening. I look at the bottle – I hope I haven't just -

Then the vomiting starts.

I've never been so glad to see so much regurgitation in my life. I turn her sideways so she doesn't choke on it and before I know it, it's over and she's crying and distressed and in shock and it's just a beautiful sound.

"…shh…it's okay…" I hold her to me. Let's both get vomit on our clothes, I don't care, "…it's okay now…"

Slowly, she comes to her senses and she looks up at me. Something fills her reddened eyes – I'm not sure what. I caress her cheek for a moment. She doesn't move my hand away.

Then I say, "You've got to get out of here."

"Wh…"

"You have to go, now, right now," I stand up and carefully bring her to her feet. "You're okay, now. Geoff called off your hit."

"But…" her eyes are full of concern now, "…what about you…?"

Damn, she's beautiful. Even though she's all muddied and dirty and vomit-stained, standing there in that dress, against the shafts of sunlight coming through from the roof – she's just a vision. I use a precious half-second to drink it in…seeing as it's one of the last sights I'll ever see.

"Emily, will you please just…"

Emily's eyes open wide as she looks past my shoulder and I know what she's seeing even before I turn around.

Sarah Jane looks very, very bad. The gut shot hasn't stopped bleeding and her entire bottom half and most of her top half is covered in crimson.

Somehow, it just makes her look even more frightening.

Especially with her Remington M24 sniper rifle and aiming scope pointed right at my head.

"Nice rifle," I say. Funny how the onset of death makes you calm. I've seen it in some of my targets over the years. Only now do I understand it.

"Thanks," she says. "Christmas present to myself three years ago. Bargain, actually, came with a handbag. Pistol on the floor."

I slowly reach into my jacket and take out the Beretta then crouch down and drop it to the floor. Then I stand up and hold my hands up. I want her to see there's no tricks – don't want to give her a reason to shoot Emily.

I can feel Emily behind me, tense, not sure where to go, what to do. She can't leave me, that's all she knows.

"Well done," Sarah Jane says, her rifle never moving an inch. "With the Jeremy thing. Good choice, good deduction. I'm proud of you, mate. You can die with your head held high. Shame that now you've proved you actually could settle down with our cheerleader over there, you're going to get your head blown off. But, hey, life can be funny like that, sometimes."

"I guess so," I shrug. Then, "Make it quick."

"Have a strawberry vodka for me when you get to wherever you're going."

There's no bravado, no mockery in Sarah Jane's voice, now. In fact, unless I'm mistaken, there may just be the faintest hint of...

...gratitude?

Every muscle in my body tenses involuntarily as I see her finger begin to squeeze the trigger. Suddenly, Emily moves.

"No!"

Sarah Jane's gunshot mixes with the word and I don't know if it's me or Emily that shouted it. The next thing I know, I'm on the floor and Emily's falling; the snow white of her dress mixing with the deep red of her blood.

I look at Sarah Jane. A hint of surprise flashes across her body language but disappears within a fraction of a second. She lines up the rifle back on my head.

For the first time ever, the idea of my life coming to an end doesn't give me a moment's pause – my only thought is for Emily. Because, having the same job training as Sarah Jane, I know what she's about to do. Once she kills me, she's going to turn her gun back on Emily and put two bullets into her head, just to make sure.

I don't know if Emily's already dead or not, but while there's a chance, there's a chance.

I see that I'm lying right next to my gun.

At first, I'm not sure if the gunshot that rings out belongs to me or Sarah Jane, it all happens so fast. I wait for my brain to catch up with the fact it's been blown out of my head.

Instead, I notice the bullet hole in Sarah Jane's rifle scope. She slowly drops the rifle away from her face. And I see that the bullet I sent into her scope carried on right into her eye and through into her brain.

Sarah Jane falls to the ground.

I sit there, gun still pointing at her body. My heart rate refuses to slow down.

I'm just there, on the ground. Bodies around me belonging to people who were alive and standing just a few seconds ago.

Familiar territory.

My eyes are fixed on Sarah Jane's unmoving body. Not so much because I'm afraid the Terminator lady might still get up from having her brain and skull cocktailed together. No, it's more because I'm afraid to look at Emily. See, if I don't look at her, she can't be dead. In fact, if I get up and leave without looking at her and I never try to get in touch with her again, then she could feasibly still be alive for years to come.

I hear a moan. It's not Sarah Jane.

"…Mike…?"

And, yes, I hold Emily and try not to cry like a baby.

thirty seven :
[agency out]

"SIR, I'M AFRAID you're going to have to turn that off, we're about to take off."

I look up at the hostess. She reminds me of that kid's story, the one about the nail soup. Some vagrant gets a bed for the night in return for making his temporary host some nail soup. All he puts into the boiling water is a nail. He also borrows just a couple of bits and pieces from his host. Some salt. Pepper. Spices. Carrots. Mushrooms. Cream. Voila. Delicious soup. And all it needed was a nail.

And I've totally lost my point.

"Okay, this is me, turning it off."

She smiles and goes on about her business, checking everyone's buckled in and sitting upright and ready to be told which door to jump out of if the plane catches fire. She doesn't wait for me to turn my phone off. Which is good, because I don't do it. I've got a conversation to finish.

Are u sure u won't reconsider?

I tap out a response.

No. I'm finished. Thanks for everything but I can't do it anymore. My days of killing are over.

I wonder what face is on the other end of this conversation. Man? Woman? Young? Old? Is it the same person I've talked with before or just some random call centre body, utilising transcripts of my past conversations to simulate an ongoing familiarity?

Well, we won't argue. Knew this day would come. We'll make arrangements for return of our equipment.

I tap out, *Regarding the Agency, my lips are sealed.*

They respond, *Don't worry. We trust you.*

- 247 -

Yeah, I'll bet. The kind of trust you get by having the most swift and lethal retribution procedures money can buy. But, still - it's nice that they think highly enough of me that they don't feel the need to point that out.

Sorry to hear about the wedding. She seemed right 4 you.

Great. Relationship analysis from an assassination agency. Can my life really get any more messed up?

I don't really know what else to send. Don't think there's anything left to say. They think so too;

If you change yr mind, whistle. We'll hear. Have a good life, Michael Shepard. [Agency out]

I can see the air hostess coming back, so I shut my cell off.

Well. End of an era.

I sit back into my seat, but I don't feel relaxed. I still feel on edge. Like the fight isn't over. Well, I guess, in a way, it isn't. Having made the decision to give up the life of an assassin, I've got to figure out how to live the life of a normal person. A life full of stuff I care about. I've not done that since I was ten years old. It's going to be tough. I don't know what I'm going to do with myself. Continue with Shepard Insurance? Start up something else? Go open a bar on some Thai island? The future's full of possibilities but that's just the problem – I'm not used to choice. I'm used to little folders of information and knowing exactly what to do, when to do it and how many bullets to use.

Where will I go? What will I do?

Frankly, my dear, I ain't got a clue.

Man, this isn't fair - where's my horse? I've got a sunset to ride off into, damn it.

Still, it's not like everything's been all sweetness and light in the wake of my change in life direction. I had to call Fraser in to get Emily to hospital and sort out what to do with Sarah Jane. He said he'd sort everything out. Her death will end up being something connected to her job, apparently. To be honest, I didn't even ask what he was going to do.

I just didn't want to know.

My mood wasn't about to be lifted by the fact that Emily didn't want me to go see her in the hospital. It was over, said the message that came back to me via Fraser. Too much had happened for us to go back. It hurt but I didn't argue. She was right. She was sore enough at me before – her disposition was hardly going to be improved by being poisoned, suspended twenty feet above the ground, forced to vomit all over her own wedding dress and then shot.

The mere fact that we managed to survive our wedding day doesn't change anything. She's best off without me and that's that.

I left the Colemans' pretty fast – I didn't want to hang around. Apart from not wanting to see or speak to Mary and Fraser, there was a steady and unending stream of wedding guests come to check if the pair of them were alright and if Emily was going to be okay and what the hell happened, anyway? Fraser's got his story all worked out for that too. Something to do with cold feet. Again, I don't want to know.

Fraser told me that since Emily was going to be okay, he'd called off the hit on me. I guess that was his version of a teary farewell on the train platform. *It's okay, I'm not going to kill you anymore. Don't forget to write!*

He also told me that Jeremy had made up with his dad – a confirmation I got from the Agency when they told me my job was cancelled. Geoff no longer has to worry about me crashing into him with a stolen car.

Sarah Jane would be pleased.

My stomach twists at the thought of her and I realise why I can't relax.

I still haven't read her letter.

I force my mind back into thinking about Emily. Which just goes to show how much I'm trying not to think about Sarah Jane's letter – since thinking about Emily is also off limits. But I can't help it. I feel all kinds of bad over what's happened to her. Everything, from the ill-fated day I caught sight of her standing near the punch.

Right up to being shot on her wedding day.

I've tried to justify it all kinds of ways. I even tried to make it okay by reminding myself she isn't exactly innocent with a father who shifts more drugs than I don't know what. But that's just sheer desperation. She's got nothing to do with that business (a business, by the way, that Fraser even hinted he and Geoff may be ready to shut down – on account of it making one of their kids run away to live in America and the other kid take out a contract on his dad's life).

Emily took off across the Atlantic hoping to find a nice, happy, *legal* life with a nice, happy legal guy. Instead, she got me. And yet, despite everything she learned about me, she was still going to marry me. When I think of how much she must have loved me to do that and how I betrayed her trust…

"Thank you for flying with us today. Here is a demonstration for your own safety. Please pay attention, even if you are a regular flyer as the procedure may differ slightly from one you have seen before."

I respond to the tannoy announcement the same way several other grizzled business people around me do. By reading the in-flight magazine.

Except the article about the woman who opened a skateboarding shop on Easter Island doesn't really sink in. I'm still thinking about the letter in my pocket.

I can't put it off forever. Sarah Jane's friend – Catherine – went to a lot of trouble to deliver it to the wedding – not that she knew what it was. She just thought it was a card. She didn't know that her friend was a psychotic assassin. A psychotic assassin that I got on real well with.

I reach into my pants pocket and take out a dog-eared envelope. I remove the card from the envelope and the folded up letter from inside the card.

As soon as Fraser had given me the card – it was addressed to me only, rather than me and Emily – and as soon as I'd opened it and found the letter, I knew what it was.

A voice from beyond the grave.

I couldn't face it, though. The thought of unfolding that piece of paper made me feel physically sick. I mean, what if it said 'you were a really good friend' or something like that? You don't shoot really good friends in the eye. It's just not nice.

Okay, I won't be able to relax until I've faced this, so let's just do it. Think of it as practice for this whole 'living with emotions' thing. Here goes;

Hi there! If you're reading this, it means you killed me, you bastard! I'm going to haunt the living crap out of you!

All the way down the runway and into the waiting dusk sky, I can't stop laughing.

thirty eight :
the letter

OKAY, JUST JOKING. Like I'm going to waste time haunting you when there's bound to be some fit angel / devil hanging about wanting to take me back to his cloud / lavapit to show me his halo / pitchfork.

Seriously, if you're reading this, then chances are, I'm dead. And I actually hope it was you who killed me. Because the only way that will have happened is if you've turned away from being an assassin. And that means Jack's dead, too.

Let me start at the beginning. If you want to go and get a cup of hot chocolate or some Baileys or something, now's your chance.

You back? Okay.

Well, as you may or may not have figured out, I was lying when I told you my husband was really still alive. When he tried to kill me, I really did kill him right back. I didn't do so well, though. I almost died and my baby was quite literally shot out of me.

That kind of thing – as I'm sure you can imagine – can do strange things to a person's mind.

See, what I thought could happen – what I had assumed – was that even though we were living this assassin's life, once we decided or realised we needed to stop, we could. If we wanted to grow up and settle down and start a family, we'd be able to. I mean, all those lads and lasses that go out clubbing and partying and fighting and vomiting all over themselves – they get to do it. Grow up, stop being such a bloody mess, settle down. Y'know, become respectable. I thought we had the same right.

Turned out I was wrong. Turned out, for thinking that, I got a divorce, an abortion and a four month stay in a hospital bed for my trouble.

And it turns out, when I got out of that bed, I wasn't alone.

See, a part of me figured that was the universe's way of telling me not to turn away from being an assassin. In fact, it was the universe's way of telling me that I should actually be *more* of an assassin. The best assassin I can possibly be. The most ruthless, most amoral, uncaring, psychopathic son of a bitch assassin that ever walked the earth. Not only would it stop me getting hurt, but it's what I was *meant* to be doing. I'd be fulfilling my calling.

Sound familiar?

So, Jack was born. From my married name, Jackson. Get it? Funny, right? Oh, whatever, you're just mardy because you never guessed it.

Anyway, Jack. Voila.

But, even as I thought that, I disagreed with it. I thought, surely it was possible to turn away from that life. And I tried. I really did try. But, somehow, I just couldn't get my emotions into gear. They'd go so far, no further. I just ended up sleeping with deadbeat after deadbeat.

But, regardless of my own personal failure to turn my life around, I did need to balance out the unmitigated evil that Jack was by now perpetrating on a regular basis. Hence the detective agency. I specialised in missing people. As I told you, I needed to try and bring people together – even as Jack was constantly ripping people apart. Was it enough to balance him out? I couldn't tell. But I had no choice. I couldn't do nothing. I just had to keep going. And all the time, I was just trying to numb the pain with drink and meaningless one night stands.

My friend, Catherine, often told me I'd end up dead in a gutter if I didn't change my ways.

Got to admit, that was kind of the idea.

And then (fanfare please) the universe brought me *you*.

An assassin who was planning on getting married. The first such fool I'd come across since – well, since myself. And didn't that just get me and Jack arguing…

I was desperate for things to work out for you because it would mean I was right – that we can settle down. But you still wanted to carry on being an assassin. That would never work and I tried to get you to realise that.

On the other hand, Jack was desperate for you to prove to me that turning away from 'our calling' was not possible. We are what we are and we have to embrace it. He wanted me to accept that you, me, everyone in our profession, we're born killers. He also wanted your marriage to end in as much blood as possible. Basically, he wanted me to see I was right to bring him into existence.

In essence, he was fighting for his life.

Now, I feel I have to take a moment out at this juncture to point out that I'm not *actually* crazy. I'm not *actually* suffering from multiple personality disorder. I didn't go all 'Dr. Jekyll and Mr. Hyde' or anything. I didn't spontaneously fall into a trance and wake up as some badass assassin with a scar over his eye and slicked back hair. This was just my way of working out all the shit in my head. Okay? The closest I am to real crazy is obsessively recording every episode of Coronation Street. (Seriously, you should watch it – it'd chill you the hell out).

So anyway, you were throwing my whole, balanced (if psychotic) world into chaos and Jack and I knew only one of us would survive. If you went my way, Jack wouldn't have a leg to stand on anymore. And if you went his, there'd be no point fighting with him. I'd chuck in the whole private eye thing and just be Jack full time. But how would it end?

Well, that'd be decided by which of us you listened to.

Jack tried to pull you one way (like at Granny Coleman's house), I'd try to pull you the other way (like, well, most of the time). And Jeremy really was a central piece to the whole thing. I wanted us to find him and reunite him with Geoff and cascade everything back to normal. Jack wanted to find him to kill or kidnap him – make sure everything stayed just like it was.

It kind of all came to a head last night. With that poisoned girl. That was Jack and me shouting at you at the same time. We were testing you to see which choice you'd make. Save a life and stay in danger – or sacrifice the girl for your own safety. When you stayed and helped the girl, it let me give a big 'Ha' into Jack's very sulky face. He was really intent on killing you both after that because he knew he'd lost the argument. Killing you was now the only way to stop me seeing the happily ever after.

As I sit here writing this, I'm hoping, *praying* even, that Gillian Gasforth will call this morning and I'll miraculously find Jeremy and get him to the church on time to stop all this. And I'm really hoping that I can keep Jack out of proceedings long enough to do that.

But, I've got to tell you, I'm still not convinced I can do that. After all, you didn't tell Emily about your job. That's a big thing in Jack's favour, no matter what else happens.

So, I don't know. I've got no idea what'll happen today. Who'll still be alive at the end of it? Me? Jack? You?

I have a feeling, just one of us.

But I'm ever optimistic, me. So I've written all this down and I'm going to ask Catherine to bring it to the wedding. If I die, it'll get into your hands. If I don't, it won't.

I really hope you get to read this. If you do, I promise I won't haunt you.

Much.

Love ya

SJ x

thirty nine :
the not so secret history of mike shepard,
act 1

JODY, WHILCE, BUD and Lianne. They all look at me in shock and disbelief.

"Fired...?" Lianne says, hurt like a child. "All of us?"

I nod my head slowly, my face is serious as stone. I'm perched on the end of a desk. All around me, the offices of Shepard Insurance have never seemed so small as they do right now. I can't wait to see the back of them forever.

"Is this because I wrote off the rental on that roundabout?" Whilce says. "Because I said I'd pay for the damage to that flower display *and* replace that old lady's dog."

"No, it's not because of the dog or the roundabout," I cock my head slightly as I look at the floor. "Or the bus stop."

"Is it because of the thing at the shopping mall with the fish?" Bud asks.

I look up. "What fish?"

"Ha ha," says Whilce with the most fake, warning laugh anyone ever angrily forced out. "Good one, Bud. Nice joke. You made him think there was a thing with fish when there *wasn't*."

"Look, it's not because of any of those things." I cock an eyebrow and look at the ceiling, then say, kind of to myself, "Well, actually... in a way, it's actually because of all those things..."

Jody steps in for the first time. "Boss, feel free to start making sense any time now."

I love her direct approach. She'll be useful, for sure.

"Well, the thing of it is," I can't hold back my smile anymore, "I'm shutting Shepard Insurance down and I want you all to come and work for me at my new company."

"*What?!*"

I'm not sure which of them said that word first, but they all said it.

"We're getting out of the insurance business." I'm loving their shocked expressions. "Come on, hands up, which of you really enjoyed selling fricking insurance for a living?"

Shrugs all round.

"See, the thing is," I say, "I've done lots of things in my life that were…well, they were not nice. Not nice at all."

"What kind of things?" asks Bud, intrigued. "Like…sex things?"

Jody buries her head in her hands.

"No, not like sex things," I say, not quite sure exactly what 'sex things' might refer to. "A lot worse than sex things. I can't tell you exactly what they were."

"Why?" jokes Lianne. "Because then you'd have to kill us?"

Everyone laughs and I laugh along with them.

"No," I smile, "Not *me*…"

Jody's the only one who suddenly stops laughing.

"Look," I say, "it actually doesn't matter what the things were. Lets say I was a balloon thief and went around parks stealing balloons from little kids."

Lianne looks kind of upset. "I don't think I like you anymore…"

"The point is," I go on, "I want to do something good for a change. Try to balance the scales."

Jody looks a little anxious. "So we're all going to become…"

She hangs it out there for me to complete.

I take a deep breath.

"…Private Investigators!" I spread my arms wide to enhance the undeniable excitement that's about to ensue.

Silence.

But it's a shocked silence. A 'let me assimilate this information' silence. Wait…

Wait for it…

"Cool!" Whilce suddenly says.

"Do I get a Ferrari?" is what Bud decides is the most pertinent question.

"Wait, wait…just one damn second…" Jodie – the voice of reason, "…what the hell do any of us know about being private investigators?"

I shrug. "I guess we don't know Jack."

Pun totally not intended. But appreciated, nonetheless.

"Seriously," I go on, "you know about as much as I do. Zip. Plus, we're going to specialise in missing persons, which is a lot tougher than photographing cheating husbands. But we can all learn together."

Lianne shrugs, optimistically. "There must be, like, courses or something."

I nod. "There you go."

"And the internet," Bud suggests, helpfully. "I bet there's loads of instructional videos on the internet."

"Well, you'd know, dude," says Whilce, "since you've already downloaded them all."

Lianne laughs but Bud just smiles a quiet, broad smile and nods slowly, like he's not even going to deny it.

Jody gestures at Bud and Whilce. "Boss, seriously?"

"Look, have you ever done something crazy?" I hold up a hand to stop Whilce as he begins to speak. "I mean *good* crazy? 'Cause if not, you need to. I learned something important while we were in England. It's easy to do the things you think you're supposed to be doing. What's hard is doing the things you really *should* be doing."

Finally, it looks like I've bumbled and stumbled my point across. They're all looking like I felt when I came up with this crazy idea about twelve minutes after finishing Sarah Jane's letter.

I remember it clearly – I was third in line for the rest room on the plane. I was shifting from foot to foot, feeling hot, sweating even – not so much from the plane, but more from the letter. At first, I'd thought it was a bad hot. Then I'd realised it was actually a good hot. An exciting hot. Suddenly, I'd recognised what it was; I'd decided to become a PI some time in the previous few minutes and I was only just realising it.

My face went kind of like the faces of the guys in front of me now.

"So…" Jody says, finally, "…what will this great altruistic venture be called? Shepard Investigations?"

"Hey, that's good," says Lianne. "That has a nice ring to it."

"Missing persons, huh?" says Whilce before raising his hands into the air, marking out a slogan. *"Shepard Investigations – we'll bring the missing lamb home."*

Everyone laughs. And I laugh. I'm sure this is going to work. I think Sarah Jane would be proud. I think Emily would be proud. But most of all, I think my parents and brother would be proud.

I just hope Whilce doesn't push for having that slogan, because otherwise I'm going to have to shoot him.

So, we push forward, we set ourselves up, we have no idea what we're doing but we do it anyway.

Four months later, and we're cooking with gas. Jody's role hasn't changed, she's still the hub of everything. Lianne, Bud and Whilce have revelled in their re-training. They've taken their natural ability to talk to folks and turned it to something more fulfilling than convincing people to part with cash. Instead, they convince them to part with information. And as much as they like to break out into spontaneous air-guitar renditions of the 'Magnum PI' theme, they're actually really, really good investigators.

And me? If I have to stand in a crowded place with a photo and ask a hundred uninterested passers-by if they recognise the person on it on the off-chance I'll strike a lucky break – then I'll do it, rain or shine.

We've got three cases on our books – one solved, two ongoing. The solved one was a teenage New York runaway who'd got exactly as far as her favourite aunt's house (I'm really not kidding). The other two are more serious – a forty-three year old father who's been missing for two weeks and a twenty-year old daughter whose been missing for nearly six months.

Every case starts with a sad story. With any luck, most of them'll end with a happy one.

We won't get rich doing this. Turns out folks who need someone finding tend not to have as much money as folks who need someone killing. Way of the world, I guess.

But we're happy.

I'm happy.

I *could* be happier…but I'm well on my way to putting the source of my lingering unhappiness behind me. Plus, I'm not greedy. After the last few decades, I'll take my happiness where I can get it.

So here I am, sat behind my desk, in my office. Everyone else is in an open plan office right outside my door. (Hey, I'm still the boss). I've got a desk big enough for husky Russian female clients to perch on the edge of while they ask for my help. It's got a buzzer on it for Jody to tell me when someone comes into the office to see me (happened four times so far – once was just the guy to read the electricity meter). I've got metal filing cabinets for all my case notes (so far, they just hold newspapers and magazines). I've even got a wooden coat stand for my trench coat and hat. Seriously, I have a trench coat and hat. I never wear them, they're kind of decoration. But knowing they're there makes me feel just that little bit more cool.

Jody shakes her head whenever I mention them and mutters something about 'giving up'.

My buzzer goes for just the fifth time ever. Did I mention I have a buzzer?

"Boss," Jody's voice is a little odd but Whilce has just finished regaling us all with what he'd get up to if he had a trench coat, so she's probably still feeling a little queasy, "there's someone here to see you. Got a case for you, so they say."

I press the button. "Send them in."

I'll never get tired of saying that.

Notepad. I'll need a notepad. There's one in my drawer. I duck down and wrestle it open (when you insist on an authentic, antique, private investigator-style desk, you have to accept that it might just be an old, banged-up, about-to-fall-apart table with warped drawers).

I hear my door open. "I'll be right with you," I say.

"I hope you can help me," says a woman's voice.

My God.

"I'm looking for the man I'm supposed to spend the rest of my life with. I last saw him on my wedding day."

I sit up.

Emily's face lights up.

"Ah, there you are! Wow, you people are good!"

I'm stunned, I can't say a word.

Emily produces two glasses from a bag and puts them down onto my desk. Then she brings out a bottle of what looks suspiciously like home-made punch.

She smiles as she pours some into both glasses. Then she sits back, her hands folded on her lap. I'm still sitting there, catching flies, not able to take my eyes off of her.

She clears her throat slightly and looks pointedly at the glasses for a second before looking back at me. She's fighting back an amused smile.

My brain kicks back into real-time and, realising what I'm supposed to do, I lean forward and pick up a glass. I pass it to her.

"Here, have some of this." It all comes back to me like it was yesterday. "I made it myself."

"Cheers," she says, taking it. She sits back, glass in hand, looking me up and down. I pick up a glass and try to resist sinking the entire thing, my mouth's so dry.

I'm getting chills all over. She was right before. Too much had happened, we couldn't just turn back the clock. So let's smash the damn clock. Let's just start again.

But this time, do it right.

"So," I say, "you're English."

"So," she replies, "you're a PI."

I nod and take a sip of punch.

"Man, that's some good punch."

"Isn't it just?" She smiles. "So, do you have a name, PI?"

I smile.

I think I'm going to enjoy the next several decades.

Also available from 88Tales Press

- Read free samples at www.88tales.com -

42872840R00155

Printed in Poland
by Amazon Fulfillment
Poland Sp. z o.o., Wrocław